THESE
TANGLED
VINES

BOOKS BY JULIANNE MACLEAN

HISTORICAL ROMANCE

The American Heiress Trilogy

To Marry the Duke
Falling for the Marquess
In Love with the Viscount

Can This Be Love Trilogy (American Heiress Spinoff)

Love According to Lily
To Annabelle, With Love
Where Love Begins

Love at Pembroke Palace Series

In My Wildest Fantasies
The Mistress Diaries
When a Stranger Loves Me
Married by Midnight
A Kiss Before the Wedding (a Pembroke Palace short story)
Seduced at Sunset

The Highlander Series

Captured by the Highlander
Claimed by the Highlander
Seduced by the Highlander

The Rebel (a Highland short story)
Return of the Highlander
Taken by the Highlander

The Royal Trilogy

Be My Prince
Princess in Love
The Prince's Bride

Dodge City Brides Trilogy

Prairie Bride
Tempting the Marshal
A Time for Love

Colonial Romance

Adam's Promise

CONTEMPORARY FICTION

A Curve in the Road
A Fire Sparkling

The Color of Heaven Series

The Color of Heaven
The Color of Destiny
The Color of Hope
The Color of a Dream

The Color of a Memory
The Color of Love
The Color of the Season
The Color of Joy
The Color of Time
The Color of Forever
The Color of a Promise
The Color of a Christmas Miracle
The Color of a Silver Lining

THESE TANGLED VINES

A NOVEL

JULIANNE MACLEAN

LAKE UNION
PUBLISHING

Published by Lake Union Publishing, Seattle

www.apub.com

Amazon, the Amazon logo, and Lake Union Publishing are trademarks of Amazon.com, Inc., or its affiliates.

ISBN-13: 9781542025393
ISBN-10: 1542025397

Cover design by Caroline Teagle Johnson

Printed in the United States of America

THESE
TANGLED
VINES

CHAPTER 1

FIONA

Florida, 2017

The telephone rang and woke me from a dream. I must have been deep in the REM cycle, because I was cognizant of the ringing, but I believed it was part of the dream, so I chose to ignore it. It was not until at least the fourth ring that I finally opened my eyes.

Rolling to my side, I flung an arm across the bedside table, picked up the telephone, and pressed the talk button.

"Hello?"

A woman with a thick Italian accent replied, "*Buongiorno*. I am looking for Fiona Bell. Is this the correct number?"

Blinking a few times into the murky dawn light, I sat up to lean on an elbow and squinted at the clock. It was not yet 7:00 a.m. "Yes. This is Fiona."

"*Ah, bene*," the woman replied. "My name is Serena Moretti, and I'm calling from Florence, Italy. I have news for you, Fiona, but I am afraid it's not good."

Inching up against the headboard, I pressed my palm to my forehead and squeezed my eyes shut. If this woman was calling from Italy, it could mean only one thing. This was about my father. My real father. The one I'd never met.

"What is it?" I asked, still groggy from sleep and struggling to rouse my bleary brain.

There was a long pause on the other end of the line. "I'm so sorry. I just realized what time it must be there. I think I miscalculated the time difference. Did I wake you?"

Heavy raindrops battered the window of my house on the Florida Panhandle, and palm fronds slapped repeatedly against the glass. "Yes, but it's fine. I should be up by now anyway. What's this about?"

The woman cleared her throat. "I regret to tell you this, but your father, Anton Clark, passed away last night."

Her words lodged in my ear, and I couldn't seem to process them, nor could I figure out how to respond.

"I'm so sorry," the woman said, speaking as if it were common knowledge, as if everyone knew that a stranger who lived in Italy was my biological father, when in fact no one knew. At least no one on this side of the Atlantic. There was not a single soul in North America who knew the reality of the situation. Not even my dad. The secret about my true parentage was my mother's parting gift to me in the hours before her death from a brain aneurysm, and I don't think I've ever quite forgiven her for that.

I sat up a little straighter and searched my mind for the proper response. I wanted to say the right thing, but it wasn't easy, because my emotions were whirling around inside me like a tornado. Of course, it was terrible for someone to die—I felt bad about that—but this man was a complete stranger to me. I knew nothing about him except that he had impregnated my mother when she and my dad spent that terrible, tragic summer in Tuscany thirty-one years ago.

I had no idea what happened between my mother and this man because Mom was heavily medicated and unable—or perhaps unwilling—to go into detail when she dropped that bomb on me. She was close to death, and she must have known it.

"Don't ever tell your father," she had said. "He thinks you're his, and the truth would kill him."

So there it was. Mom had told me nothing about my real father except his name and nationality, and she had forced me into a vow of silence when I was eighteen and convinced me that if I ever asked questions about the circumstances of my conception or let something slip, I would be responsible for my father's demise.

For the past twelve years, I had been keeping her secret because I believed her—that the truth would indeed kill my father. I still believed it, because with Dad's health issues, every day was a challenge as well as a blessing. That's why I had buried my mother's secret deep in the darkest hollows of my consciousness. I had forced myself to forget what she had told me. I'd purged it from my brain. Pretended it wasn't true, that it was just part of a nightmare.

But now, a woman was calling from Italy, and she knew things.

"I'm sorry to hear that," I said. "What happened?"

"It was a sudden, massive heart attack," the woman explained. "He was gone before the paramedics even arrived, and there was nothing they could do. I hope it will give you some comfort to know that he went quickly. He was in his own home. He wasn't alone."

I swallowed uneasily. "I see." *His own home.* That made him seem real to me suddenly—an actual physical person who had existed all my life, but now, he was gone. Just like that. He was no longer alive on this planet. He would be lowered into the ground. Buried. And not just figuratively in my consciousness. I would never lay eyes on him.

"Well . . . that's a blessing, at least . . . that he didn't suffer."

An awkward silence ensued, and I felt ashamed of the absence of grief in me, but what could I do? All I felt was confusion and a somewhat morbid curiosity, as I wondered if it truly was too late to see him. I didn't even know what he looked like. Would there be a wake?

Then it dawned on me—that my real father had known about my existence and had deemed me important enough to be informed of his passing. I had always assumed my mother had kept it secret from him too.

"I'm sorry," I said, desperate to fill the silence. "What's your connection to my . . ." I could barely get the word out. "How do you know my father?"

"I apologize again," she said. "I should have explained myself. I work for the legal offices of Donatello and Costa. We were your father's legal team in Italy, which is why I'm calling."

I sat up straighter against the pillows, feeling more awake now.

"Your father named you as a beneficiary in his will," she explained, "and we're going to need you to sign some papers."

"Wait a second . . . he what?" My heart seemed to plummet into the pit of my belly.

"The funeral is on Monday, and there will be an official reading of the will with family members on Tuesday. I realize it's short notice, Fiona, but could you arrange a flight?"

I felt a sudden, rapid rush of heat to all my extremities at the prospect of traveling to Europe on my own to meet the family of a man I'd never wanted—or expected—to know. Whatever he left to me, I didn't want it, because this man had caused my mother discomfort and shame on the day she died. I'd recognized it when she told me the truth. As she lay on her deathbed, she could barely speak of it. Whatever happened between them was not a pleasant memory for her.

Besides that, how would I ever explain it to Dad? To the loving father who raised me? I couldn't possibly confess to more than a decade of dishonesty. It would break his heart to know that I wasn't really his and that I had kept such a monumental secret from him. And he had been through enough. Suffered more than enough loss.

I shifted uncomfortably on the mattress. "Um . . . this is a lot to take in. I'm not sure . . ." I swallowed hard. "Is it really necessary for me to be there in person? I mean, it's a long way to travel, and I'll be honest—I wasn't close to . . ." Again, the word *father* got stuck in my throat, so I managed a quick pivot. "I'm not sure how much you know about the situation, Ms. Moretti, but I've never even met Mr. Clark. I always assumed he didn't know about me. He certainly never made any attempts to contact me, which is why this comes as a surprise. I don't know his family at all, so it might be awkward for me to be there. And I don't like to be away from my father. He needs me here. Is there any way we can do this through email or fax?"

Ms. Moretti went silent for a moment. "I am aware that you weren't a part of Mr. Clark's life, but he was very explicit in his instructions about the will. I won't be coy, Fiona. He left you some property, which is why I think you need to come here and see it, sign for it, and then decide what you want to do with it."

"Property." My eyebrows pulled together with bewilderment. "In Italy? How much, exactly? I mean, how much is it worth?" I shut my eyes and shook my head. "Oh God. I'm sorry. That sounded very greedy. I'm not a greedy person. I'm just surprised, that's all. And confused. I wasn't expecting this."

"Please don't apologize," Ms. Moretti said. "I caught you off guard. And I wish I could tell you more about your inheritance, but I don't know anything beyond what I've already said. It's a bit complicated. Your father was a British national, so he had a British will. There's a lawyer coming tomorrow with the actual documents. I'm just the messenger, trying to get everyone gathered here locally to hammer out the details."

He was British? I'd always imagined him to be Italian.

Pressing my fist to my forehead, I tried to think this through. I had just been told that I was inheriting property in Italy from a virtual stranger. I had no idea how much it was worth, but I'd be a fool to turn it down. Heaven knew we needed the money. It wasn't cheap, taking care of Dad.

So there it was. I had to accept the fact that I would need to book a flight to Italy straightaway, get time off work, and figure out how to explain all of this to Dad.

"Okay," I said. "I'll try and get on a flight today. Where am I going, exactly? What city?"

I heard papers shuffling on the other end of the line. "You should fly into Florence. I'll arrange for a driver to pick you up and bring you to Montepulciano. Do you have an email address where I can send you some information and contact numbers? And do you have a cell phone number I can put in the file?"

"Yes." I relayed all my contact information, and Ms. Moretti promised to send me a message in the next few minutes.

I ended the call and set the phone down in the cradle. For a moment, I sat on the bed, staring wide eyed at one of my paintings on the wall—the one that made me feel as if I were standing on the edge of a high, rocky coastline, staring out at the vast, stormy sea. I had painted it a year ago, shortly before Jamie and I split up. A chill seeped into my bones, and I shivered.

My biological father was dead, and for some reason, he had remembered me in his will.

I turned my face away from the painting and tossed the covers aside. Then I rose from bed, deciding that I would need coffee before I opened my laptop and started searching for flights. As I donned my bathrobe, the wind howled like a beast through the eaves, and I felt a dark cloud of sorrow settle over me.

He wasn't *really* my father, I tried to tell myself, because what did blood tests and DNA results have to do with parenthood? I'd had no personal connection to the man, no love or loyalty, which were the benchmarks of a normal family. Ms. Moretti had used that word on the phone. She said, "There will be an official reading of the will with family members on Tuesday." This included *me*.

I didn't even know who these people were. His other children? My siblings, possibly? A wife? His brothers? Sisters? Cousins? I had no place among them, unless there might be other illegitimate children in attendance, like me. Perhaps then we might have something in common. But I had no idea. I knew nothing.

~

"You're up early for a Sunday," Dottie said when I entered the kitchen.

Dottie was our night shift nurse. She had been with Dad and me for many years, and I adored her because she was always cheerful. She sang show tunes while she worked, dyed her hair pink and purple, and flirted playfully with Dad, which always made him smile, even on the worst days. All our caregivers had been wonderful, but none, other than Dottie, ever lasted more than a year or two at most. They came and they went, which wasn't entirely surprising. It was a tough gig, looking after a quadriplegic.

"Yes. Did you hear the phone ring?" I asked.

"I did, but you picked it up before I could get to it. Who in the world was calling at seven a.m. on a Sunday?"

Somehow, I managed to think on my feet. "My boss. But before I tell you about that, how's Dad doing? Did he sleep okay last night?"

The last few nights had been rough, as he had a mild chest infection. "Like a baby."

"That's good," I replied, "because today's movie day."

Dad loved movies and live theater, and it was important for him to get out of the house now and again. Once a week, Jerry, our weekend caregiver, took him to a matinee. That's when I liked to seize the opportunity to disappear into my makeshift studio in the garage and paint something. It was my only true escape.

At least Dad was lucky in that he had partial use of his wrists and hands. All our nurses over the years had worked with him diligently to maintain the muscle tone. Because of that, Dad was always able to use a computer and voice-recognition software to write. He had been a successful thriller novelist at one time and had three books published, but lately, he wrote articles for the foundation he and Mom had spear-headed in '96 to raise money for spinal cord research. It had been years since Dad wrote any fiction, other than a few short stories. I think the novels took too much out of him, but honestly, I don't believe the novels sold very well. The first one did, but the second and third books were a disappointment to his publisher.

I can only assume that must have been difficult for Dad at the time. Writing was the only thing he thought he could do.

Outside of that, he was the bravest person I'd ever known. The accident that injured his spinal cord happened before I was born, so I had no knowledge of him as a man who could walk or get around on his own. All I ever knew growing up was that he loved me and cher-ished me more than anything in the world. I never considered him to be deficient in any way compared to other children's fathers. I knew our situation was different, but I never felt deprived, and there were all sorts of reasons for that.

For one, when I was small, he would let me sit on his lap while he sped around the house in his power wheelchair, spinning in circles until I shrieked with laughter. The chair moved at the touch of a button, and he controlled it with a joystick, which he gave me license to use at far too young an age. Together, we caused all sorts of havoc when I drove us into tables and knocked over lamps and teetering piles of books. *Oops* was his favorite word back then, and we both knew it rankled my mother, who had to clean up the messes we made, and that was before we had full-time caregivers. Mom did everything for him, and her devotion rubbed off on me. Until the age of eighteen, I'd believed we were the closest family on earth because of the challenges we faced every day, especially when Dad was in and out of the hospital for any number of infections that could have killed him. He was very vulnerable then. He still was.

But then Mom died unexpectedly of a brain aneurysm, and I learned about secrets and lies. That's when I discovered that people weren't always what they pretended to be. Except for my dad, of course. He was always real with me. All I ever wanted to do, after Mom died, was protect him and keep him happy and healthy. I couldn't lose him too.

Hence the keeping of my mother's secret.

"So about that phone call . . . ," I said to Dottie as she dropped a slice of bread into the toaster for me.

"What in the world did your boss want?" she asked. "I hope it was important."

"It was," I replied. "She asked if I could fill in for her at a sales conference in London this week. She was supposed to give a presentation, but she came down with a stomach bug, so she asked if I could go in her place."

Dottie faced me. "Seriously? To London? England? Where the queen lives?"

I chuckled. "Yes, that's the place. I'll have to take a red-eye tonight or tomorrow."

"And you said yes?"

"Of course. What kind of idiot would I be to turn down a free trip to London?"

I had considered the invention of a fictional conference in Italy, which would have been closer to the truth, but I was afraid to mention Italy to Dad because that was where he had his accident. It was the worst trauma of his life, so it might make him uncomfortable to talk about it or imagine me traveling there. London was a far better fabrication to avoid the subject of Tuscany altogether.

"You guys will be okay while I'm gone?" I asked, facing the toaster, keeping my back to Dottie.

"Of course. What an amazing opportunity. Any room in your suitcase for a stowaway? I could curl up very small, teensy tiny."

I smiled as I waited for my toast to pop. "That would be fun."

"Your father will be thrilled for you."

"I hope so," I said as I buttered my toast, "because I'll feel terrible leaving him."

Dottie spoke firmly. "Don't say that, Fiona. You deserve to get away, and you're not allowed to feel guilty about it. If anyone feels guilty, it's him for making you feel as if you need to keep watch over him every minute of the day. We were perfectly fine when you moved out last year. He was happy for you, remember?"

I found a jar of strawberry jam in the refrigerator and carried it to the breakfast bar, where I sat down beside Dottie. "Yes, he was happy for me in a way, but we both know he never really liked Jamie."

"No, he didn't," she replied, "but I told him that you needed to live your own life and that he had to let you do that. It took some convincing, but he agreed in the end."

"Thanks for that," I said, giving her a warm and grateful smile. "Even though it didn't work out."

Dottie sipped her tea. "I'm sorry that it didn't."

"Me too," I replied. "I wish it could have turned out differently, but Jamie was just too . . . I don't know . . . materialistic, I guess. It's better that I realized that before the wedding and not after. I'd hate to be paying for a divorce lawyer right now."

It was money that had become the main source of tension between Jamie and me. He hated it when I helped Dad out financially, but what else could I do? Money was tight. The proceeds from Mom's life insurance policy were nearly exhausted, and Dad's novels were all out of print. They stopped paying royalties years ago. He had some income from his disability insurance and other government assistance, but that alone wouldn't cover three full-time caregivers and the payments on the new van and wheelchair we bought for him last year.

Jamie had wanted us to save for a down payment on a house and buy a nicer car, but I had to share my income with Dad, so I never had any extra savings. In the end, it seemed as if Jamie and I were always arguing about how we spent money, and he finally gave me an ultimatum. It was him or Dad. I didn't appreciate that, so I made my choice. It was Dad.

And now . . . Italy.

I had to go. I had to find out what I had inherited from the father no one knew about. I didn't want to get my hopes up, but what if the value of the property was substantial? It could make such a difference in our lives.

"Jamie was handsome, though," Dottie added. "I can't blame you for falling for him. He had those gorgeous blue bedroom eyes."

I chuckled again as I ate my toast. "Yes, he did. But charm like that . . . it can only go so far."

I finished my breakfast and rose from the stool to put my plate in the dishwasher. "I should go look at flights." Dottie stood up, and we hugged each other. "What would I do without you?" I asked.

She drew back and held my face in her hands. "Your father's a lucky man to have a daughter like you. You're his whole world, Fiona."

Dottie's words caused an unexpected tightening in my chest. It had been happening a lot lately, ever since I broke up with Jamie and moved back home. Of course, I wanted nothing more than for Dad to be happy and well cared for, but it wasn't always easy. On the bad days, it was imperative that everyone around him remain positive. We worked hard to bolster his spirits. There was a lot of pressure that came with that, so I couldn't deny that I was looking forward to getting away for a while, having a little time to myself.

"If I don't see you before I leave for the airport," I said to Dottie, "have a great week, and take good care of Dad, will you?"

"I always do. Say hello to the queen for me when you get to London."

"I will." Doing my utmost to conceal my readiness to get away, I went to my room to open my laptop.

After a thorough search on Expedia, I chose a connecting flight through Frankfurt because it was cheapest. As soon as I received the confirmation from the airline, I sent the information to Ms. Moretti, who responded immediately with detailed instructions about what to expect upon my arrival in Tuscany.

CHAPTER 2

FIONA

The journey from Florida to Florence was an ordeal that I had not anticipated. I had no one to blame but myself for the horrors of my itinerary, because I was not a seasoned traveler and had selected two long layovers in New York and Frankfurt, which resulted in twenty-six hours of travel time.

Foolishly, I'd imagined I would sleep on the plane as it flew over the Atlantic, but I was seated in economy, at the back of the aircraft, in the second-to-last row on the aisle, next to the lavatories. The noise was a constant disturbance during the night. I envied the woman beside me, who had nodded off as soon as the meal trays were collected, but she had taken a sleeping pill. Smart woman. I wished I'd thought of that, because the woman snored the entire time and I only managed to doze in brief spurts. By the time the aircraft touched down in Frankfurt, I understood why those flights were called red-eyes. I felt like a member of the zombie apocalypse.

Next, I was faced with another exhausting eight hours of layover in Frankfurt before I flew to Florence, where I arrived after dark and had to wait yet another hour in a slow-moving lineup at passport control. By this time, I truly was a member of the walking dead. All I wanted to do was brush my teeth and find a soft place to collapse for the next ten to twelve hours.

When the Italian officer stamped my passport and waved me through, I wheeled my carry-on suitcase past the baggage carousel, keeping my eye out for a driver holding up a sign with my name on it, but there was no such person at arrivals. My heart sank because I didn't have the mental or emotional stamina to determine how to get from Florence to Montepulciano in the darkness when I didn't even speak the language.

With a sigh, I dug into my purse for my phone and searched for Ms. Moretti's email, hoping she had provided a number to call. All I remembered was that she'd told me I would be staying at Anton Clark's place of business, a winery that included an inn on the premises, but for the life of me, I couldn't remember the name of the winery.

I was scrolling through the messages in my inbox when someone tapped me on the shoulder.

"*Scusa*. Ms. Bell?"

I swung around to find myself facing a weathered-looking forty-something Italian man in loose-fitting jeans and a plaid shirt.

"Yes," I replied. "Are you Marco?"

"*Sì!*" He held up the sheet of paper with my name on it. "I am your driver. Welcome to Italy."

"Thank you."

He reached for my suitcase and picked it up. "Here, we say *grazie*, and I will say *prego*. You're welcome."

"Thank you for my first lesson in Italian," I replied good-naturedly, hurrying to keep up with him. "Or I should say *grazie*."

He smiled broadly. "Very good. *Molto bene*."

I followed him out of the terminal to a black Mercedes sedan parked at the curb. He opened the back door for me, and I climbed onto the leather seat, wondering if Marco would consider it rude if I were to lie down and fall asleep as soon as he hit the gas.

Without missing a beat, Marco shut the trunk, got into the driver's seat, and started up the engine. "How was your flight?" he asked, glancing at me in the rearview mirror.

"Long. I'll be glad to get to a warm bed."

"I understand. The drive will take about an hour and a half. Rest if you like."

"I might do that." I turned to look out the window. "It's too bad it's dark outside. I was hoping to see something of Florence."

"It's a beautiful city," he replied, "but overrun with tourists."

We drove through brightly lit streets beside an ultramodern tram that had also left from the airport. Marco pointed to the right. "Look over there. You will see the Duomo."

"What's the Duomo?" I asked.

"The Cathedral of Santa Maria del Fiore. The dome is lit up. Do you see?"

Sitting forward, I identified the historic cityscape in the distance. "Oh yes, there it is. It's beautiful. I'll have to google it. Maybe I'll get a chance to visit while I'm here."

"You can climb up the tower," he said, "but the lineups . . . very long. Book in advance."

"Thank you for the tip. I mean *grazie*," I said with a smile.

Before long, we merged onto a freeway, and Marco accelerated to a fast clip. I rested my forehead against the window, hoping to finally drift off, when Marco spoke softly. "I see resemblance."

Again, our eyes met in the small space of the rearview mirror. "I beg your pardon?"

"You look like him," Marco said with a touch of melancholy. "Like your father."

I sat up a little straighter. "You knew him?" I'd assumed Marco was just an anonymous airport limo driver.

"*Sì.* I was Mr. Clark's driver for six years."

I froze for a second or two, my ears still ringing from all the noisy takeoffs and landings. Or maybe it was something else, a sudden awareness that the father who was a stranger to me—a man I thought of in the way one might think about a stone statue—had lived a full life with close friends who knew him intimately. People who worked for him, people who cared for him.

Of course, rationally, I knew that he must have had friends. Thanks to Ms. Moretti's email, I knew for a fact that he was survived by a wife and two children. It was surprising how quickly I devoured the information in her email, even though I had never wanted to know anything about him before. All my life, I had preferred to think of my biological father as not quite human. A one-dimensional villain, if you will. Not a person I would ever wish to know or care about.

Perhaps the reason I didn't want to know anything was because I feared it might lead to a desire to meet him. Then I would have to travel a great distance to satisfy my curiosity, and I couldn't do that to Dad. It would have felt terribly disloyal.

"Did you enjoy working for him?" I asked Marco, finally removing the chains from my curiosity. I was in Italy for one week only. I might as well surrender to it.

Marco laughed. "I don't think anyone enjoyed working for your father. He was . . . how do you say in English? *Oppressore? Tiranno?*"

"A tyrant?" I offered.

"*Sì!* Tyrant!"

I sat back, feeling strangely relieved to hear that. If he was, in fact, a horrible person, that might soften my regrets in the future. I might be grateful I'd never met him. "Really."

Marco laughed again. "But we loved him. We would have done anything for him. I don't know why."

I inclined my head. "Who's 'we'?"

Marco shrugged. "Everyone. He had a certain . . . how do you say?" Marco gestured with a hand. "Power. A way to charm anyone into doing anything."

I gazed out the window again and wondered what would have happened if I'd traveled here when Anton was still alive. It might have been interesting to witness his alleged charisma for myself. He had, after all, seduced my mother into cheating on a husband she deeply loved. If that's what happened. I wasn't actually certain that *seduction* was the right word. It might have been something far less romantic, a situation she couldn't control, based on the anguish on her face when she told me.

Feeling a little sick at the thought, I tapped my finger on my knee and realized that the curiosity I had managed to bury for the past twelve years was waking up like a sleeping dragon. I was eager to reach Montepulciano.

~

Marco was a confident driver, but he liked to speed.

"You must know these roads pretty well," I said, waking from a nap and running my fingers through my hair as I took in our surroundings. We seemed to be in the middle of nowhere, careening through dark and twisty country roads.

"*Sì.* I've lived here all my life."

I wished I could see more than the leafy foliage closing in on us from either side of the narrow road.

"It's foggy," I mentioned, being tossed suddenly to the left as Marco maneuvered around a hairpin turn at a breakneck speed.

"Fog is common in Tuscany," he replied. "Lots of hills and valleys where it likes to worm its way in. Almost there. Not far now."

I reached into my purse for some gum and rubbed the pad of my finger under my eyes to wipe away the smudges of yesterday's mascara.

It was 10:00 p.m. local time, and I prayed I would be reaching a soft bed soon. Or a hard one. It wouldn't matter. I just needed to be horizontal.

Marco hit the brakes and turned onto a gravel road with a big sign that said **MAURIZIO WINES**. The road snaked through a forest and sloped steeply uphill. I bounced on the seat as Marco hit the gas on the final approach toward a tall wrought iron gate flanked by massive brick columns. He stopped, retrieved a key fob from the console, and pressed the button, and the gate slowly opened, creaking on hinges in need of oil. He pulled onto the gravel parking lot in front of a large, medieval-looking stone building.

Did Anton own all this?

"We are here." Marco shut off the engine and unbuckled his seat belt, then hurried around the car and opened my door for me.

As I stepped out, a fresh scent of damp earth and the chill of the thick, briny fog sneaked through the fabric of my jean jacket. Marco carried my suitcase, and I followed him into what appeared to be the reception area of a B and B type of establishment. A young Italian woman greeted us at the desk.

"Ms. Bell?" she asked.

"Yes, that's me."

"I'm Anna. It's nice to meet you." She bent to retrieve a key card from under the counter. When I whipped out my credit card, Anna held up a hand. "No need for that. It's all taken care of. You're in room number seven, on the top floor. Up those stairs, to the left. Breakfast is in the dining room just through there from eight thirty to ten thirty. And you'll find the Wi-Fi password on a card in a basket in your room."

"Thank you very much, Anna." I took the key card and was surprised to see Marco already carrying my suitcase up the worn black marble steps.

The building seemed ancient, with thick plastered walls and heavy exposed beams on the ceilings. I paused to inspect framed photographs on the staircase walls with celebrity guests. George Bush had visited the inn, as well as Tom Hanks and Audrey Hepburn. I felt a little like Alice going down the rabbit hole.

Marco led me to a dark mahogany door on the fourth floor. I inserted the card into the key reader, pushed the door open, and found a light switch that lit up a massive hotel suite with antique furniture, velvet drapes on the windows, and a king-size bed with luxurious white linens. I could have wept with joy at the sight of it.

Marco set my suitcase down inside the door and moved to switch on the light in the bathroom. "You should be comfortable here. It's the best room we have."

"It looks wonderful." I peered in at a gigantic bathroom with black and white tiles, a deep soaker tub, a stand-up tiled shower with glass doors, and a bidet, which I studied curiously for a moment.

Marco moved to the door and pulled a business card from his shirt pocket. "Here is my cell number in case you want to be driven anywhere. You'll definitely want to visit Montepulciano. Cars aren't permitted in the town, but I can drop you off at Piazza Grande, and you can walk everywhere from there. There are lots of good shops with leather goods. I can recommend some restaurants. Tomorrow you'll meet the family."

His mention of the family caused a sudden nervous tremor in me because I had no idea what to expect. Visions of *The Godfather* sprang to mind.

Marco turned to leave, but I stopped him with a question. "Wait. Do you mind if I ask . . . ? Is my presence here going to be awkward? I mean, Anton had a wife and children. Do they know who I am? Have they always known?"

Marco regarded me steadily for a moment, and I sensed a measure of sympathy in his expression, which I wasn't sure how to interpret.

"It was a shock to them," he finally admitted.

"They didn't know?"

"Not until the other day."

I let out a breath. "I see. Were they very upset? Because I've been worried that I might be walking into a hornet's nest."

He rubbed at the back of his neck and chewed on his lower lip. "I can't guarantee that you won't be. It depends what the will says."

"The will . . ." I paused. "Do you know anything about that?"

He shook his head. "No one does, but there's been plenty of talk around here the past few days. Anton was a wealthy man, so there are many expectations."

My poor brain needed sleep, and I couldn't seem to form a response. It had been less than forty-eight hours since I learned that Anton owned a winery and the inn I was staying in. Exactly how wealthy was he?

Marco tried to leave again.

"Wait." I grabbed hold of his sleeve. "Do you know who will be there when the lawyers read the will? I'm assuming his other children. What are their names?"

"Connor and Sloane," Marco replied. "Connor is the younger one. He's here on his own. Sloane is here with her two children, but her husband stayed behind in America."

I tried to process this. Connor and Sloane would be my half brother and sister. The children would be my half nieces and nephews. As I'd grown up as an only child, it was a strange thing to conceive of.

"There is also Mr. Clark's ex-wife," Marco added. "Mrs. Wilson. She came for the funeral as well."

"They're divorced?" I asked. "Since when?"

He shrugged. "Not sure, exactly. They separated before I started work here, when the children were very small. I met Mrs. Wilson for the first time at the funeral today. Maria would know more about all that."

"Who's Maria?"

"The housekeeper at the villa. Her father-in-law, Domenico Guardini, was the vineyard keeper when Mr. Clark bought the winery years ago. Now her husband, Vincent, takes care of the vines."

"I see. And where is the villa? Will Maria be there in the morning when the lawyers come?"

"*Sì*, she will be there. It's at the top of the hill, end of Cypress Row, easy walk from here. But you should sleep now, Ms. Bell. You had a long journey. No need to worry."

"Thank you. But please call me Fiona."

He nodded and was quick to leave, as if he had a dozen other things to attend to. I sensed he was an efficient person.

Closing the door behind him, I turned to look at the gigantic bed and sighed with exhaustion. After that, I must have set a record opening my suitcase and changing into my pajamas.

~

I groaned at the sound of my cell phone alarm. Reaching across the soft pillow, I hit snooze and wondered what fresh new hell this was. My body felt like a block of lead. I tried to calculate what time it was back home in Tallahassee. Two in the morning?

Almost instantly, I fell back into a deep, dense slumber.

The shriek of my phone woke me again nine minutes later. Knowing that more sleep was out of the question, I rolled onto my back and forced myself to rise because I didn't want to miss breakfast. More importantly, I wanted to find my way to the villa early to get the lay of the land before the lawyers arrived.

Groggily, I shuffled across the wide-plank floor to the window, where I pulled the heavy velvet drapes aside. Expecting sunlight beyond panes of glass, I was instead presented with oak shutters that blocked out the light completely. I jimmied the latch and pulled one shutter open, then let out a gasp of shock. The view . . . was this even real?

Before my sleepy, squinting eyes, a medieval castle town stood high on a lush green mountaintop. The stone buildings and towers were framed by blue sky. Low to the ground, a misty white ribbon of fog crept across olive groves and grape vineyards. Bells began to chime from a cathedral somewhere on the hilltop, and a flock of swallows fluttered out of the tall cypress tree near the swimming pool below my window.

I was awestruck and couldn't speak for a few seconds. No wonder famous people had stayed here. This was a million-dollar view. It was like waking up in the middle of a live-action Cinderella movie.

Letting my eyes fall closed, I breathed in the fresh scent of the September air, the grass and dew, and urged myself to appreciate this week of total freedom. I would not let myself worry about Dad back home. Dottie had everything under control. I needed to remember what she had said—that I deserved a week off.

The bells in town stopped ringing, and then all I could hear was the calming whisper of a breeze through the olive grove. Eyes still closed, I inhaled another deep, cleansing breath, then finally forced myself to step away from the window and head for the shower.

A short while later, I made my way downstairs to the dining room, where a buffet breakfast was laid out with pastries, yogurt, cereal, eggs, and a platter of sliced meats and cheeses. A long table, large enough to seat thirty people for a formal dinner, was dressed up with a white tablecloth and bouquets of fresh flowers. As soon as I reached the sideboard to pick up a plate, a young woman from the kitchen approached me. "*Caffe?*"

"*Sì, grazie*," I said. "I'll have an Americano, if you have it?"

She smiled and nodded and returned to the kitchen. I then filled my plate and sat down across from a young couple.

"Good morning," I said as the server returned with my coffee and set it down in front of me.

"Good morning," the young woman replied. From the sound of her accent, I speculated she was from the southern US. "Have you tried the cappuccino yet?" she asked. "It's delicious."

"Not yet. I'll give it a try tomorrow."

We made small talk, and I learned they were on their honeymoon. They'd started in Rome, and now they were on their way to Venice to board a private schooner and sail around the Mediterranean.

After they left, an older couple—also American—walked in and ordered cappuccinos before filling their plates with eggs, toast, and sliced meats. I chatted with them as well. They were recently retired and making the rounds in Tuscany, touring a different winery every afternoon, but this was their home base for the full two weeks.

"We love Montepulciano," they explained. "And the wine here . . ." The man kissed his fingertips with a flourish. "Simply the best."

"I'm not much of a wine connoisseur," I quietly admitted, keeping my head down as I stirred my yogurt. "I always go for the same label at home—a California merlot that hits all the right notes when it comes to the price tag."

They laughed and nodded with understanding. "You'll enjoy trying these old-world wines. There's a very different flavor here."

"In more ways than one," his wife said with a smile as she gazed across at her husband. "There's just something about Europe."

They seemed very happy. "How long have you two been married?" I asked.

"Going on forty years," the man replied.

"You're lucky you found each other." I sipped my coffee and set it down, cupping it in my palms. "This is just what the doctor ordered. I'm still a bit jet lagged."

"That will pass," the woman said. After a pause, she asked, "Are you traveling alone?"

"Yes, though I'm not really 'traveling,' so to speak. I'm here for a funeral."

"Oh, that's a shame. We saw everyone heading to the church yesterday. Our condolences."

"Thank you." I finished my yogurt and changed the subject before they had a chance to ask about my relationship to the family. "I might try to walk around Florence for a few hours before I head back," I said. "Have you been there?"

"Yes, and do try," the woman said. "Pitti Palace is worth a visit. The gardens are impressive. And walk across the Ponte Vecchio. It's an old medieval bridge with shops. Mesmerizing at sunset. Of course, go and see *David*. You can't visit Florence without feasting your eyes on *that*."

I laughed. "I'll make sure to get there."

After breakfast, I returned to my room to brush my teeth, then ventured downstairs to the reception desk to ask the clerk how to get to the villa. It turned out to be Anna, the same young woman who had checked me in the night before.

Anna pulled a colorful map out from behind the counter and used a red Sharpie to circle a building, dead center. "We're here at the inn. Go out the front door to the parking lot, turn right, and walk up the gravel road between this building and the new winery facilities. When you get to the top, turn right at the chapel and follow Cypress Row up the hill, past the cemetery to the big iron gate. Here's a fob to open it, and you might as well hold on to this while you're here so that you can come and go as you please. It's about a two-minute walk from the gate. The family's up there now, so the front door should be open. If it's locked, just ring the bell. Maria will answer. She'll take good care of you."

I thanked Anna, then walked outside and crossed the parking lot to overlook a vast valley of fields, forests, and grape vineyards with neat, straight rows on sloping terraces. Olive trees to the east shimmered like silver in the sunlight, their leaves pale next to the darker pines of the forest.

I could have stood there for a while, but the lawyers were due to arrive at the villa soon, and my nerves were getting the best of me. I was under no illusions that the family members would be happy to see me. I was an outsider, an illegitimate child, a skeleton in the closet who had emerged at the worst possible time—to claim a piece of their inheritance. Undeserving, of course, because I had never expressed any interest in meeting them or the father who had sired me.

I still couldn't believe I was even here. Why in the world had Anton included me?

Dread filled my insides as I turned and walked slowly up the steep gravel lane toward the villa, all the while wishing that I had brought a trusted friend with me so that I wouldn't have to face the family alone. But I had never confided in anyone about my mother's secret. It was mine alone to bear.

I continued past the chapel and what appeared to be a small medieval hamlet halfway up the hill, then turned onto Cypress Row, a straight dirt road lined with towering evergreens. At the end of it, I came to an iron gate and pressed the key fob button. The gate swung slowly open, and I passed through it. A few steps farther, over a gentle rise, the enormous stone villa came into view.

My breath came a little short at the sight of it, and I stopped and stared. It was a Renaissance-style mansion, butter colored with a six-column, Palladian-style portico at the entrance and a massive stone terrace surrounding the entire building. There were formal Italian gardens to the left and tennis courts to the right.

Suddenly intimidated, I felt my heart begin to thump in my chest. I had learned from Ms. Moretti's email that Anton owned a winery, but I had no idea it would be anything like this. Marco had said he was a wealthy man. How wealthy, exactly, and what in the world had he bequeathed to me, and why? What had he been thinking when he added my name alongside his other two children as a beneficiary? Would anyone here know the facts behind that decision?

Inhaling a deep breath, I strode forward purposefully, my feet crunching over white gravel. The stone steps took me up to a wide terrace and a massive medieval door with an ancient lion's head for a knocker. I was about to take hold of it and rap a few times when I noticed an electronic doorbell to my right, wired and fixed to the stone facade. I pressed the black button and heard a bell chime. A moment later, the door opened.

An older Italian woman with gray upswept hair in a loose bun greeted me with a smile. "*Buongiorno*. You must be Fiona?"

"*Sì*," I replied, grateful for this initial warm welcome. It calmed my nerves slightly, at least for the time being.

"I'm Maria Guardini, the housekeeper." She opened the door wider. "Please, come in."

I stepped over the threshold onto a wide terra-cotta tiled floor in a brightly lit central foyer. A large wrought iron chandelier hung over a round table with a vase full of fresh flowers, and the plastered walls were painted cream. Straight ahead, the foyer opened onto a large reception room with a bank of french doors, all flung open, toward the back terrace.

"How was your flight?" Maria asked.

"Long," I replied. "It was hard to wake up this morning."

"I don't doubt it. Can I get you anything? A cappuccino or espresso?"

"No, thank you. I just had coffee at breakfast."

She stared at me for a moment, and I felt suddenly self-conscious. If I were a turtle, I would have retreated into my shell.

"Marco was right," she said. "You do look like him. In his younger days."

I swallowed uneasily. "Do I?"

"*Sì*." Maria checked her watch. "The lawyers won't arrive for about twenty minutes. We have time to get acquainted. Would you like to come into the reception room?"

"Yes, thank you."

She led me to the expansive space at the back of the villa, which housed a few cozy groupings of sofas and chairs on area rugs. A grand piano was nestled at the far end of the room, and the walls were adorned with oil paintings that looked like they should be kept in a museum.

I followed Maria to a sofa in front of the large stone fireplace. "You must have many questions," she said.

"I do, actually."

"We do as well," she replied.

There was a tightening in the pit of my belly, and I cleared my throat nervously. "I'll be honest, Maria. This is very awkward for me. I'm not sure how much you know about the situation, but Mr. Clark wasn't a part of my life. My mother only told me about him an hour before she died, more than a decade ago, and she revealed very little. Even my father doesn't know I'm another man's child. So you see, it's complicated."

"*Oh, mamma.*" Maria's eyes held a puzzled look. "You know nothing about your mother's relationship to Anton?"

Nothing except for the fact that she had turned her face away in shame and despair when she made her deathbed confession.

"I'm not even sure if it was an actual *relationship*," I explained, "because my mother was happily married to my father when they spent a summer here, thirty-one years ago. That's why I wasn't told that Anton was my real father, at least not until she was dying. I guess she just wanted me to know for some reason . . . maybe in case there were ever any medical issues in the future? That's the only reason I can think of for why she wanted me to know. But she begged me not to tell my dad because it would have broken his heart, and he has enough to deal with. He's a quadriplegic, and he needs twenty-four-hour care."

"*Santo cielo.*"

I lowered my gaze to the floor. "Pardon me. I'm rambling."

"Not at all."

I took a deep breath. "I just have so many questions."

Maria sat back. "I wish I had answers for you, but this is as much of a shock to us as it must be to you. We only learned about your existence from Anton's legal team in London a few days ago. They're the ones who are coming here this morning with the will that he updated recently."

I frowned with uncertainty. "How recently?"

"Two years ago. In 2015."

I considered that. "Was that when he found out he had a heart condition, maybe?"

She shook her head with regret. "He wasn't aware, as far as I know. He seemed healthy as a horse."

A door slammed somewhere in the house, and I turned to the sound of a woman's heels clicking briskly down a flight of stairs. Maria rubbed her temples. "*Porca vacca*. I apologize in advance for what is about to happen."

A tall, beautiful Italian woman with long black hair, an ivory complexion, and full red lips stormed into the room. She wore a black Armani pantsuit and began ranting in Italian, shouting an endless wave of complaints while gesturing wildly with her french-manicured hands. I couldn't understand a single word she said, but I suspected it had something to do with the lawyers' visit.

Maria held out a hand to try and calm the situation. She spoke slowly to the woman in Italian. All I could do was sit and watch.

Another woman stormed into the room. This one was blonde and older, possibly in her early sixties, but she looked fantastic. It was obvious to me that she'd had some work done.

"She won't leave!" the blonde woman shouted.

"I won't leave because I live here!" the Italian woman countered.

"No. You were a guest here, and now you are no longer welcome."

The younger woman shot back with a firestorm of emotion, hollering in Italian, until the other threw up her hands in defeat. She turned to Maria expectantly, waiting for her to intervene and say something to diffuse the situation.

"Ladies!" Maria said. "This must wait. We cannot make any decisions about who stays and who goes until we know what the lawyers have to say."

"See?" the Italian woman snapped. "I told you!"

"They won't have anything to say about *you*," the blonde woman said. "Anton drew up his will two years ago, and he didn't even know you then."

The Italian woman snapped her fingers in front of her face three times. "You think you have all the answers, but you don't. You know nothing. Anton loved me. He told me so. You don't know what he was thinking before he died. He might have added something. A letter. I don't know how these things work."

"No, you don't know anything, because you have lipstick for brains."

"And you are an arrogant cow! You're only here for the money! You didn't care about him! If you did, you would have come to visit him before he died, but you didn't. And who was here, making sure his last days were beautiful?"

Maria stood up and spread her hands wide, like an orchestra conductor. "*Tacete!* We'll talk about this later. I must introduce you to Fiona. She just arrived."

They both fell silent and turned their fiery gazes in my direction.

The younger Italian woman stared down at me as if I were a snake in the grass. "This is she?"

I stood up and tried to smile. "*Buongiorno.*"

"This is Kate Wilson," Maria said to me, gesturing toward the older blonde woman, "Anton's ex-wife. She's here from California. And this is Sofia Romano . . ." Maria struggled for the right words. "A friend of Anton's."

"I was more than a friend," Sofia replied. To my surprise, she swept her anger aside and held out her hand with a smile. "It is a pleasure to meet you, Fiona. I see the resemblance. You have his eyes."

"That's what everyone keeps telling me." I shook Sofia's hand.

Mrs. Wilson stepped forward as well. "It's rather unsettling, actually. So much for the suggestion that you're not really his daughter."

Maria let out an uncomfortable laugh, for it was a clear shot across the bow.

Mrs. Wilson's cool green eyes swept over me from head to foot. I had the distinct feeling that the woman found me lacking in every way, especially regarding my wardrobe choices. I wore skinny jeans and a light tank top under a black cardigan—a polyester-and-spandex blend, purchased at Walmart because I was on a very limited budget.

"You certainly came a long way for this," Mrs. Wilson said with a note of accusation in her tone.

"You did as well," I replied. "Maria mentioned you live in California?"

"Yes." Her arched eyebrows pulled together. "And you're from . . . ?"

"Tallahassee, Florida."

She let go of my hand and stepped back. "I've never been to the Panhandle."

"It's nice. You should visit sometime."

Mrs. Wilson chuckled lightly.

By now, Sofia was marching out of the room and stomping back up the stairs.

Mrs. Wilson turned to Maria. "She's not invited to the meeting, is she?"

"No," Maria replied. "She's not on the list."

"Good. I'll need you to buck up and help me get rid of her afterward. Unless Anton did something foolish in his final days. God help us if he did, but it wouldn't surprise me." She glanced briefly at me again before she left the room.

Maria sank onto her chair. "*Mi dispiace.* I apologize."

I sat down as well. "It's not your fault. Was Sofia . . . ?" I pointed a finger at the empty doorway.

"*Sì.* Anton's mistress. Not the first one, but she got lucky, being the one who was with him at the end. Honestly, I can't imagine that he would have left her anything. He wasn't a fool, and he gave her plenty while he was alive. There was some talk about a necklace that would pay for a flat in Rome for an entire year. I suppose she did deserve something for sticking around when he was cantankerous. She certainly was devoted. Although . . ." Maria shook her head disapprovingly. "The motivation is suspect, if you understand my meaning. He wasn't a young man, and you saw her."

"You think she was hustling him?"

"Possibly."

Not wanting to presume anything or pass judgment, I looked down at my hands in my lap. "His ex-wife didn't seem to like me very much."

Maria waved a hand dismissively. "Don't worry about Kate. She's heading into her third marriage, and the second husband was even richer than Anton, so she has nothing to complain about."

"What about the children?" I asked, point-blank. "Are they going to hate me?"

"Definitely," Maria replied, giving me a look. "But it doesn't matter what they think. The will is what it is, so just take whatever he left you, and walk away."

Surprised by the woman's candor, I blinked a few times. "I appreciate the advice."

Maria sighed in defeat. "You wouldn't stand a chance otherwise, because this family has a talent for making life far more difficult than it has to be. Everything is a battle."

"I wouldn't know anything about that."

"No, of course you wouldn't." Maria toyed with her earring and studied me for a moment. "Whatever happens this morning, don't take it personally. They haven't had a chance to come to terms with the fact that their father had another child. But really . . . I don't see how they could be surprised. Their mother took them away to America thirty years ago. It's not as if their father was a monk. He had many women in his life."

Something about that statement troubled me, because I didn't want to think of my mother as one of his many conquests. At the same time, I didn't want to suggest anything untoward the day after the man's funeral. But I had my suspicions.

I sat forward again. "Marco said your father-in-law, Domenico, worked in the vineyard before you and your husband took over. Would your husband's parents know anything about what happened between Anton and my mother?"

"They might have known something, but they're both deceased. Vincent and I came here to take over the vineyards in 1988. When was your mother here?"

"It was the summer of '86." When that line of questioning provided no results, I shifted direction. "What about Anton's driver before Marco? Where is he now?"

"His name was Gordon Nucci, and he was with Anton for many years. He was living in the villa since before I started, so he might have known something as well, but he died a long time ago, which was when Marco was hired."

Before I had a chance to ask any more questions, the doorbell chimed.

"That must be the lawyers." Maria rose from her chair. "Stay here while I go and greet them and get them settled."

As I watched her leave the room, my stomach flipped over at the thought of what was about to happen in the next few minutes—my first meeting with my half siblings, who probably hated my guts for being named a beneficiary in their father's will. Nevertheless, I was curious to know what Anton had left me and how much it was worth. Judging by what I'd seen of this property so far, it could be something significant. Or not. Either way, I'd be glad to get this meeting over with.

CHAPTER 3
SLOANE

Shortly before the lawyers rang the doorbell, Sloane Richardson was having an epiphany. It happened around the back of the villa, in the vegetable garden, where the sun shone most brightly in the mornings. Perhaps it was the glorious peal of church bells ringing on the hilltop that brought it on. Or the fresh country air feeding oxygen to her brain instead of foul exhaust fumes that gave her a headache whenever the Los Angeles freeway was gridlocked and their driver couldn't get them out of it.

"Kids, come and look at this," she said to her children, Chloe and Evan, who were following at a distance.

Evan was ten and Chloe was seven. Neither looked up from their phones.

"Evan! Chloe!" she shouted.

"What?" Evan shouted back.

"Put your phones away, please. It's a beautiful day. Come and see what I found."

Chloe rolled her eyes as she followed her older brother along a row of tomato plants.

Sloane pointed at the dirt. "Look, it's a lizard."

They both crowded in. "Cool," Evan said.

The lizard scurried away beneath a patch of leaves and disappeared.

"Can we catch one?" he asked.

"I suppose," Sloane replied, "if you're quick enough. Maybe we could come out later with a bucket. But if we catch one, we have to let him go when we're finished looking at him, all right?"

"Can we bring him in the house?" Evan asked.

"No way, Mom!" Chloe shouted.

"Hmm," Sloane said. "Maybe your sister's right. Maria might not like it very much if a lizard gets loose in the kitchen."

"I'd keep him in my room, under my bed," Evan promised.

"We'll see." Sloane squeezed his shoulder, then sighed with defeat when they both returned their attention to their cell phones.

As she led them out of the tomato patch toward the olive grove, she felt as if she were walking alone. The story of her life lately.

A memory came to her then, like a fresh breeze across the hilltops. It took her back to her childhood, when she and Connor and their cousin Ruth used to play hide-and-seek in the cool, musty wine cellars. What fun they had, exploring the dark spaces between the gigantic wooden barrels full of aging wine. Sometimes they were put to work, pruning the vines in July and weeding the vegetable gardens. Maria always had something interesting for Sloane to do in the kitchen. She remembered kneading bread, standing on a chair to stir something in a big pot, or bottling plum jam. Sloane remembered all of it fondly, until it became colored with regret. The feeling caught her off guard and left her a little shaken.

Clearly, her father's funeral had been more difficult than she had anticipated. The deep melancholy in the wake of her nostalgia came as a surprise to her, because she and her father had hardly spoken in years, nor had she visited the winery since before her children were born. Whenever she traveled, she took them to London to visit her cousin Ruth, who was more like a sister than a cousin to Sloane, and Ruth had two young children of her own, which made it fun for Evan and Chloe. For that reason, she had expected to arrive in Italy, say her final good-byes, lay the past to rest forever, and move on. But seeing this place again reminded her of another time in her life when everything was so much simpler.

People say you can't return to the past, but why can't you? she wondered with frustration, looking around at the familiar landscape. Here it was, exactly as she remembered from her childhood.

Some things in the past were gone forever, of course. She had grown apart from her father in recent years, and she would never see him again. Even if he were still alive, she couldn't imagine how she could ever go back to the way things were and be close to him. Her parents had separated when she was only five and Connor was three, and an ugly divorce had followed because their father cheated on their mother. That's why she took them out of Italy, where they were born, and dragged them back to her family in California. The custody agreement specified that Connor and Sloane would spend four weeks each summer with their father in Montepulciano and one week at Christmas. They'd enjoyed it when they were young children, when they considered it an adventure to spend a month on what was essentially a working farm, where they could get dirt under their fingernails and chase chickens. But when the teen years came, there were arguments and doors slamming over the issue of their visits, when all they'd wanted to do was remain in LA with their friends. Their authoritarian father had never budged an inch, and he had forced them to present themselves each summer until the age of eighteen, when he finally relented and allowed them to make their own choices.

Unsurprisingly, Sloane and Connor elected to remain in LA most of the time, and their mother always took their side over their father's. If they traveled, it was to their London house, where they enjoyed a social life with Ruth, who took them to parties. With every year that passed, they saw their father less and less. They spoke to him on the telephone once a year on their birthdays, when he called to catch up.

A bumblebee flew by. Sloane turned to look back at her children. Their eyes were glued to their phones, and she sighed heavily, wishing they would show some interest in their surroundings.

Another wave of regret washed over her. Was this how her father had felt when she and Connor visited him in the summers, surly and resentful, complaining about what they were missing back home?

Catching sight of someone in her peripheral vision, Sloane turned and shaded her eyes from the morning sun. It was her brother, Connor, walking briskly toward her with his hands in the pockets of his blue chinos, his white shirtsleeves rolled up to the elbows, his mirrored sunglasses reflecting the blinding glare.

"I've been looking for you," he said, ducking out of the path of a dive-bombing dragonfly. "What in God's name are you doing out here?"

"Showing the garden to the kids," she explained.

He glanced back at them. "Looks like they're loving it. A couple of gifted green thumbs you've raised there, sis. Congrats on that."

"Oh, shut up," Sloane said.

Connor pulled out his phone and checked the time. "It's almost ten. The lawyers will be here any second, and you're out here playing peasant games in the vegetable patch."

"Cut it out." She turned away from him because she couldn't bear for him to lay waste to the enchantment of her childhood memories just now, which he would definitely do if she spoke of them. He would crack some stupid sarcastic joke like he always did.

"This is good for them," she said. "They need to experience other cultures."

Connor laughed mockingly. "For pity's sake, it's not like we're visiting a developing country. Didn't you notice they buried Dad in a gold Rolex?"

"No, I didn't, but I'm not surprised that you did."

He checked his phone again. "You need to lighten up. This will all be over soon enough, and we can take the money and run."

She kicked at the grass with the toe of her shoe, then glanced back at her two children, who were now sitting on a bench under an olive tree. They were still swiping. Always swiping.

"Do you think I allow them too much screen time?" Sloane asked.

Connor glanced in their direction as well. "Please. You're not going to turn into one of *those* mothers, are you? Back to the land? Will home-schooling be next?"

"Of course not," she replied. "I just wonder how this generation is going to turn out. I mean, look at them. They hardly talk to each other. What's going to happen when Chloe grows up and has a baby? Will she be pushing a stroller down the street and looking at her phone, ignoring her child? What about language skills? How will babies learn to talk when their mothers are barely present? Chloe could be sitting on a park bench in a playground with her eyes on her phone, sucked into an endless stream of cat videos, and someone could abduct her toddler, and she wouldn't even notice until it was too late."

"What is *wrong* with you?" Connor asked. "She's *seven*!"

"I know, but look at her. Clearly, she's addicted. They both are. Alan didn't want to give them phones until they were older, but all their friends had them, so I couldn't say no. Now I think he was probably right. It's going to melt their brains, and heaven help me when they hit the teen years."

"Listen to you," Connor said affectionately, wrapping an arm around her shoulders and giving her a tight squeeze. "What a good mama you are, all concerned about their welfare."

"Just wait until you have kids."

He raised both hands in the air. "Oh no. Not me. I'm never having kids."

"Oh, right. I forgot," she replied. "You'd have to enter into a committed, loving relationship in order for that to happen."

He wagged a finger at her. "Not so. I could follow in Dad's footsteps, have a few illegitimate rug rats, and never even have to meet them."

Sloane laid her hand on the tree trunk and frowned. "Do you think there were others, besides Fiona?"

"Who knows?" Connor replied. "Dad was a spectacular cornucopia of secrets."

They were quiet for a moment, standing in the shade of the olive tree. Sloane shrugged out of her blazer. "Have you seen her yet?"

"No, but the girl at reception said she checked in last night. They put her in room seven. Fourth floor."

"*Did* they now?" Sloane draped her blazer over her arm. "What do you think he left to her, anyway? The lawyer said it was a piece of property."

Connor slowly paced around on the grass. "Your guess is as good as mine. I don't even know what else he's accumulated lately. He was always picking up vineyards here, there, and everywhere in different regions, adding to the brand. Maybe he left her a little patch of something in Chianti territory. A cute little yellow house with green-painted shutters. Or maybe he left her a flat he bought for one of his mistresses. Or it could be one of the London properties."

Sloane frowned. "No. He wouldn't have. Do you think?"

Connor shrugged. "I don't know. He rewrote the will in the UK. Maybe that's why."

Sloane's mouth fell open slightly, and she inclined her head. "Connor. You don't think he would have left her the Belgravia house, do you? Where would we stay when we went there? Ruth lives all the way out in Richmond. Not with Aunt Mabel, surely. I'd rather stick needles in my eyes. Dad knew that."

Connor removed his sunglasses and polished the lenses. "Do you know what Aunt Mabel's house needs?"

"What?"

He put his sunglasses back on and squinted up at the sky. "A wrecking ball."

Sloane felt a little guilty for chuckling. "I can't disagree. At least it would get rid of the embarrassing eighties vibe she's got going on in the kitchen."

Connor looked down at the grass. "That would be cruel, though. Poor Aunt Mabel loves that moldy old dump."

"Some people just can't be helped."

Chloe laughed out loud and inched closer to her brother to show him something on her phone. Evan glanced at it, was unresponsive, then returned his attention to his own screen.

"Look, how adorable is that?" Connor said. "They're sharing. See? They're not complete social misfits."

"You're a skunk."

"No. That would imply that I smell bad, and we both know that I smell great today."

"Do you?" Sloane replied. "What is that you're wearing? Eau de Gigantic Inheritance?"

Connor sniffed his wrist and held it out to Sloane, who also sniffed it. "It's nice, you have to admit."

"Sure." Sloane glanced back at the villa, which stood majestically against the blue sky, and stared at it for a long time.

Connor watched her with some concern. He snapped his fingers in front of her face. "Earth to Sloane. You're not going to get all sentimental on me, are you?"

"And change my mind about selling?" she asked. Keenly aware of his scrutiny, she chose not to answer the question.

"Sloane!"

She turned to him. "What?"

"I don't like the look on your face."

"Why not?"

He narrowed his eyes, as if warning her, and she surrendered with a sigh of defeat.

"Are you sure about this?" she asked. "What if it's a mistake? Maybe we should think about it before we call the sales agent."

"No. We're not doing that. Are you insane?"

She shrugged. "I don't know . . . we had some good times here, didn't we? When we were kids? Don't you remember when Dad used to let you drive the tractor around the vineyards? And Maria . . . she was always so good to us. It was nice to see her after all these years. She looks good, don't you think? She put on a little weight, but otherwise she's aging well."

Connor placed his hand on Sloane's shoulder and squeezed it, none too gently. "You're just emotional after the funeral. Trust me, it will pass."

"Will it?" She raised an eyebrow as she touched the soft leaves of a low-hanging olive branch. "What if we keep the winery and run the business together? Think about it, Connor. It's a well-oiled machine with all the managers in place. His driver—what's his name? He said it would be business as usual without Dad here. They have everything under control. If we keep it, we could come here whenever we want, and our kids could get away from LA and learn something about farming and wine making and Italian cooking. It would be so much fun for them."

"You keep forgetting that I don't have kids," Connor said. "And if fun is what you want, you can use the proceeds from the sale to buy Chloe and Evan their very own theme park. It would be a hell of a lot closer to home, and you wouldn't have to deal with jet lag."

Sloane gave her brother a brutal stare. "I don't want to buy them a theme park."

"No? Then buy them a hobby farm or a petting zoo. Something where we don't have to work so hard to manage it. Come on, Sloane. Don't be an idiot. You hate having to work."

"Maybe. I don't know. It just makes me feel kind of dirty, liquidating our father's life's work for cash. Part of me would like for Chloe and Evan to come here for their vacations, like we did when we were their age."

"Sloane. We hated it here."

"Only when we were teenagers."

"Seriously, when was the last time you came here by choice? Right. Never. Dad always said there was an open invitation, but neither of us ever took him up on it."

"That's because *he* was here, and I was still mad at him about the divorce and what he did to Mom. But now he's *not* here."

"Ooh!" Connor laughed. "That was cold. So much for feeling sentimental."

"That's not what I meant," she said, covering her face with her hands. "What I meant to say is that . . . I regret that we let things fester, and now he's gone and there's no way to fix it. But that's beside the point." She lowered her hands to her sides.

"What is the point, exactly?"

"That I don't think we should rush into selling, and if you insist on it"—she paused and folded her arms—"I might have to fight you, because I feel like this winery should stay in the family."

Connor's head drew back in surprise. "Wow. I'm impressed. Is this big sister playing hardball?"

"Maybe."

He inclined his head. "You're assuming he left us equal portions. Maybe he left the winery to me and the Belgravia house to you. We don't know."

His crooked smile aroused in Sloane an irrepressible urge to smack him on the ear and fight like they used to do when they were children, when he'd yank her hair and she would scream at him, and they would end up wrestling on the floor until someone pulled them apart.

Sloane checked her watch. "We should probably go inside."

"Yep. It's time to cash in our chips."

Sloane called her children to follow them back to the house but found herself looking around with wonder at the rolling hills and valleys and the ancient stones on the back terrace as they made their way to the door.

She'd never truly appreciated any of this before. Admittedly, she'd been blind to it in her youth and had taken it for granted. And she had never really considered the yearly income from the wine business. She was aware that some of her father's bottles sold for $600 in LA restaurants. She was always quite proud of that, and Alan enjoyed mentioning it to his colleagues at business dinners—that Maurizio Wines belonged to his father-in-law.

Maybe it would make more sense financially to hold on to the winery. It would be more of a long-term plan.

With age comes wisdom, she thought to herself and wondered what ancient philosopher had said that. She would have to google it.

CHAPTER 4
FIONA

By the time Maria returned to the reception room, I was on my feet, looking at a display of black-and-white framed photographs on the table behind one of the sofas. I was quite certain I had identified my half siblings, Sloane and Connor, as children in one of the photos. They were posing in front of a row of grapevines with the sunlight at their backs, smiling. I wondered if Anton had taken the picture. All the other photographs were of people I didn't know and couldn't guess at. Many were headshots from the 1970s.

"Fiona, can you come with me now?" Maria was wringing her hands in the doorway.

With unsteady nerves, I followed her through another door that took us across a small outdoor courtyard. We crossed to the other side and reentered the house into a large reception room that overlooked the formal gardens on the east side of the villa. At the far end of the room, people were seated at an oval dining table. Everyone sat in silence.

I halted on the spot when all eyes turned to me and stared.

Unflinching, Maria approached the table and pulled out the last two empty chairs. "Everyone, this is Fiona Bell. Sit down here, Fiona, next to me."

I remained standing for a few seconds while Maria began introductions. "This is Connor, Anton's son."

My half brother.

He was slouched low in the chair with his head tipped back, staring up at the ceiling, looking bored. At the mention of his name, he lifted his head to offer me a salute from across the table, then stared up at the ceiling again.

Maria continued, gesturing to the attractive dark-haired woman sitting next to him. "This is Sloane, Anton's daughter."

"Good morning," Sloane said with a slight lift of her chin. She took in my overall appearance with eagle-eyed scrutiny.

"You've met Mrs. Wilson," Maria said. "And here, we have Anton's sister, Mabel, who is visiting us from London." Mabel was an elderly woman in a wheelchair. "Beside her is Ruth, her daughter."

"It's a pleasure to meet you, Fiona," Ruth said warmly.

"It's nice to meet you too," I replied.

Ruth leaned close to her mother and shouted in her ear, "She looks just like him, Mummy!"

Mabel frowned. "You don't need to shout!"

"These are the lawyers," Maria continued. "John Wainwright and Karen Miller."

"A pleasure, Fiona," Mr. Wainwright said. "Please take a seat, and we'll get started."

"Thank you." I sat down next to Maria at the table.

The lawyers arranged their papers in front of them and shut off the ringers on their phones. My heart began to pound as I felt everyone's eyes on me, staring with venom.

"Let's get started, shall we?" Mr. Wainwright said. "First of all, please accept our sincere condolences on the loss of a great man. He will be missed by everyone who knew him."

"What a beautiful sentiment," Connor said. "Thank you very much. We're incredibly touched."

Sloane slapped him on the shoulder, and I sensed an unease from everyone around the table. Even the lawyers seemed caught off guard by the interruption.

Mr. Wainwright cleared his throat and continued. "Mr. Clark's will is dated December seventh, 2015, and it was completed by me, in the presence of Mr. Clark at our offices on Fenchurch Street in London." He flipped a page. "So let us begin with the London properties. The house in Chelsea has been left to you, Mabel, along with three million pounds cash."

Ruth squeezed her mother's hand. "There, Mummy. Everything's going to be all right."

"The house on Eaton Square in Belgravia has been deeded to Connor and Sloane, as equal co-owners."

"Oh, thank God," Sloane said, her head falling forward onto the table with a noticeable clunk.

"See?" Connor said. "He knew how much you loved that house."

"I guess he did," she replied, sitting up again. "I can't tell you how relieved I am." She looked sharply at me.

Mr. Wainwright turned to Maria. "As for the properties here in Tuscany . . . Maria Guardini, you have been bequeathed the house in which you currently reside, along with six hectares of land and two hundred thousand euros."

Maria stared at him with wide eyes. "*Oh, mio Dio!*"

"Really? You're kidding me." Connor seemed taken aback but also strangely amused. "Way to go, Maria. That's awesome for you. Congrats."

Sloane pushed a lock of hair behind her ear. "That's wonderful, Maria. Well deserved."

Ruth handed Maria a tissue, which she used to dab at her tears.

"Connor and Sloane," Mr. Wainwright continued. "Out of the UK investment portfolio, your father has left you each three million pounds."

"Excellent," Connor said, sitting forward to rest his forearms on the table, his hands folded.

"Mrs. Wilson, he left you the Caravaggio painting that hangs over the fireplace in the main reception room."

Kate laughed bitterly. "Really. I begged him to give me that in the divorce settlement, but he flat out refused."

"Don't complain, Mom," Connor said. "You got it in the end."

She sat back and folded her arms. "Well, I'm glad to finally have it. I'm the one who suggested that he bid on it."

Mr. Wainwright flipped another page. "As for the business of Maurizio Wines, which includes the winery and all its inventory, buildings, and equipment, nine hundred hectares of land in Tuscany, and all its cash holdings—this has been bequeathed to Fiona Bell."

What did he just say?

The room fell silent, and my mouth went dry.

"What?" Connor shouted.

As if in slow motion, Mr. Wainwright picked up another sheet of paper from his stack of notes and flipped it over. In a bewildered daze, I stared at that sheet, like a leaf floating on air.

Connor stood up and pressed his open hands to the top of his head. "Tell me you didn't say what I think you said. I don't think I heard you correctly."

The lawyer repeated himself, and everyone continued to stare at me.

"That can't be right," Sloane said, unconvinced. "Why would he leave everything to her?"

I sat motionless, unable to utter a single word.

Connor glared at me maliciously. "What the hell did you do?"

"What do you mean?" I asked, still not accepting what was happening here. There had to be some mistake. Anton wouldn't have left me *everything*.

"You heard me," Connor replied. "What did you do?"

"I didn't do anything," I blurted out, defensively.

He turned his attention back to the lawyers. "This can't be right."

"I'm afraid it is," Mr. Wainwright replied. "Your father was very clear about his final wishes."

"With who?" Connor asked. "You? Were you there personally when he arrived at this decision?"

"No, but he was clear about it when he came to my office."

Connor shook his head with disbelief. "Was he drunk?"

"No, he was altogether sober and in his right mind, I assure you."

"How do you know that? Are you a doctor?"

Mr. Wainwright remained stoic. "I would testify in a court of law that he was in full possession of his faculties."

Connor turned to look at his mother, who sat across from him. "Mom. Do something. This can't be happening."

She blinked a few times. "What do you expect *me* to do? I'm just as shocked as you are. Your father never mentioned anything to me about changing his will, and I certainly didn't know anything about an illegitimate child he had." She glared at me accusingly. "How old are you? What year were you born?"

"Nineteen eighty-seven," I replied.

Mrs. Wilson scoffed heatedly. "We were still married then. We weren't yet divorced."

I fumbled for words. "I'm very sorry. I don't know what happened back then. All I know is that my mother spent a summer here—with my dad, her husband—and I was born in the United States after they went home."

Mrs. Wilson scoffed. "Unbelievable. Although I shouldn't be surprised."

"Of course you shouldn't," Sloane said. "You knew he was sleeping around when you were still married. It's why you left him."

They all looked at me again, as if it were my fault that their father was a depraved philanderer.

"Don't look at me," I finally said. "I'm innocent in all this."

"Are you?" Connor said. "I find that pretty hard to swallow."

"Why?" I asked. "Your parents divorced decades ago, and there's a woman upstairs right now who is just one of his recent girlfriends. The only thing that surprises me is that I'm the only illegitimate child sitting at this table this morning."

Mrs. Wilson stood up. "How dare you. He's not even cold in his grave."

I laughed out loud. "Seriously? I'm sorry. This is *really* weird."

She sat back down and turned to speak sweetly to the lawyer. "John. Surely you can understand that there's a problem here. If I had known it was going to turn out like this, I would have brought my own lawyers."

"It wouldn't have made any difference," Mr. Wainwright replied, matter-of-factly. "The will is valid."

She gave him an almost flirtatious sidelong glance, as if she could charm him into shifting things in her favor. But he remained silent, not swayed in the least.

"Did he tell you why?" she asked, her cheeks flushing red with frustration. "Did he explain why he would disinherit his own children for the sake of a child he never met?"

"He didn't disinherit them," John informed her. "He left them three million pounds each and the London house."

Mrs. Wilson exhaled sharply and laid a hand on her chest, as if she'd been insulted.

"That was pocket change to him," Connor informed everyone. "This winery is worth way more than that."

I was more than a little curious to know how much it was worth, exactly, but I didn't dare ask the question. It would be best, for the time being, to sit quietly and keep my mouth shut.

Connor sat back down. "We're going to fight this."

"I suspected as much," Mr. Wainwright said.

Sloane waved her hand frantically. "Wait a second. I'm sure this can be cleared up quite easily. It's my understanding that there are laws in Italy about what children must inherit. My husband looked into it before I got on the plane. He said it was called forced heirship, or something like that, and that we have to get at least sixty-six percent of his property in equal shares." Sloane pointed at me. "She's not an heir. She's illegitimate."

I was beginning to hate the sound of that word.

"That is true," Mr. Wainwright replied. "The Italian Civil Code protects close family members, but there was an EU law passed in 2015 that allowed your father, as a British national, to state that the laws of his own country would apply to his will. In the UK, a person is allowed testamentary freedom, meaning that he can do whatever he pleases with the assets of his estate. He could have left everything to charity if he wanted to."

Connor held out a hand, gesturing toward me. "Behold our charity case."

"Excuse me?" I said.

Maria took hold of my hand under the table and squeezed it. I met her gaze, and she shook her head at me.

"What I don't understand," Connor said to me, "is what happened between my father and your mother. Was she blackmailing him? Or were you?" His eyes bored into mine.

"Of course not!" I replied. "I never spoke to him once in my life!"

"Then how are we supposed to accept this?" Connor asked. "We never heard of a woman he knocked up thirty years ago. What was her name?"

"Lillian Bell," Mr. Wainwright said.

Connor turned to Maria for clarification. "She wasn't a part of his life, was she?"

Maria shrugged. "Not that I'm aware of."

The lawyer spoke matter-of-factly. "According to your father, there were letters."

Connor frowned. "Letters? What are you talking about? Love letters?"

"I don't know. He wouldn't say," Mr. Wainwright replied.

With a sudden burst of anger, Connor flung himself out of his chair, knocking it over, and strode to the window, where he stood with his hands on his hips, looking out. Everyone sat in silence, except for Sloane.

"He didn't give the letters to you for safekeeping?" she asked. "As evidence or something?"

"Evidence concerning one's final wishes isn't required for the writing of a will," Mr. Wainwright explained, doing his best, I thought, not to sound condescending.

"But he kept everything," Sloane replied. "Didn't he, Maria? I don't want to use the word *hoarder*, but he had trouble throwing things away. Obviously, these letters must have been important to him. They must be here somewhere."

Connor turned to face Mr. Wainwright. "What if this woman, Lillian Bell, *was* blackmailing him? That would be grounds for us to contest the will, wouldn't it?"

Mr. Wainwright turned in his chair. "Yes, it would be if that were the case. But you would have to prove it."

Connor strode forward. "If it's not blackmail, what other grounds would be necessary to overturn it? Undue influence? Duress? Fraud?"

"Yes, to all of those," Mr. Wainwright replied, "but your father gave no indication that he was being manipulated."

"Maybe he didn't realize it. Or if it was blackmail, he would have wanted to keep it under wraps for whatever reason."

Mr. Wainwright faced him squarely. "Connor, you can't contest a will with allegations like these simply because you feel it's unfair. There must be a valid legal reason, and to suggest what you are suggesting . . . you would need evidence to prove it. Compelling evidence."

"But you just said there were letters," Connor replied as he turned to everyone at the table. "I can tell all of you right now—I'm going to start asking some tough questions around here. Someone must know something." He pointed at me. "She probably does."

"I don't," I replied.

He chuckled bitterly. "Even if you did, you wouldn't tell us, not when you stand to inherit all of this." He gave me a seething look before he headed for the door. "I'm calling my lawyer."

Sloane stood up too. "That sounds like something I should be doing as well." She followed him out of the room.

Maria let out a breath. "Here we go." She sat forward and turned to the lawyers. "May I ask, Mr. Wainwright, if this will is overturned . . . is there an earlier will that would take its place?"

"Yes, there is," he replied. "It was filed about ten years ago."

"And did the children get the winery in that will?"

"Yes."

"I see." She paused and fiddled with an earring. "Please forgive me. I don't know how to ask this question without sounding self-serving, but in that version of the will, was the little villa left to me? And the money?"

He paused. "I'm afraid it was not. That was a recent addition made in the current will."

Her shoulders slumped a little, and in that moment, I suspected I had an ally, because Maria would not wish to lose what Anton had bequeathed to her. For the first time since my arrival in Tuscany, I didn't feel quite so alone.

CHAPTER 5

SLOANE

"How could he have done this?" Sloane asked when Connor ended the call to his lawyer and pitched his cell phone onto the sofa in his bedroom. "We're his own children. She's just some person he never even met. Did he hate us, Connor? Is that it? Is he punishing us because we didn't visit him often enough? Or was he trying to get back at Mom for what he lost in the divorce? Because she did take him to the cleaners. She admits it with pride."

Connor paced. "It's not as if Fiona came here to suck up to him. No way. There's something else going on here. She's coming off way too innocent." He thought about it for a moment, then waved his hands in the air and spoke in a high voice. "Oh, look at me. I'm a purehearted angel who knows nothing about my mother's slutty life before I was born. I don't know why in the world your father would leave everything to little ole me." Connor sneered. "Give me a break."

"She did seem overly defensive," Sloane replied. "She had a guilty look in her eye." Sloane sank onto a chair, buried her face in her hands, and exhaled heavily. "This isn't how I thought this day would go. I thought I would have a soft place to land in case things don't work out with Alan. You know what it's been like lately. I thought I could pack up the kids and move here to live, maybe travel back and forth between here and London. Start fresh."

Connor swung around. "Oh, come on. You're never going to leave Alan, and you know it."

Feeling like she had nothing left to lose, Sloane lifted her watery gaze. "I think he's having an affair."

Connor stared at her for a few seconds, then laughed. "Seriously, Sloane? Like this is a surprise to you?"

"Don't be a jerk."

"I'm not being a jerk. You knew he was a womanizer when you married him. And you must have known he was marrying you for *this*." Connor gestured toward the vineyards outside the window. "So don't pretend to be some innocent little virgin housewife who didn't know any better."

He was right. Even on her wedding day, Sloane had felt smothered by doubts and fears, and she had cried in the bathroom that morning before the hairdresser arrived. But she was so madly in love with Alan—rich, handsome Alan—and she wanted desperately to be loved and married and to have children and a beautiful, perfect life that all her friends would envy. It was what her mother wanted for her too. Her mother had walked into the bathroom and wiped Sloane's tears away and convinced her that everything would be fine. It would be different once they were married, her mother had said, and then she'd convinced her to go through with the ceremony.

Since then, Sloane felt her world continually caving in around her, because there were always other women. Last week she had dreamed of a thunderstorm where the roof of her house was struck by lightning and her attic was exposed.

"Why do you always have to be so mean?" she said to Connor. "Even when we were kids, you used to throw spiders at me."

"I'm not being mean," he said. "I'm being honest. And if divorcing Alan is what you have up your sleeve, why should you care that Dad cut us out of his will? Are you just insulted by the principle of the thing? Because you'll get at least twenty million in a divorce settlement, easy. I know how much Alan is worth."

"No, I won't," she replied, morosely. "I signed a prenup."

Connor frowned at her. "Are you joking? You didn't tell me that. You said he didn't want one."

"I lied."

"Sloane! What the hell?"

"Please stop. You're not helping. My life is imploding right now, and I thought this was my escape hatch. This morning, I had visions of leaving all the gossip about Alan behind in LA and coming here, where Maria would cook traditional Tuscan meals for the kids, and they would help harvest the grapes every September and learn how to speak Italian, and I wouldn't have to see or hear what Alan was doing with other women."

Connor pinched the bridge of his nose. "Oh, please, Sloane. You wouldn't last five minutes without your therapist and your personal trainer."

"Yes, I would," she insisted. "I think that's half the problem. I expect too much from myself. I keep paying other people to make me perfect and happy. But maybe there's no such thing as perfect, and I think I just need to eat some pasta and not worry about it."

Connor sat down and pressed the heels of his hands to his eyeballs. "I can't deal with this right now."

"Fine," Sloane said, standing quickly. "I'll go and take the kids for another walk."

He watched her head for the door. "You say that like it's a threat. *Oh no! I have to stop my poor sister from this terrible self-inflicted torture where she takes her kids outside to play!*"

"Like I said. Jerk." Sloane walked out.

Returning to her own room, she found Evan and Chloe sitting on opposite sides of the sofa, staring at their phones.

"Hey, you guys!" she sang cheerfully, smiling. "How about we go outside and see if the grapes look ready to harvest? Maybe we could help pick some."

Evan glared at her with contempt. "They don't need our help, Mom. And we don't know anything about grapes."

"But wouldn't it be fun to learn?" she suggested, full of enthusiasm.

"No." He looked back down at his phone.

"Chloe, how about you?" Sloane asked with a smile, speaking in a singsong voice, trying desperately to tempt her. "Want to go check out the vineyard?"

"Mom! We did that this morning," Chloe replied in that whiny tone of voice that made Sloane want to rip her own hair out.

What was wrong with her daughter? Didn't she understand how important it was to be charming and charismatic?

"Fine." Sloane turned on her heel. "I'll go and see what's cooking in the kitchen."

She left the room, ever hopeful that they would suddenly realize what they were missing out on and change their minds. But no one ever followed Sloane when she said *fine* and stormed out of a room. Alan especially. He always just let her go.

CHAPTER 6

FIONA

As soon as the lawyers packed up and left, Ruth rolled Mabel's wheelchair away from the table. She said they had a plane to catch and pushed her aunt out the door without a single glance back in my direction.

"They're not happy about this either," I said to Maria. "I can hardly blame them. No wonder they want to fight it."

"Yes, but you heard what Mr. Wainwright said. They can't fight it without clear evidence of blackmail or fraud or undue influence."

I leaned back in my chair and sighed. "My mother would never blackmail anyone. You should have seen how she cared for my dad every day of her life. She was a saint."

"Except for the fact that she was unfaithful to him," Maria gently reminded me. "Maybe you didn't know her as well as you thought you did."

I had no choice but to accept that Maria was right. "I don't know anything anymore," I said. "I didn't expect this to happen today. I thought I was just going to inherit some dinky little plot of land somewhere, maybe half an acre with a little house on it. Not the whole kit and caboodle." I sat forward again. "How much is this winery worth, anyway? The lawyer said there were nine hundred hectares. Is it all vineyards? Because that sounds like a lot of grapes."

"It's one of the largest and oldest wineries in Tuscany," Maria replied. "My husband said it's probably worth close to a hundred million euros."

I blinked a few times, then lost my breath. "What did you just say?"

"That's why Connor and Sloane want to fight this new version of the will. They've grown up thinking they would inherit the mother lode. Three million British pounds is a pittance compared to what they were expecting."

I barely heard a word Maria was saying about Connor and Sloane. I was too busy doing the math in my head.

One hundred million euros?

I had no idea that Anton Clark—my actual biological father—was worth *that* much money. Imagine what I could do with a windfall like that! I'd never again have to worry about falling short when it was time to pay Dottie or Dad's other home care workers. I'd give Dottie a raise so that she would stay with us forever. I could even have a life of my own, maybe get my own house and buy a new car. I could definitely pay off the wheelchair-accessible van we just purchased and get Dad a new computer with the very latest voice-recognition software. I'd get him all the bells and whistles. Maybe I would take him on a trip. His biggest bucket list item was to see Billy Joel in concert at Madison Square Garden. I could afford front-row seats!

I was starting to hyperventilate. I'd always felt a little guilty for keeping such a big secret from my dad all these years, even though it was for his own good, but surely this made it worthwhile. Never mind how I would explain the sudden change in our financial situation to Dad and Dottie when I got home. I'd figure out something.

Maria touched my shoulder. "Are you okay?"

"I'm not sure. I think I'm in shock."

"Me too," she replied. "I'll admit, I'm surprised he left you everything."

I looked up. "But why in the world would he do that?"

This was too much. *One hundred million euros.* I had to be careful. I couldn't let myself fall into the trap of thinking that I'd just struck it rich, only to learn later that it was all a big mistake and I was poor again. Certainly, it was fun to dream about buying a new house and taking Dad to see Billy Joel, but I needed to keep my feet on the ground in case this fell through in a few days' time.

Even if it didn't, wouldn't it make sense to share it with Connor and Sloane?

"The letters that the lawyer mentioned . . . ," I said.

"Maybe they explain what Anton was thinking," Maria suggested. "Maybe he really did love your mother. Maybe she was the great love of his life."

I shook my head at that notion, because I remembered the look on my mother's face when she told me I was another man's child. It was a look of regret and shame. At best, what happened between them was a one-night stand.

"Mom was only here for a summer while Dad was researching his book," I explained. "Wouldn't she have told me if she actually loved the man who was my real father?"

"Maybe not. Maybe she didn't want you to think she loved your father any less. The one who raised you, I mean."

"Fair enough." I stood up and moved toward a large gilt-framed portrait of a Georgian family on the wall. "But if Anton really loved her, wouldn't he have tried to fight for me or get to know me? Unless he never found out about me until . . ."

"Until your mother died," Maria suggested. "Maybe that's when she finally wrote to him, in those final hours, when she told you. Maybe that's the letter the lawyer was talking about."

"She wasn't well enough to write a letter," I replied, "and I was with her the whole time. Besides, the lawyer said 'letters,' which suggests there were more than one." I stared down at my open palms. "Either way, why would he cut his own children out of the bulk of his estate? Didn't he love them? I just don't understand it."

Maria stood and joined me in front of the painting. "I could probably shed some light on that part of it."

"Could you?"

"*Sì.*" She hesitated, and her cheeks flushed with color. "I don't like to gossip, Fiona, and who am I to judge? But I'll be honest . . . Connor and Sloane weren't exactly what I would call loving children. They were darlings when they were little, and I enjoyed having them come to stay, and I could forgive them for not wanting to visit when they were teenagers. They didn't want to leave their friends. That's natural. But I can't forgive them for staying away so completely as adults."

"There must have been some reason why they didn't want to visit."

"All I know is that Anton made every effort to stay in touch. He called and invited them, but they were too busy all the time. With what, I don't know. Neither of them has a job. But they didn't even humor him by suggesting they'd try to fit in a trip some other time. The only time Connor ever called was to ask for money. It was hard on Anton, and I believe he might have been testing them over the past few years. He gave them every opportunity to come and learn about the winery, but they always said no. I suspect that just confirmed to him the fact that they didn't care about him or this winery."

I turned to Maria. "So you think he might have wanted to teach them a lesson by giving everything to me? Or that he was being vengeful?"

"He certainly could be vindictive sometimes. He was ornery in the end. Reclusive."

"But why not teach *me* a lesson?" I asked. "Because I certainly wasn't a loving child."

Maria gave me a look. "Maybe it wasn't you he was thinking about when he rewrote the will."

I rubbed at the back of my neck. "You think it was my mother, for whatever reason. Guilt, maybe. Atonement?"

Maria shrugged. "Someone around here must know what happened between them."

I walked back to my chair, sat down, and drummed my fingers on the tabletop. "How did they even meet?"

I thought about Connor's accusations suddenly and felt a surge of panic. He was, at that very moment, calling lawyers and probably private detectives to help him prove his claim—that some crime had been committed, which would overturn the will.

What if my mother had threatened Anton in some way? What if this was going to get ugly and Connor was going to drag my mother's past into the spotlight or paint us as gold diggers? Maurizio Wines was a big name. It could be a juicy story back in the US.

Poor Dad. It would kill him to learn the truth that way.

"I feel a little nauseous," I said and put my head between my knees.

"Can I get you anything?"

"No. I think I just need to find the letters the lawyer was referring to. I need to find out what really happened." The sick feeling in my belly was still there, but I forced myself to sit up regardless. "Maybe you could help me with that?"

"*Sì*. I want to get to the bottom of it too." Maria began to tidy up the water jug and glasses. "Let me show you around the villa today. You should know what you've inherited. Later, I'll ask my husband to take you around the vineyards and show you the wine cellars."

"Thank you, Maria. I feel like you're my only friend right now."

She glanced at me meaningfully. "No one should be without friends."

After gathering the water glasses onto a tray, she carried them out of the room.

For a long while after she was gone, I sat alone, staring at the wall, thinking and reflecting. What were Connor and Sloane doing at that moment?

Probably not retreating. Not when there was €100 million at stake.

A terrible wave of guilt washed over me. What right did I have to take away their inheritances? Even if they were horrible, selfish children, I certainly wasn't any more deserving.

I really needed to understand what was happening here. Those letters needed to be found.

CHAPTER 7
LILLIAN

Tuscany, 1986

In the decades following that tragic summer in Tuscany, Lillian Bell often wondered: What if she'd had a crystal ball? Would she have canceled the trip? Or never suggested it in the first place? Or would she have given herself over to fate, regardless of the consequences?

In the spring of 1986, Lillian and Freddie Bell were living in Tallahassee, Florida, and heading into their fifth year of marriage. Admittedly, when Lillian had first met Freddie, she didn't have it all together. She had suffered a difficult upbringing with parents who were alcoholics in dead-end jobs they both hated. They stayed together "for the sake of the baby" when they should have split up at the outset, early into the marriage, because all they ever did was scream and fight and drink, then scream and fight and drink some more.

Lillian's father finally left when she was ten. She never saw him again, but rather than feeling frightened and abandoned, she'd wished he had left sooner. Or that her mother had been the one to leave.

Maybe it was something in her mother's DNA that made her stick by her husband, year after year, enduring verbal abuse and backhanded smacks to the face.

Or was it love? Lillian often wondered. Because her mother did have romantic feelings about Lillian's father, at least in the beginning. Her mother often reminisced about picnics in the park, chocolates and flowers, and a marriage proposal on a sandy beach at sunset while foamy waves rolled in.

Lillian had no idea if any of that ever really happened, but she cherished those stories regardless, because they made her believe in a fairy-tale world where grown-ups were happy together. That belief carried her through the dark times when her parents were smashing things in the kitchen at night and Lillian was hiding under her bed, whispering soothing words to her baby doll. "Don't be scared. I'm here. I'll protect you."

Later, after her father was long gone and Lillian began to date in high school, her mother advised her to avoid ham-fisted alpha males. "Marry someone soft," she said. "The kind of man who wouldn't hurt a flea."

And so, after a number of years dating the types who fell into the "hard" category and liked to smash things (like Lillian's face against a wall), she met Freddie Bell on a vacation in Florida. Disney World of all places. After standing in line for an hour to ride the Space Mountain roller coaster with two friends, she had been relegated to sit alone in the seat behind them. At the last second, Freddie hopped in beside her.

"Looks like we're a matched set of third wheels," he said with a shy smile. He was handsome and adorably boyish, and it felt like fate, and heaven knew she was a sucker for the idea of destiny. Why? Maybe, deep down, she relished the notion of not taking responsibility for major decisions. It was easier sometimes to go with the flow and simply let fate carry you along. Then you couldn't blame yourself when the river got angry and threw you up against a rock. It was simply your lot in life.

She and her friends spent the rest of the week in Disney World with Freddie and his group. A month later, she quit her waitressing job in Chicago and moved to Florida to be with him. She felt fortunate because he was gentle and endearing and he passed the all-important litmus test: he had slender hands that were made to hold a pencil, not punch a hole in a wall. He was creative—an intellectual who read books and wrote poetry. He'd even gone to college to study English.

Lillian was, to put it plainly, astounded by her good fortune. She had once heard that women often married carbon copies of their fathers, but she had vowed never to fall into that trap. After a few regrettable, abusive relationships in her teens and early twenties, she'd begun to dream about the polar opposite of her father. At long last, she had found it in Freddie.

Things moved quickly after that. She got pregnant (they thought they were being careful), so they tied the knot before anyone found out about their inability to use birth control effectively. Sadly, however, a month after the wedding, Lillian lost the baby.

A terrible year of grief followed in which she blamed herself for not protecting her unborn child, and she considered it the worst failure of her life. At one point, she told Freddie that she would understand if he wanted to part ways and start over with someone else, since they'd only gotten married because of the baby.

Freddie gaped at her in shock. "Lil, don't say that. I could never live without you." His face went pale, and he nearly worked himself into a panic.

Then Lillian remembered that he had his own issues with loss because his mother had walked out on his family when he was five, and he had never truly gotten over being left behind.

Lillian realized her mistake in suggesting such a thing and took him into her arms. "I'm sorry. I didn't mean it. I promise I won't ever leave you."

Her words reassured him, and over the next few years, she soldiered on, working the front desk at a local hotel, supporting them financially while Freddie pursued his lifelong dream of writing a bestselling novel.

But by 1986, Lillian couldn't escape the old familiar longings. She had always wanted to be a mother, but she had pushed that dream away after her miscarriage. Perhaps now the deep cut in her heart had finally healed enough to allow her the courage to try again.

She brought it up with Freddie on their fourth wedding anniversary, when they sat on a blanket on a beach in Tallahassee, watching the waves roll in. "So what do you think?" she asked.

Freddie thought about it for a moment before responding. "I don't know, Lil. It's a pretty big step. A huge responsibility."

"Kids usually are," she replied.

"But don't you think . . . I don't know. I feel like I should finish my book first. We don't even own a house."

Her heart squeezed with disappointment. "A house would be nice—I'd love that—but we can't afford it on my salary right now, and if we wait for everything to be perfect, we might end up waiting forever, and it'll be too late. I'm thirty now, and you know how much I've always wanted a baby."

"Of course I know." Freddie looked down. "And I want to have a family with you. I just want to be responsible about it. I want us to be ready for it financially."

"Money isn't everything," Lillian argued, feeling grim and not caring if she was being irresponsible. She wanted a baby more than anything, and she'd wasted so much time being afraid. "We'll figure it out somehow. We could get by."

"I don't want to just get by," Freddie replied. "I want to be able to support you and give us a good life, but how am I supposed to write if we have a baby to look after? You'd have to quit your job, and if I have to go to work, I'll never finish the book." He shook his head. "We've come so far. I'm almost there. If you could just be patient a little while longer, I'll get published, and then everything will fall into place. You'll be able to quit your job and be a stay-at-home mom, and we can live off the advance and royalties while I write another book."

Lillian watched the colors change in the sky over the Gulf. Freddie's dream was a lovely one, but how could she be sure it would ever come true? What if no one wanted to buy his book? Ever?

"I'm just afraid," she carefully said, "that it might take a while for you to find a publisher. You know I believe in you, but you've been working on your book for almost three years. You're only half-way done. Maybe we could just start trying and see what happens, and if I get pregnant, you could work super hard and finish before the baby comes. Maybe you just need a deadline. It might even help."

He was quiet for a moment, and she worried that she had just stomped all over his lifelong dream.

"I wish I could write faster," he said. "I wish that more than any-thing, but you know how it is. I spend so much time researching, and I can't skip that—otherwise, when I sit down at the typewriter, the words just won't come. The setting has to come alive for me." He shook his head in defeat. "Maybe I should just give up. I don't know anything about Italy. I'm starting to feel like a fraud."

Lillian inched closer to him on the blanket and linked her arm through his. "You're not a fraud. You're brilliant."

"You don't know that," he replied. "Maybe I'm just a no-talent hack."

She worked hard to lift his spirits and bolster his confidence. "Not a chance. And I'd be able to tell you for sure if only you'd let me read it. Just a few pages?"

He often talked to her about the plot, and she helped him brainstorm whenever he got stuck, but he had never let her see the words on the pages.

Freddie shook his head. "No. It's not ready for anyone to look at. It's a first draft, and it's rough, but I need to finish it completely before I can start polishing."

Lillian hugged her knees to her chest and tried to think of a way to help him finish faster.

"What if we went there?" she suggested, on a whim. "To the actual places where your scenes are set."

He looked at her with surprise. "To Italy?"

"Why not? I could ask my boss for a leave of absence, and we could spend the summer in Tuscany. I could get a seasonal job there. Imagine how amazing that would be." She thought about it for a moment and began to feel a sudden rush of excitement because she had never been to Europe before. She began to imagine castles and cobblestones . . . red wine with bread and pasta. And wasn't this the perfect time to travel? Before they settled down with children? "If my boss says no, it wouldn't matter. I could quit and find something else when we got back. There are lots of hotels around here."

"I don't know, Lil . . ."

She squeezed his shoulder and shook him. "Come on! Let's be adventurous! Wouldn't it help you to breathe in the atmosphere and walk the streets where your book is set? Imagine how confident you'd be when you sat down to write. You could finish it so much faster. Then we could start the life we've always wanted, with kids and a house and a real writing career for you."

He looked at her with disbelief. "Are you nuts? How would we pay for the flights?"

"My credit card," she replied. "I've kept up with the payments, and they keep increasing my limit. And we'll be getting the deposit back on our apartment when we finish the lease in May. It's almost as if the stars are aligning for us—as if this is meant to happen."

He regarded her with amazement. "You'd actually do that for me? Give up your job and max out your credit card?"

"Of course I would, because I believe in you, and I want you to finish the damn book so we can get pregnant." She nudged him playfully.

They sat and watched the sun dip below the horizon.

"This is crazy," Freddie said.

"Maybe it is," Lillian replied. "But something about this feels right, don't you think? Can't you feel it?"

"I don't know . . ."

"It's the setting for your book, which means everything to you," she reminded him. "You need to go there, Freddie."

"Maybe." He exhaled. "I'm just worried about how much it'll cost and how much work it'll take to organize a trip like that."

"Don't worry about any of that," she said. "I work in the hotel industry. I know a bunch of travel agents who can help us. I'll take care of all the details." She gazed out at the water and watched the whitecaps in the distance. "I don't know why, but I have a really good feeling about this. I think it's going to speed things up for you."

She couldn't deny that she had her own ulterior motive—to help him feel more ready to start a family. To beat down the excuses.

Freddie leaned toward her and kissed her on the cheek. "I'll make a promise to you right now. If we go to Tuscany and I finish my book, you can go off the pill the minute I type 'The End.'"

Lillian laughed. "I'm going to need that in writing."

She tackled him on the blanket and straddled him for a kiss.

~

Two months later, Lillian was bent over a gigantic map on her lap, trying to make sense of the narrow, twisting Tuscan roads as they found their way from a tiny apartment in Montepulciano to her new job at Maurizio Wines. It was her first day of training as a tour guide and front desk clerk at the inn. She had landed the job as soon as she and Freddie touched down in Rome, jet lagged from an overnight flight. While he was waiting for their bags at the carousel, she had wandered sleepily toward a bulletin board near the exit doors.

There it was—an advertisement for the most perfect job on the planet. Maurizio Wines was looking for an English-speaking American or Canadian for the summer season to cater to the North American tourists. Lillian knew right away that she was the perfect person for the job, having worked the front desk at a resort in Florida for the past four years. She ripped off the phone number, found a pay phone, and called for an interview.

The manager at the winery asked her a few questions and hired her without even checking her references. She ran back to Freddie, who was lifting their bags off the carousel, and shouted, "I got it!"

Three days later, they were on their way to the winery in a second-hand car they had purchased from an old repair shop.

"Take the next left," Lillian said, looking up from the map and scanning the rolling green countryside. They had just circled around the medieval hilltop town of Montepulciano and were now barreling down another twisty road at a terrifying speed. "And slow down!"

"It's not my fault," Freddie replied, glancing repeatedly into the rearview mirror. "It's that knucklehead behind me. He doesn't understand the concept of personal space."

The knucklehead—who drove a shiny red European sports car—roared into the opposite lane, ignoring the fact that they were on a curve. He sped past them and disappeared around another bend.

Freddie took his foot off the gas pedal. "Good riddance to you, buddy."

"He's going to get himself killed," Lillian said.

They continued up a steep, sloping road overlooking vineyards in all directions until they spotted what appeared to be a cluster of stone buildings at the top of the hill.

"That must be it." Freddie craned his neck to see out the side window, and that was all it took—a moment's distraction as they reached another hairpin turn.

"Freddie!"

He was too slow to respond. He didn't make the turn in time and overcompensated with a desperate tug at the steering wheel. Their tires skidded across the pavement, and they flipped sideways. Over they rolled, tumbling and bouncing down the steep, grassy mountainside.

Lillian was belted in, but she felt as if she were being flung about in dizzying circles. Glass shattered and steel collapsed all around them. Surely, the entire world was exploding in a violent, thunderous end to all existence.

When at last they slammed into a grove of poplars and the world went quiet and still, it took a few seconds for Lillian to wake from the shock of the crash and become aware of her heart pounding against her rib cage.

"Freddie?"

She felt no pain. Was she bleeding? No. She was alert. Hyperalert, in fact. Sparks of adrenaline shot through her veins like bullets.

"Freddie!"

He was slumped forward over the steering wheel, and his face was covered in blood. Fearing the worst, she reached out and touched his arm.

He lifted his head and groaned.

"Are you okay?" she asked. "Look at me."

He turned his befuddled gaze in her direction and cupped his nose with both hands. "I think I broke my nose."

The fact that he was speaking to her in full sentences was a good sign, so she unbuckled her seat belt, opened the car door, and found herself looking straight down the nearly vertical side of the forested mountain. Her stomach spun like a wheel.

"Oh my God. We have to get out on your side. Hurry. Get out!"

He fumbled to unbuckle his seat belt and fought to open the driver's side door, but it was mangled from their trip down the hill and wouldn't open. Overwhelmed with panic, he slammed his shoulder against it, but that only made the car rock back and forth, creaking and groaning.

"Stop!" Lillian shouted. "Don't move."

Just then, the back door on the driver's side swung open, and a man peered in at them. "Is everyone all right?" He spoke with a British accent.

Lillian was never so happy to see another human being in all her life. "I think so, but we can't open the door."

He glanced over the exterior of the vehicle, then peered in at them again. "Right. That door's finished. Can you climb over the seat, into the back, and come out this way?"

The man looked at Lillian as he spoke, but Freddie was first to scramble out of the driver's seat, crawl into the back, and spill out onto the steep slope at the man's feet.

Lillian crawled out next, her thoughts ablaze with the terrifying possibility that the poplars would bend and snap and the car would tip sideways and fall over the edge of the mountain before she could make it to safety.

"Give me your hand," the man said. "That's it. You're doing fine. Out you come."

She fell onto her hands and knees, never so happy to see blades of grass up close. Fisting big clumps of them in her hands, she shut her eyes, pressed her cheek to the ground, and breathed in the heady scent of the earth.

A hand came to rest on her back. "Are you hurt?"

She sat back on her heels. When she finally lifted her gaze, she saw Freddie rising unsteadily to his feet beside her and realized she was shaking uncontrollably.

The man who had come to their rescue knelt beside her. His green eyes studied her with concern. "Can you stand?"

"I think so. I'm just a little shaken up."

"No wonder." He helped her rise, then spoke to Freddie. "Are you all right as well?"

"I think so."

The man glanced up the steep slope. "My car is up there. Can you both make it up the hill?"

"I can do it," Lillian replied.

"Me too," Freddie said.

The man remained at Lillian's side, helping her stay balanced as she made her way up to the road and finally to a silver Mercedes convertible parked on the shoulder.

Lillian hobbled toward Freddie, who had reached the top first. "Are you okay?"

"I don't know." He was cupping his bloody nose.

"We should get you to a hospital," she said.

The man stayed close. "I can take you. It's not far. Hop in."

Lillian got into the front seat, and Freddie slid into the back. As the man turned the key in the ignition, Lillian shaded her eyes and pointed at the buildings on the hilltop. "That's where we were going. I'm supposed to start work there today."

"At the winery?"

"Yes."

It was madness to worry about her job at such a moment, when Freddie's nose was bleeding all over his trousers, but she obviously wasn't thinking clearly.

The man spoke with understanding. "It won't be a problem. That's my winery." He pulled onto the road. "What's your name?"

Lillian's heart skipped a beat, and she stammered, "Oh . . . that makes you my boss. I'm so sorry about this. I'm Lillian Bell. This is my husband, Freddie."

The man glanced at Freddie in the rearview mirror. "It's good to meet you both. I'm Anton Clark."

Lillian exhaled heavily. "Well, this is awkward, Mr. Clark. I swear, we weren't speeding or anything."

"No need to apologize," he replied as he turned the car around to head back toward Montepulciano. "You're not the first to run into trouble on this curve. I'll call a tow truck for you, but I think your car's probably beyond repair."

Freddie spoke with defeat. "Wonderful. We just spent everything we had on that car, Lil. We can't buy another. How am I going to do my research if I can't get around Tuscany?"

Mr. Clark interjected. "Where are you living?"

Lillian turned to him as he picked up speed, and the wind blew her hair in all directions. "We just rented an apartment for the summer. It's near the train station on the other side of Montepulciano."

Seeming unconcerned about their commitment to the landlord, Mr. Clark waved a hand. "It won't be a problem. You can stay on the property, at the winery. The shed is usually empty."

Freddie gave Lillian a quick look. "A shed?"

Mr. Clark looked at Freddie in the rearview mirror again and tried to explain. "It's not an actual 'shed' in the literal sense. We just call it that because it was part of a farm in a previous century, but now it's expanded and renovated for tourists. We usually keep one suite empty for overbookings or emergencies like this one. You're welcome to it, if you like. You'll be able to walk to work, Lillian, and Freddie, we might have a car you can borrow for your own purposes, until you make other arrangements."

Lillian turned in her seat to look at Freddie, who was wiping blood from his nose. "That sounds wonderful," she said. "Thank you."

"It's not a problem. I'll make a phone call and arrange for you to start tomorrow, Lillian, instead of today, if you're up to it."

"Thank you so much. I really appreciate this." She settled into the leather bucket seat and looked at the dashboard with fascination. She'd never been in a Mercedes before.

"I'm so sorry about all this," she said as Freddie buckled his seat belt behind her. "I'm sure you had better things to do today."

"Nothing that can't wait," Mr. Clark replied as he shifted gears and took them back toward town.

CHAPTER 8
FIONA

Tuscany, 2017

All I wanted to do was find those letters that my mother had allegedly written to Anton Clark, but Maria wanted to take me on a tour of the villa first. It began in the kitchen on the main floor, where Maria introduced me to the cook, Mrs. Dellucci. She was a heavyset woman in a white dress, a black apron, and white leather nurse's shoes, and she was busy kneading dough on a stainless steel worktable in the middle of the kitchen.

"This is Anton's daughter from America," Maria said. "Fiona Bell— the new owner of Maurizio Wines. Basically, Nora, she's our new boss."

Mrs. Dellucci stopped her kneading and spoke with disbelief. "He didn't leave it to the children?"

"She is one of his children," Maria reminded her. "We just didn't know about her."

Mrs. Dellucci turned to me with her arms outstretched. "What a happy day. It's so good to meet you." She pulled me into a snug embrace and didn't let go.

Maria touched Mrs. Dellucci's arm. "Easy, Nora, you're going to frighten her off."

"*Spiacente, spiacente*," she replied, smiling as she backed away.

Later, as Maria led me up a wide marble staircase, I asked, "Was I mistaken, or was Mrs. Dellucci relieved to hear that Connor and Sloane didn't inherit everything?"

Maria continued walking. "You're not mistaken. Everyone who works here was speculating about what would happen if the children took over. Most of the workers expected them to sell to the highest corporate bidder—who would immediately carpet-bomb all the vineyards with chemical insecticides. But if they had decided to keep it and run it themselves, I'm not sure who would have stayed around to work for them."

I paused at the top of the stairs. "They weren't popular, I take it?"

Maria shrugged. "They never kept in touch." She continued along a red-carpeted corridor and pointed at a closed door. "This is the entrance to the south wing," she whispered, "which is where Mrs. Wilson and the children are staying. It's always reserved for them, so we won't go that way this morning. Not while they're in there."

I didn't argue, but I slowed down to listen as I passed by the door. Connor and Sloane were speaking in hushed, angry tones, about the contents of the will, no doubt. I felt inclined to tiptoe softly down the rest of the corridor.

We came to another closed door at the end, and Maria put her ear to it as she knocked. No one answered, so she knocked again. "*C'è qualcuno lì dentro?*" Before she opened the door, she turned to me. "This was your father's room."

I felt a deep shudder from within. I had never met my real father in person, but I was about to step into his private bedroom, where he had slept every night of his life.

"Just so you know," Maria whispered respectfully, "this was where he died. He got out of bed in the morning, not feeling well, and collapsed on the floor. Sofia was with him."

"His girlfriend . . . ," I said.

"*Sì*, but now we'll need to find a polite way to get rid of her, since she wasn't mentioned in the will." Seeming unfazed by that notion, Maria knocked again as she opened the door. "Sofia, are you here? It's Maria and Fiona."

The room was empty, but Sofia's clothes were strewn all over the floor and upon the four-poster bed, as if she had just tried on every outfit she owned and tossed all the rejects aside. Perfume bottles and makeup brushes covered every available space on the mirrored vanity in the corner of the room. It smelled of hair spray.

"I gave up trying to pick up after her," Maria said, stepping over high-heeled shoes and silk scarves on the floor. "She's a grown woman, not a child."

"Where do you think she went?" I asked.

"Probably shopping. If we're lucky, she went shopping for another man to support her."

I moved to the bed and ran my fingers along the heavy oak foot-board. My gaze fell to the mattress beneath a crimson comforter and half a dozen decorative pillows. Had my mother spent time in this room? Was this the place of my conception?

"It's strange to be in here," I said.

"No doubt." Maria couldn't seem to help herself. She began to pick clothes up off the floor and hang them neatly in the wardrobe.

I moved to one of the bedside tables and opened a drawer. Inside, I found scented lotions, a cell phone charger, a nail file, and a book of matches. I bent to peer deeper into the back of the drawer.

"Looking for something?" Maria asked.

Feeling like a criminal, I shut the drawer. "Sorry. I shouldn't be snooping."

"Don't apologize. It's your house," Maria reminded me.

"I suppose it is. At least for now."

While Maria tidied up, I opened a few more drawers and rifled through an old shoebox on the top shelf inside the wardrobe. It contained store receipts.

"Sloane said that Anton was a hoarder," I mentioned. "But this room doesn't seem that bad."

Maria responded with a dismissive scoff. "Sloane was exaggerating. I'll admit, Anton's study could be a catchall for books and papers. It was always a challenge to dust in there, and his studio hasn't been cleaned out in decades, but for the most part, he was fairly organized."

"His studio?" I asked. "What sort of studio?"

I jumped as my cell phone rang in my back pocket. Quickly, I pulled it out. "It's a local number. Hello?"

"Is this Fiona Bell?"

"*Sì.*" I wandered to the window and gazed out at the pristine Italian gardens below and the rolling hills and mountains in the distance.

"*Ah, bene.* I'm calling from the Mancini Bank in Montepulciano. We just received a copy of your father's will. I'm very sorry for your loss. We understand that you arrived in Italy yesterday?"

"Yes, that's correct."

The gentleman paused. "Just to be clear, we're not the bank he used for his financial accounts, so that's not what this is about. I am calling because he kept a safety-deposit box here with us, and we have instructions to contact you about the contents in the event of his death."

A spark of adrenaline lit in my veins. "Do you know what's inside the box?" *Is it the letters?*

"No, I don't have that information," he replied. "It was a private box, but I do have the key, which I've been instructed to turn over to you. When do you think you might be able to come by?"

I checked my watch. "How about this afternoon? Where are you, and what time do you close?"

"We've just closed for lunch," he explained, "but we reopen at three. We're in Montepulciano, not far from Piazza Grande." The gentleman provided the street address, which I repeated to Maria.

"It's not far," she said. "Marco can drive you."

"Perfect." I made an appointment for three o'clock, then Maria insisted that I come down to the kitchen for something to eat before I left.

~

"Cars aren't allowed into the town," Marco said, "so I'll drop you off here." He pulled over in front of a restaurant with an outdoor patio. "If you walk straight ahead, you'll reach the piazza. Turn right and go down the hill next to Contucci Palace. You have your map?"

"Yes, thank you. I should be able to find it." I opened the car door and got out.

"Take your time," Marco said. "I'll wait right here."

I thanked Marco again and started walking, careful not to stumble across the cobblestones while I gaped in awe at the magnificent stone architecture on either side of the narrow lane.

When I reached Piazza Grande, I stopped and wanted to pinch myself, for I stood before the Palazzo Comunale, an impressive town hall with an imposing clock tower, and Santa Maria Assunta, an ancient cathedral to my right. Children played games in the center of the square, and sidewalk cafés were busy with tourists.

"Is this even real?" I said to myself as I crossed the sunlit square.

Beyond Contucci Palace, the cobblestone streets were narrow, steep, and winding. It was easy to lose my sense of direction, but I soon found my way to the little bank and ventured inside.

It wasn't anything like the banks back home. The tellers stood behind an ornately carved walnut counter, and the floors were stone. I felt as if I'd stepped into another century.

"Hello," I said to the first teller who looked up and smiled at me. "I'm Fiona Bell. I'm here about a safety-deposit box."

The young woman perked up. "Ah, *si*. You're Anton Clark's daughter. I'll tell the manager you're here."

She disappeared into a back office, then reappeared with an older gentleman wearing a suit and tie. "Ms. Bell. What an honor. Thank you for coming at such a difficult time." He laid a hand over his heart. "Your father entrusted me personally with the task of guarding the key to the box and handing it over to you." He passed me a small envelope. "If you will follow me, I'll take you to the vault."

Other than the letters, I hadn't considered what else might be inside the box. The fact that I'd received the phone call from the bank so quickly after my arrival in Italy made me wonder if Anton had predicted Connor's and Sloane's combative reactions and had taken the necessary steps to ensure that the letters didn't fall into their hands. With such a tremendous amount of money at stake, he must have known they would make every effort to repeal his wishes. But who knew what else might be inside the box?

I followed the bank manager down a set of steep stone steps to a vault on the lower level. He removed the steel container from a locked cubbyhole and placed it on a table. "I will leave you alone," he said, amiably. "When you're finished, you can lock the box again and leave it here on the table. I will wait just outside."

"*Grazie*," I replied.

He walked out and closed the door behind him.

For a moment, I stared at the box. It was rectangular, long, and flat. Not very large but certainly big enough to hold a stack of letters.

Burning with curiosity, I reached into the envelope for the key and unlocked the box. I raised the lid on squeaky hinges but found it to be empty.

I spoke in a low voice. "Anton. Maybe you're getting back at me as well—for ignoring you all these years."

Lifting the box to carry outside to the manager—to let him know that it was empty and to ask if anyone else had a key—I noticed that something went clank at the back. My heart did a flip, and I reached deep inside to feel around. Right away, my fingers touched upon a cold, hard object. I pulled it out.

It was another key—a wrought iron, medieval-looking work of art.

I shook the box to make sure there wasn't anything else I had missed, but this was it.

"You couldn't have included a note with this?" I whispered to the ghost of my late father and wondered what keyhole it belonged to.

~

A short while later, I returned to Piazza Grande and found Marco waiting for me in the shiny black Mercedes.

"How did it go?" he asked as I got into the passenger seat and shut the door.

"Fine," I replied. "He left me this." I pulled the key out of my purse and passed it to him. "Do you have any idea what it's for? Maybe an old chest? A secret room?"

Marco held it in his hands and examined it closely. "This is a very old key, Fiona. Too big for a chest, I think. It does not look familiar, but I was just Anton's driver." He handed it back. "Maybe Maria will know. Or her husband. Or Connor or Sloane."

I slipped the key back into my purse. "If you don't mind, I'd rather not mention it to Connor or Sloane. We're not exactly playing on the same team right now, if you get my drift."

Marco started the engine. "I do. They're not happy about the will. I won't say a word."

"Thank you, Marco. I appreciate that."

He turned the car around, and we drove back down the hillside.

CHAPTER 9

LILLIAN

Tuscany, 1986

"The shed" was one of three stone buildings that each contained luxurious guest suites. Lillian and Freddie would occupy suite number two—a two-bedroom, two-level apartment with a kitchenette, two luxury bathrooms, and a sitting room. There was a small car park outside beneath an overhang, an olive orchard on a terrace below, and, from the kitchen window at the back, a magnificent view of the hilltop town of Montepulciano, high in the clouds. The suite also came with weekly maid service.

After the accident, Mr. Clark had dropped Lillian and Freddie off at the hospital, then handed Lillian a business card with a phone number for the winery's shuttle service, which would pick them up whenever they were ready to leave the hospital.

Now, at last, after a long, exhausting day, they were finally settled into bed for the night.

Lillian lay on her back, gazing up at the ceiling fan. "I feel like we were given a second chance today, and we can't take it for granted."

"How do you mean?" Freddie asked.

She wondered how he could not recognize the magnitude of what they'd just experienced.

"I mean"—she propped herself up on an elbow—"we could have been killed this morning. Do you know how lucky we were that those trees were there? If not for them, we would have gone straight over the edge and down five hundred feet."

Freddie rolled onto his side, facing the other direction. "But it didn't happen. We're fine and it all worked out, so you shouldn't worry about it."

Did he think she was complaining?

"I'm not worrying," she replied defensively. "I'm thankful."

"Me too. But can we put it behind us? I really don't want to think about it, Lil. Would you mind turning off the light?"

She stared at him for a moment, frustrated and dissatisfied, then said, "Sure."

Lillian rolled over to tug the little chain on the lamp. As soon as darkness descended, she lay with her back to Freddie, listening to the sound of crickets chirping in the grass outside the open window. The fresh scent of the country air filled her with a strange, unfamiliar euphoria as she gazed out at the full moon.

She didn't want to think about the accident either. It had been a terrifying, harrowing experience. But she *did* want to think about how lucky they were to be alive. What a wonder it was—that she was lying in a cozy bed with no broken bones, no skin lacerations or internal bleeding. Freddie's nose wasn't broken. He was just a little banged up. Lillian was comfortable and warm, gazing up at a dazzling moon and a bright, starry sky.

A fresh breeze billowed the white, gauzy drapes, and she let out a sigh, for the world was more beautiful to her than she had ever known it to be. Whether it was some sort of spiritual awakening brought on by the accident or simply the beauty of this place, she didn't know. Either way, she was inexplicably overcome by the night's magic.

~

Lillian began her first day of training the morning after she and Freddie moved into the shed. From there, it was an easy walk up a gravel lane through the forest to the main winery facilities, where the gift shop served as a reception area for tour guests.

The senior tour guide was a handsome young Tuscan by the name of Matteo. He was happy to have an American take over the English-language tours, which never went well for him due to his thick Italian accent and his tendency to speak too quickly.

After a week, Lillian felt only somewhat confident in her basic knowledge of the wine-making process, but Matteo assured her it would be adequate for the majority of tourists, who knew very little about it.

"What happens if I get a professional winemaker from Napa who knows more than I do?" she asked.

"All you can do is your best," Matteo replied. "If you can't answer a question, be honest and refer that person to me. But if he's in the business, Mr. Clark will probably want to meet him anyway, so just pass him up the chain, and we'll take it from there."

"Got it."

When Lillian finally began conducting daily tours on her own, Freddie established a habit of driving to Florence and Siena to visit churches and art museums, then write in different coffee shops. At night he sat at the desk in the upstairs bedroom, clicking away on his portable electric typewriter, working on revisions, until well past midnight. It was wonderful that he was so focused and inspired, and Lillian knew enough not to disturb him when the creative juices were flowing. She brought him meals on a tray, and she kept the volume low on the television.

She didn't mind doing those things. She was pleased and proud of Freddie and wanted to support him, because all she'd ever wanted over the past few years was for him to finish his book so that they could start living a normal life. Now, at last, he was getting somewhere.

He slipped into bed one night and shook her awake. She had been up early that morning and realized she had fallen asleep with the lights on.

"Lillian," he whispered, leaning over her. "You were right. Coming here was the best thing ever. It was exactly what I needed. The plot's really coming together. There's just something about this place. Don't you think?"

She rubbed her eyes and fought her way out of sleep. "Yes. Definitely. I'm glad it's working for you."

"It is. Love you." He gave her a quick peck on the cheek, then rolled to his side, facing away from her. "Could you shut off the light? I want to get an early start tomorrow."

"Sure." Lillian tugged the little chain on the lamp, and the room went dark.

~

After two weeks on the job at Maurizio Wines, Lillian had not seen or encountered the owner, Anton Clark, since the day he'd rescued her and Freddie from the wrecked car. Then one day, seemingly out of nowhere, he appeared in the vineyard and joined a tour group just as she was beginning her talk.

The sight of him caused her belly to burst into nervous flames because she wasn't completely confident in her position yet. There was still so much she didn't know about wine making. She wondered if she should introduce him to the group. She was about to do just that when he raised a finger to his lips and shook his head, as if to say, *Shh.*

"This particular vineyard," Lillian said without missing a beat, "is thirty years old. The grapes are Sangiovese, which are used in many of the winery's most popular blends."

She continued her memorized speech about the time it took to grow and harvest the grapes, then answered questions and led the group out of the vineyard and up the steep gravel lane toward the chapel and cellars.

"If you'll follow me this way," she said, "we'll step inside the ancient Maurizio wine cellars, which have been used for the aging of red and white wine in oak barrels since the medieval period, when the family acquired the estate."

There was a murmur of anticipation from the group. As she continued along, a young man wearing a red leather jacket, with too much gel in his spiky hair, pushed his way to the front to ask a question. "How much wine do you sell in the US?"

"That's an excellent question," Lillian replied. "In total, the winery produces about five hundred thousand bottles each year, and most are sold in Europe and the UK. Only about ten thousand are shipped to America."

"Cool," he replied. "I've never heard of this wine before, but now that I've been here, I'll look for it. My girlfriend likes red wine. Do you sell any in Arizona? That's where I'm from."

"I'm not sure about that," she replied. "What's your name?"

"Bobby."

"It's nice to meet you, Bobby. I can certainly find out for you after the tour is over. But when you get home, take a look around your local wine shops and request it if you don't see it. It can easily be ordered from any reputable distributor. Or you can buy a bottle while you're here and take it home with you on the plane. I'll recommend something very nice for your girlfriend."

"Cool," he said.

Lillian remained focused on the tour group, even while she was unnerved by her boss following along, listening and watching, taking mental notes, judging her performance. She wanted to do well and prayed she wouldn't receive any difficult questions she couldn't answer.

When they reached the door to the wine cellars, she unlocked it and directed everyone down a set of circular stairs. Mr. Clark was the last to enter, and he nodded as he passed by.

"Excellent tour so far," he said.

She felt some of the nervous tension come loose in her shoulders and let out a breath of relief. Then she followed the group down to the damp gloom of the wine cellars with their vaulted stone ceilings, moldy walls, and gigantic oak barrels.

"Smells musty down here," Bobby said as Lillian moved through the group to begin the next portion of the tour.

"Yes, but that's a good thing," she replied, pointing at the black ceilings. "The walls are covered in mold, but don't worry. It's not toxic. It's caused by the evaporation of the wine from the barrels." She moved to one of the oak barrels and laid her hand on the side of it. "Here, we age the wine for two years. In this room, we have Austrian oak barrels, which give a spicy finish to the wines, while the French oak barrels in the next room give a vanilla flavor. When we bottle the wines, we can blend them, then we store the bottles in another area of our cellars to age them longer still."

"How long?" an older man asked.

"It depends on the type of wine it is," she replied, "and what we use it for or how patient we are. Sometimes it's difficult to wait for something that gives you pleasure. Wouldn't you agree?"

A few members of the group chuckled softly.

She described the bottling process, answered more questions, and then took the group into the wine library. "Here we have the family's private collection. Some of the older bottles are from 1943, made from grapes that were harvested at the beginning of World War Two. It is being kept for its historical value."

"Why are all the bottles so dusty and moldy?" a young woman asked, looking horrified. "Can't you get someone down here to clean them?"

"We don't clean them," Lillian replied, "because we want to keep them still so that the sediment doesn't move around inside the bottle. That would affect the flavor. But when it's time to open a bottle, we clean it up and put a clean label on it so it's just like new."

She finished the tour and led the group up another circular stone staircase to a medieval-style tasting room. Lillian presented three bottles of different red wines from the collections, described each one, poured a glass for each member of the group, and taught them how to swirl the wine, look at it and identify the "legs," then stick their noses into the glass and attempt to describe the aromas and flavors. She did not sample the wines herself. She had done that during her training, but Mr. Clark sipped the wines while he listened to everyone's comments and reactions.

After the final bottle was emptied and the guests began to socialize, Mr. Clark discreetly left the room through the side door. Lillian exhaled heavily, thankful to have made it through his impromptu performance review.

Later, after she sold a few cases of wine in the gift shop and said good-bye to each member of the group, she balanced the cash register, tidied up, and prepared to close the shop for the day. She was just about to leave when Mr. Clark entered through a door at the back.

"Well done today," he said, causing her to jump. "I'm sorry, I didn't mean to startle you."

"You didn't. I mean . . . yes, you did, but it's fine."

He approached the counter, and Lillian slung her purse over her shoulder.

"I appreciate you coming," she said, "although I will be the first to admit that you made me a little nervous."

"It didn't show. You did well. Have you been all right since the accident?"

"Yes," she replied. "And Freddie's fine too. We were just a bit stiff and achy for a few days."

He watched her move out from behind the counter. "And is the guest suite working out for you?" he asked. "Do you have everything you need?"

"Yes. It's more than we could ever ask for. Thank you so much for letting us stay there and for what you did for us that day."

"I was happy to help. And the car's working out fine?"

"Good golly, yes. Freddie's absolutely thrilled and driving all over Tuscany, writing up a storm."

"Writing?"

She wished suddenly that she hadn't said that. She didn't want to bore Mr. Clark with details about her personal life. "Yes, it's why we're here," she explained. "So that he can finish a novel he's been working on. It's set in Tuscany."

"A novel. Interesting," Mr. Clark said. "I had no idea he was a writer. Does he have a publisher?"

"Not yet," she replied, "but he's working on that, waiting to hear back from a couple of agents who requested the full manuscript. He just needs to finish it so that he can send it to them."

"Good luck to him."

"Thank you."

They stood on the carpet in the middle of the gift shop for a few seconds.

"Do you have to go back now?" Mr. Clark asked. "Is he waiting for you?"

Slightly unnerved by the question, Lillian inclined her head. "Um . . . no. Freddie went to Siena for the day. He probably won't be home until after dark. Why?"

Mr. Clark studied her face. "Because I'd like to show you a few things that we could add to the tour narrative. Maybe tailor it to the Americans. You're from Florida, correct?"

"Yes," she replied, "but from Chicago originally."

"Even better. Do you have some time right now to learn a bit more about wine?"

She pursed her lips. "Will this involve drinking it? Because I'm still on the clock." She tapped a finger on her watch. "I'm not sure if the boss would approve."

A slow grin played at the corners of his mouth. "I can have a word with him if he complains. Maybe pull a few strings."

Lillian laughed. "In that case, I'm always eager to learn."

"Right then," he replied with enthusiasm and a strong clap of his hands. "Let's start in the vineyard."

She followed Mr. Clark outside, where he took her in a southerly direction across a fragrant rose garden with a stone fountain in the center. On the far side of the garden, they walked up a set of ancient stone steps to a higher terrace, where they looked up at a steep slope containing straight, narrow rows of young vines. The top of the field was nearly two hundred feet higher than the spot on which they stood.

"The vineyard where you start the tour," Mr. Clark said, "was planted by the Maurizio family. It produces quality Sangiovese grapes. No question. But this one is all mine. It's new, and it's a merlot."

Lillian considered this with confusion. "Merlot . . . isn't that a French wine?"

"Yes. And I have cabernet sauvignon planted on the southwest-facing field over there." He pointed. "But what does it matter if it tastes like nothing you've ever experienced? And this was the perfect spot for it, with good soil, plenty of minerals, and cool breezes in the afternoons. It was a risk, I admit, but I wanted to try something new."

He knelt and scooped up a handful of dirt, rubbed it into his open palm, then sniffed it. He stood up again and held it out to Lillian. She sniffed it as well.

"There's a lot of clay here," he said, "which is why the family ignored this plot. But we'll see what we can do. It'll be an interesting harvest this year. The workers are placing bets about it."

Lillian chuckled. "Can I get in on that?"

He smiled in return. "If you like."

The sun touched the horizon in the distance. An evening mist was beginning to roll into the valley.

"You keep referring to the Maurizio family," Lillian said, "and every day I show their private collection to the tourists, but you're obviously British. I know that you own this winery, so if you don't mind my asking, what is your relationship to the Maurizios?"

She and Mr. Clark started back toward the rose garden. "Nothing, really," he said, "except that I purchased the winery from the last living relative five years ago, after the owner passed away. Sadly, he outlived all his children, so there was no one to take over, except for the employees who had been managing the operation for years. They were happy to have a new buyer on the scene, to keep the business running."

"You're not tempted to change the name to Clark Wines?" she asked. "Or to put your own stamp on it somehow?"

"That's exactly what I'm doing with that new vineyard I just showed you. So I will put my own stamp on it, but I won't change the name. This winery is an important part of Italy's history."

They returned to the main parking lot and continued walking up the hill toward the chapel.

"What about your family?" she asked. "Do you have children to help you run things?"

"I do have children," he replied, "but they're too young to help out. They're only two and four years old."

"Oh. That's wonderful. They must love living here."

He shrugged. "I don't know yet. They're in California with my wife. She's American, and she prefers LA over Tuscany. I can't seem to convince her to stay here more than a few weeks at a time."

Lillian considered this and watched his expression as they walked slowly up the hill. "But you prefer it here? Even though you're from the UK?"

He gazed up at the sky. "That's another story altogether, and it requires wine. We should go and get a couple of bottles out of the cellar. I want you to taste something outside of the current inventory. I want you to have a better understanding."

"A better understanding of what?" she asked, wondering if he was going to share more about what had brought him to Italy.

"Wine," he replied, as if she had missed something.

She followed him through the pinkish glow of the setting sun toward the wine cellars across from the chapel. Together, they descended the circular staircase to the cavernous gloom belowground. Mr. Clark switched on the lights. The air smelled of oak and wine.

"What do you think?" he asked. "We could try something from a decade ago or go back even further, maybe to the 1950s. It's risky, though. About twenty-five percent of those old bottles are no good. We'll be taking our chances."

He inspected a few different sections of the wine library and selected two bottles. Then he moved deeper into another area and stopped outside a medieval-looking arched door.

"The tour groups don't come in here," he told Lillian with a sly grin as he dug into his pocket for his key ring. He unlocked the door, which creaked on ancient hinges as he opened it. Then he led her into a small room and switched on a light. A few hundred dust-covered bottles were stacked up against each wall, resting on wooden slabs.

"I didn't know this little cellar existed," Lillian said.

Mr. Clark gave her a moment to look around, then spoke in a quieter voice. "When you're leading the tour out there and you talk about the family's private collection, that's just for show. This is the *real* private collection."

Small wooden plaques hung on the walls above each stack. The plaques indicated a name and a year.

"These were gifts for the Maurizio children," Mr. Clark explained. "Whenever a child was born, one hundred bottles were set aside from that year's harvest. The intention was for them to begin aging so that the child could enjoy the wine later in life, on special occasions. As you can see, some of the children enjoyed their wine quite a bit while they lived. But look at this one." He pointed at the largest stack. The plaque said **LORENZO, 1920**. "All one hundred bottles are still here. I looked into it, and this man lived to be fifty-seven, but he never opened a single bottle. I wonder what he was waiting for."

"Maybe he didn't drink," Lillian suggested. "Or maybe he was a wayward son who wasn't close to the family. Either way, it's sad. Especially for the father, to have outlived all his children and to know that they didn't get to enjoy every last drop of the wine he had left them. Or that they chose not to enjoy every delicious drop of life when they had the chance."

"Exactly," Mr. Clark said.

Suddenly, Lillian felt a shiver run down her spine. She rubbed at her arms to warm herself. "It feels like a tomb in here."

He turned to her. "You're right. It does. Maybe I shouldn't have presumed . . ."

"No, don't apologize. I'm glad you brought me here. I'm honored to see it, especially after . . ."

She stopped herself, because she didn't want to become maudlin or overly philosophical about the car accident. Freddie certainly hadn't wanted to talk about it. He kept shutting the conversation down whenever she brought it up.

"You're thinking about what happened to you when you went off the road," Mr. Clark conjectured.

Lillian dropped her gaze. "Is it that obvious?"

"Maybe. To me, anyway." He shrugged a shoulder. "Maybe that's why I brought you here. Because I've been thinking about it myself, quite a bit."

"Really? Why?"

"I'm not sure. There was just something about the way you fell to your knees when you climbed out of the car. You seemed so grateful to be alive. It was . . . I don't know . . . humbling to see that. We should all be so grateful. Every day."

She felt a rush of emotion. "Yes, and I *have* been feeling immensely grateful. More than that. I feel different. Like it changed me somehow. Now I can't seem to take my eyes off the moon at night or the way the mist rolls between the hills in the early hours of the morning. Just looking at the world makes me feel euphoric. I've never felt such joy before. I can't begin to explain it."

He smiled with understanding. "I once read that people who are going through cancer treatment sometimes feel like the disease was a gift, no matter the outcome, whether they beat it or not, because they feel like their spirits are awakened." He grew quiet and contemplative for a moment. "I'm not sure if I would consider it a gift, myself, because I already feel in awe of the world most of the time, and I don't want to leave it anytime soon. But who knows what I have yet to learn? Socrates believed that true knowledge exists in knowing that you know nothing. So I guess I'm still just a student of life. Always will be."

Lillian marveled at the way he spoke about spiritual awakenings and true knowledge. Freddie never spoke that way, even though he considered himself to be a poet. He was very good at rhythm and rhyme, but she couldn't say that he ever wrote deeply about the heart or the soul. A touch of guilt struck her suddenly for comparing Freddie to Mr. Clark, but she supposed none of that had occurred to her in the past because she had never been terribly spiritual herself. At least not before now.

"I'm learning too," she said.

Mr. Clark moved closer to Lorenzo's section—the tallest stack of bottles, which had never been touched by the man who was no longer alive to claim them. "Maybe we should drink one of these."

Lillian glanced all around. "Are you sure?"

"Why not? They'll just go to waste otherwise."

"Have you ever opened any of these?"

"Not yet. I've owned the winery for five years, but I couldn't bring myself to touch them. I always felt like it would be a violation of the sanctity of this room. But life is meant to be enjoyed, don't you think? As long as we're not hurting anyone."

"Yes, I believe it is," Lillian replied. "And I think that if Lorenzo were here, he would tell us to drink up his wine and not squander it. Not to squander anything. You can't take it with you, right? And you never know when it will come to an end, in the blink of an eye."

Mr. Clark considered that. "Why do we always wait for traditional special occasions to enjoy good things? Maybe we just need to create our own special occasions."

Lillian made a face. "You know, I've always objected to Valentine's Day, because I don't think a day like that should come only once a year. *Every* day should be Valentine's Day. People should say *I love you* all the time or show their love, even in small ways."

He nodded. "We're in agreement, then. It's decided. Let's celebrate the fact that we woke up this morning."

She laughed. "And we'll raise our glasses to Lorenzo, wherever he is."

Mr. Clark held up the two bottles he'd already selected. "My hands are full. Will you pick one of them?"

"I'd be honored." She tried to inspect the labels. "They're so dusty I can't tell what's what, so I'll just close my eyes and trust the hands of fate."

A short while later, they were sitting down on the leather sofa in the tasting room. Mr. Clark opened all three bottles and poured three small glasses for each of them—for sampling, just like she did with the tour groups.

"Now we wait for it to breathe," he said, sitting back and resting his arms along the back of the sofa. "To pass the time, I'll ask you about your family, Lillian. Any brothers or sisters?"

She sat back also and told him that she was an only child. Then she opened up about her parents' volatile relationship and how she had spent most of her childhood hiding under the bed when they were shouting and smashing things.

"During my teenage years," she told him, "I was a textbook case when it came to relationships. I dated boys who treated me exactly like my father treated my mother, because it seemed normal to me. But thankfully, my mother's lecturing finally sank in."

"What sort of lecturing?" he asked.

"After my father left, she apologized for not doing a better job protecting me. I think she'll take that regret to her grave. And then she warned me about boys with bad tempers—her way of protecting my future, I suppose. She told me to run in the opposite direction, even if they were handsome and charming. Then I met Freddie, and he was the exact opposite of what she was talking about."

Mr. Clark studied Lillian's expression. "He's good to you, I take it?"

"Very. He would never hurt a flea. Those were my mother's words. It's what she told me to look for in a husband." Lillian sighed. "So that's why I'll never take Freddie for granted. I'll always appreciate how good he is. And someday, when we have children, I'll be protective of them."

Mr. Clark sat forward on the sofa. "Where is your mother now?" He picked up the first glass of wine and swirled it around.

"In Chicago—with a new man these days. She finally followed her own advice. He wouldn't hurt a flea either. He's an older man. A retired math teacher."

Mr. Clark gestured for Lillian to pick up her glass. "Shall we? We can toast to your mother."

"Yes."

The first sample was a Brunello from 1962. Lillian was no expert when it came to wine. She was only just beginning to appreciate the experience of tasting different blends and vintages and to understand something about the variety of what existed in the world.

Each wine they tasted was different, delicious in its own way, and Mr. Clark was wonderful about helping her to identify the flavors and aromas. They sampled everything and talked more about her life back in the US, her childhood and work experiences. She'd been holding down jobs, at least part time, ever since she was fifteen.

"These bottles have been amazing," she said. "I hate to admit it, but I think I might be a little drunk."

Mr. Clark chuckled softly. "But clearly you're a happy drunk, which speaks volumes about you, Lillian."

She wondered if her cheeks were flushed. She felt very warm suddenly and shrugged out of her sweater.

The building was dark and quiet after hours, except for the clock ticking on the mantelpiece. Lillian leaned back against the sofa and looked up at the frescoed ceiling.

"That's very beautiful. We don't have old painted ceilings like that back home. This house would be a museum if it were in Tallahassee. But you *live* here. You get to look at these beautiful paintings every day." She lifted her head off the back of the sofa and frowned slightly. "I've never seen the ceiling of the Sistine Chapel. Have you?"

"A few times." His eyes glimmered with amusement.

"I haven't been to Rome yet," she said, "or to the Vatican, but I'd like to go."

"You should."

"Freddie wants to see it as part of his research for the book, so he'll probably go without me."

"Why would he do that?" Mr. Clark asked with surprise.

"Because I have to work, and he won't want to wait. When he gets inspired with an idea for a scene, he wants to go and research it right away, that very second. He has no patience. Off he goes. I've learned not to hold him back when inspiration is striking, because it never seems to strike twice in the same place. Or so he says."

"You can take time off, you know," Mr. Clark told her. "Just arrange it with Matteo."

"Thank you," she replied. "I would do that, but it's difficult because I can't plan in advance. Freddie wants to go when he wants to go." She sat forward and took another sip of wine. "But that's enough about Freddie. I sound like I'm complaining. I'm not." The room began to spin a little, so she set down her glass. "I should stop now."

"Are you all right?" he asked.

"Yes. I probably should have eaten something, though. What time is it?" She checked her watch.

"Almost eight," he replied.

She listened for sounds. People in the building. Voices. There was nothing but the clock ticking and the crickets starting to chirp outside the windows as the moon began its rise.

"Everyone's gone home," she said.

"Yes. We seem to be alone."

They stared at each other for a moment, and she felt the effects of the alcohol in her blood—the way it made all her muscles relax and her eyelids grow heavy. Through the gigantic windows, she watched a moth flitting about, bouncing off the glass, wanting to reach the light inside.

Mr. Clark was stretched out on the sofa, his long, muscular legs crossed at the ankles. Silence floated around them like the belts of fog in the Tuscan valleys. She realized he was right—they were very alone here—and she felt a touch of discomfort, as if she were doing something wrong. Drinking too much wine with her employer, a man who was handsome and interesting. He was as intoxicating as the wine.

Was he the type of man who had a temper that he covered with good looks and charm, like her father had done in the early days of her parents' relationship?

Lillian certainly felt charmed, and she began to wonder with some unease if she might have walked into a situation she wasn't entirely equipped to handle.

CHAPTER 10
FIONA

Tuscany, 2017

After the trip to the bank, Marco drove me back to the villa. We entered through a side door on the lower level and walked to the kitchen, where we found Maria helping Mrs. Dellucci reorganize the pantry cupboard.

"How did it go?" Maria asked.

"I'm not sure," I replied, setting my purse on a stool. "The only thing in the box was a very old key, which looks like something to keep Rapunzel in the tower." I dug it out of my purse and handed it to Maria. "Do you recognize this?"

Maria shook her head. "I'm afraid I don't, but it could belong anywhere. There are all sorts of old buildings on the property. I can't think of any locks here in the house that would require a key of this size, but my husband might know something. Will you come for dinner tonight? You could ask him then."

"That would be lovely," I replied. "Thank you." I dropped the key back into my purse. "And there's something else I need to ask you. When we were upstairs in Anton's room earlier, just before my cell phone rang, you mentioned a studio?"

"*Sì*. Anton used to paint when he was younger."

"Really?" I was astonished and momentarily thrilled to learn that my desire to brush colors onto a blank canvas was an inherited gene, but in the very next second, I felt an emptiness well up inside me—a feeling that I had lost something precious that I could never get back. "I didn't know that. Was he any good?"

Maria made a face. "I don't know. I'm not a good judge of that sort of thing. I only go into the studio to dust, very infrequently. A couple of times a year."

I pushed a strand of hair behind my ear. "Could I see it?"

"Of course. I'll take you now."

Marco's cell phone rang. He answered it, spoke a few words in Italian, and ended the call. "It's Sofia. She wants me to pick her up."

"Where did she go this afternoon?" Maria asked, curious.

"I don't know. Somewhere in town. I'll be back shortly." He flipped the car keys around his finger and walked out.

I watched him go, then followed Maria out of the kitchen and up the main staircase. We walked past the south wing, where the family was staying, and down the long corridor to a room at the end of the hall, across from Anton's bedroom.

Maria pushed the door open but stopped abruptly on the threshold. I nearly bumped into her.

"Connor," Maria said. "What are you doing in here?"

I peered over Maria's shoulder and suddenly understood why Sloane had called their father a hoarder. The room was not a studio. It was storage space for junk. Old chairs were piled on top of each other, along with ladders, easels, toppling stacks of books and magazines on tables, jars full of dried-up paintbrushes, cardboard boxes full of heaven knew what, hundreds of rolled-up posters . . . or were they canvases?

"What do you think I'm doing?" Connor replied, groaning as he lifted a heavy cardboard box off the floor and dropped it with a loud thwack onto a table. "I'm looking for those scandalous love letters Fiona's mother wrote. I hope they don't make me blush."

My stomach turned over with nervous apprehension.

Connor glanced at me briefly. "It's kind of gross, don't you think? Who wants to read about your father's sexual exploits from days gone by? But I suppose we all have to make sacrifices when the family business is at stake."

The box was damp and moldy. As soon as Connor tugged at the flaps, it collapsed in limp defeat, and all the papers spilled onto the floor.

"Great," he said, resting his hands on his hips.

I moved quickly, traipsing through a tight, twisty path between junk piles, and dropped to my knees at Connor's feet. I wasted no time sorting through the contents of the box, because if private letters from my mother existed, I wanted to be the one to find them.

Connor stood over me. I felt the scorching heat of his malicious stare on the back of my neck but chose to ignore him as I picked up an envelope and inspected the return address. It was nothing familiar.

Finally, Connor dropped to his knees as well and grabbed a bunch of envelopes before I could examine them.

Maria approached. "Look at the two of you, digging through trash for the family jewels. Your father wasn't stupid, Connor. He wouldn't leave something so important in here to rot."

"I beg to differ," Connor said. "He was stupid enough to let a woman from Tallahassee, Florida, trick him into handing over his entire fortune."

"I didn't trick him," I insisted.

"I was referring to your mother," Connor replied, bitterly.

I said nothing and continued to search through the papers.

Connor sat back on his heels, rested his hands on his thighs. "You really have no idea what happened between them, do you."

"No, I don't."

"Well, I know something," Connor said.

My eyes shot to meet his. "You do?"

"Yep. I did a little digging today and found out that your mother worked here at the winery for a summer. She was a tour guide in 1986."

I had known that Mom and Dad spent a summer in Tuscany to research Dad's first book, but I'd had no idea she actually worked for Anton. I sat back as well. "She was?"

He regarded me with derision. "Your mother must have been a real proper southern lady, sleeping with the boss."

His sarcasm grated on my nerves, and I returned to the task of digging through the pile of papers on the floor. "Please don't insult my mother. She was a good woman."

"Oh, I'm sure," he replied as he rose to his feet and looked around at all the clutter. "Maria, I need a drink. Would you fetch me a vodka martini? Grey Goose if you have it. And make it a double." He let out a sigh. "I need to self-medicate."

Maria glanced at me with a look of apology. "Would you like something?"

"No, thank you."

She stepped around a crate full of empty wine bottles as she made her way toward the door.

"Bring it in a proper martini glass!" Connor shouted after her. "Three olives!" He squatted next to me, and his mouth curled into a sinister grin. "I must be my father's son, because I like my martinis like I like my women. Dirty. *Really* dirty."

I knew he was just trying to get a rise out of me, but I had no intention of taking the bait. "Do you mind?"

"I'm just teasing."

"And I am not amused." I got to my feet and found another box on a shelf to sort through.

"Fine. Be like that." He turned and dug through a dusty pile of magazines.

We worked in silence until Maria returned with the drink on a small tray. She walked carefully to keep her balance as she inched around a stepladder to deliver Connor's martini.

"Thank you, Maria," he said. "You are the cat's meow." He picked up the drink, sniffed it, and took a sip.

Maria passed me on the way out. "Eight o'clock?" she whispered. "Come around to the back."

I nodded.

Connor sat down on an old ottoman splattered with different colors of dried paint and sipped his drink. "Did she invite you to dinner?"

"Yes."

He sighed. "I'm trying not to feel heartbroken that she didn't invite Sloane and me, considering how she used to mother us when we were kids, but I suppose her loyalty has always been with the person who writes her paychecks, whomever that may be."

I chose to ignore him.

"Don't worry about us, though," he added, stirring his martini with the toothpick and olives. "Sloane and I have dinner reservations in town. Don't get me wrong. The food's great here. That lady in the kitchen does a bang-up job with pancakes."

"Her name is Mrs. Dellucci," I informed him.

"Dellucci. Good to know. Very important information." Connor sat back and watched me move a heavy box from one stack to another.

"We should lay out some ground rules here," he said. "If either of us finds something, we should share it. Don't stick it in your pants and make off with it."

I said nothing as I ripped open another box.

"I'm getting a read on your mood . . . ," Connor added. "What I'm hearing is this: *Share it? Screw you, Connor Clark.*"

"I never said that."

"No, but you're thinking it, and I can't blame you. It's certainly what I'd be thinking."

"No doubt," I replied, "but you and I are nothing alike."

He chuckled at that. "Maybe not today, because all this must seem very surreal to you—the big Italian villa, the wine business, truckloads of cash in the bank. But wait until you start spending that cash. Trust me, you're going to enjoy it far more than you ever imagined, and you'll do just about anything that's necessary to hold on to it."

"Is that what's happening here?" I asked. "You're going to do whatever's necessary? Should I be worried?"

Connor laughed softly as he downed the last few drops of his martini and sucked the olives off the toothpick. "Where to next?" He looked around.

I dug an old wallet out of a box and searched through it, but it was empty.

"You'd be surprised," Connor said, "how money can make people do terrible things."

"Not me."

"No?" He moved a little closer. "Tell me then, sweet sister Fiona. What are you going to do with this inheritance if fate rules in your favor? Are you going to sell the winery and donate the proceeds to charity? Use the proceeds to go on humanitarian missions to Africa? Cure cancer? Save the whales?"

All I could do was shake my head at him.

"You must have thought about *something* you want to spend the money on," he said. "Come on. What's on your bucket list?"

I glanced at a yellowed brochure for a symphony performance in Rome that happened years ago and set it aside. "I'll spend it on my father. The one who raised me, I mean."

"Why would you do that?"

"Because he's a quadriplegic, and he needs constant care."

My response was met with silence. It was the first time my half brother, Connor, had seemed the slightest bit flustered. "You didn't mention that."

"You didn't ask."

Connor cleared his throat and shifted uneasily. "Was he born like that?"

"No, it was a spinal cord injury. It happened before I was born."

Connor chewed on his bottom lip, and it was obvious that he was uncomfortable. People often were when it came to my dad. They stared at us when we went places.

"What happened?" Connor asked.

"He was hit by a car. Here in Italy, actually."

Connor bent to look at something on the floor, his hands resting on his thighs. "Wow. Now I understand why dear old Dad never let us walk to town. Not a lot of sidewalks around here."

"And lots of twisting, turning roads," I added.

We worked for a while in silence until curiosity got the better of me. "So what was Anton like as a father?"

"Oh, you know . . ." Connor stumbled over a box on the floor. "Basically, your everyday, garden-variety tyrannical monster."

I raised my eyebrows. "Sounds like I didn't miss out on much."

"Lucky you. You got the gain without the pain."

I regarded Connor with a frown of concern. "Was he really that bad?"

He shrugged. "Oh, I don't know. I didn't spend much time with him after he and Mom divorced. But that's why I got cut out of the will, apparently. If only I'd known it would come back to bite me in the ass. I would have done my duty. I would have come here and played the part of devoted son."

"No pain, no gain," I said.

"Hardy har har," Connor replied. He finished searching through a shoebox and tossed it aside. "It wasn't all my fault, though. Do you know that song 'Cat's in the Cradle'?"

"Yes."

"Well, Dad was basically Harry Chapin. My mom wanted to move back to the US, but he wouldn't budge. He chose his winery over his family. So why should we come running when old age slowed him down and he finally wanted to spend time with us?"

"What about the women?" I asked. "I thought they divorced because of your father's affairs. My mother being one of them."

"Icing on the cake," Connor said. "Apparently, Dad was a real charmer. He knew exactly how to make a woman believe that he'd 'never felt like this before.'" Connor made air quotes with his fingers. "I'm telling you . . . this must have been the ultimate bachelor pad. He'd seduce them with his classic vintages, get them drunk, make them think it was true love, then boom—straight into the sack."

I held up a hand. "Please."

Connor laughed. "What? Just ask Sofia. She's half his age, but she was completely infatuated. Or maybe it was just the money that she loved. Who can blame her?"

I sorted through the box in front of me. "If money was the source of the attraction, maybe she seduced *him*."

"Touché," Connor replied. "It probably was the money, especially at the end, when he probably couldn't get it up."

Feeling a little disgusted by the conversation, I tried to change the subject. "None of this helps me understand what happened between him and my mother. All I know is that she would never have gone after Anton's money. She wasn't like that."

"Yet here you are," Connor replied, "by some miracle, the prime beneficiary. Something does smell fishy about that."

I finished searching through a box, set it aside, and opened another.

"Look at you . . . ," Connor said. "What a busy bee. I'll bet you'd pay a million bucks right now to find a box full of perfume-scented valentines so that you could put a stamp of approval on that bogus will."

"It's not bogus," I replied. "The lawyer said it's valid."

"That lawyer's a hack who doesn't know anything about what was written in those letters. I can't believe he even mentioned them to us. He must have known I'd turn this place upside down looking for them. But what do I know? Maybe he's sipping brandy on a plane back to London right now, laughing his ass off."

"I doubt that's the case," I said.

"You have such sweet faith in people. It's hard to believe we're related."

"I can't argue."

Connor sat down again. "It's getting late, and I'm hungry. How about this for an idea? We'll call a truce for today. I'll leave if you will. I've had enough of this musty old studio anyway."

I looked around at the remnants of my father's artistic life—the paintbrushes in jars, old tubes of oils, and rolled-up canvases in boxes, which I couldn't wait to look at. But Maria was expecting me for dinner.

I checked my watch. "I do have to get changed."

Connor stood. "Excellent. We agree on something at last. It's quittin' time. Let's go." He clapped his hands. "Chop-chop."

He watched my every move as I closed the last box. Then he followed me out.

CHAPTER 11

LILLIAN

Tuscany, 1986

"Forgive me, Lillian," Mr. Clark said, sitting forward on the sofa and smiling charmingly. "I've poured too much wine."

"No," she replied, "it was wonderful. They were good wines, I must say."

He raised a glass. "Thank you, Lorenzo, wherever you are."

The weather outside had grown hot and humid, and Mr. Clark raked a hand through his hair. Lillian couldn't seem to look at him directly. She gazed at a painting on the wall, studying its composition and colors, but this was a ruse to hide the fact that she was aware of her boss's every movement, even the rise and fall of his chest as he breathed.

They sat in silence, not talking, just listening to the crickets chirping in the cool grass outside. Feeling the pleasurable effects of the wine, Lillian tilted her head back and looked up at the frescoed ceiling again. She wondered about the artist. He must have been a spiritual person, passionate about his work. How wonderful it must be—to love your work in such a way . . .

She supposed Freddie was like that. Sometimes his desire to write was all-consuming. Whenever he was sitting at his desk, hunched over his typewriter, and she carried a supper tray into the room, she felt like an unwelcome disturbance. At the very least, she felt invisible. Sometimes he would hold up a hand to signal that she shouldn't speak, because if she did, she would interrupt his creative flow and pull him out of his imagination.

She respected Freddie's focus. It was a natural, God-given gift that he could transport himself to another world—as if he were leaving his physical body—and tell a story about that world of his creation.

"Why don't you come for dinner tonight?" Mr. Clark suggested, surprising Lillian with the invitation.

She sat forward. "Dinner? Where?"

"At the villa." He checked his watch. "Mrs. Guardini sometimes gets her nose out of joint when I work too late in the evenings. I should head up there."

Lillian felt a touch of disappointment at the notion that he considered this to be work. For her, it was pure pleasure.

"She'll have the table set by now," he continued, "and everyone will be sitting down shortly."

"Everyone?" Lillian grimaced. Heaven help her, the wine had clouded her brain. She couldn't seem to form a complete sentence.

Mr. Clark began to name names. "Matteo, Domenico—that's Mrs. Guardini's husband, who runs the vineyards for me—and Francesco, my driver and right-hand man. You could invite your husband to join us if you like, if he's back from wherever he went today. You could call him from the villa."

Lillian's stomach had been growling for the past hour. "I am hungry."

Mr. Clark stood and held out his hand. "Well then. Up you come."

She allowed him to pull her to her feet.

"But first, we should clean up after ourselves," he added. "Let's take the glasses to the kitchen and recork these bottles. We'll bring them to the table and finish them off. Domenico will be thrilled."

Lillian helped him with those tasks. Then they carried the bottles out of the tasting room to the stone terrace and up a set of worn marble steps to the iron gate outside the formal gardens.

The villa came into view. It was dark, but the moon was full. It cast a bright, bluish glow on the garden path, lighting their way. Their footsteps crunched over the white gravel while they talked and laughed. Moon shadows were everywhere.

During her training, Lillian had seen the villa from afar, but she had never set foot inside the enormous Tuscan mansion. Mr. Clark led her to a narrow side door, where they entered into a lower level.

"This must have been a servants' entrance at one time?" Lillian asked.

"Actually, I believe this was a 'door for the dead.' In medieval times, it was considered bad luck to bring your dead out the front door, so homes often had a smaller door somewhere."

"Interesting." The door looked wide enough for a coffin but not much else.

Mr. Clark showed her to a telephone in the hall, which she used to call Freddie at the shed. She let it ring more than five times, but he didn't answer, so she finally hung up.

Mr. Clark then escorted her through a wide stone corridor with graceful arches. It took them past a large kitchen, recently modernized, where delectable aromas of basil, pasta, and roasted meat roused Lillian's senses.

"It smells scrumptious in here," she said.

Another corridor brought them to a back door that opened onto a patio beneath a green arbor. Covered in thick, tangled vines, it was a cozy space with tiny white lights strung overhead. A long dinner table beneath a floral tablecloth held countless platters of food, vases of fresh flowers, and candles that burned in old straw-covered Chianti bottles.

"Anton, you're late!" a man shouted in good spirits as he turned in his chair. "And who is this lovely creature you have brought with you this evening? Welcome."

An older woman slid her chair back and stood. "I'll get another plate," she said before disappearing into the house.

Mr. Clark began the introductions. "Allow me to present Lillian Bell, our new American tour guide. Lillian, this is Domenico Guardini, the vineyard foreman, and that was his wife, Caterina. She'll be back in a moment. You know Matteo, and this is Francesco. He's a Renaissance man. He does everything for me."

Francesco held his hand over his heart. "With pleasure, Anton."

Caterina returned with a plate and utensils, which she laid out while Matteo leaped up to fetch another chair.

Lillian took a seat at the table. "It was very nice of Mr. Clark to invite me."

"Lillian, please. You must call me Anton," he said.

"I see you brought wine," Domenico interrupted with delight, rising from his chair to investigate the labels. "*Meraviglioso*, Anton. Finally. Let's enjoy it, shall we?" He turned and winked discreetly at his wife.

Lillian suspected they had been discussing, in private, the wine that had been locked away in the secret Maurizio room for decades—bottles no one was permitted to appreciate.

"Everyone, eat," Caterina said, sitting back down and passing a large platter of antipasto to Lillian. "But save room for the roast duck," she quietly added, leaning close. "It's my special recipe."

"I could smell it cooking when I came in," Lillian replied, her mouth watering. "It smelled delicious, and this looks unbelievable. Thank you so much for having me."

"It's our pleasure," Domenico said, raising a glass to her.

Lillian helped herself to an array of crostini—mini toasts with various toppings like bacon with caramelized onions and ricotta with fresh pesto sprinkled with red pepper flakes.

"What a lovely table you've laid out," Lillian said to Caterina. "Is this a special occasion?"

Caterina laughed. "Every night with good friends is a special occasion."

Anton, who was seated at the head of the table, poured himself some wine. "Lillian and I were just talking about that very thing earlier." He spoke to her directly. "And you asked why I prefer Italy over my home country these days. I'm not sure if I ever gave you an adequate answer, but this is precisely why. Tuscans love to celebrate." He turned to Caterina. "You have a food festival for everything, isn't that right?"

She laughed. "*Sì*, we like to have fun, and what is more fun than enjoying delicious food and wine under the light of the moon at the end of a long day?"

"Cheers to that," Anton said, raising his glass.

By this time, Mr. Guardini had already poured another glass of wine for Lillian, so she raised it and joined in the toast, then helped herself to a few more of the delicious crostini.

Next came a massive bowl of pasta—tagliatelle with fresh mushroom sauce—which was passed around the table until it was empty. Vigorous conversation and laughter filled the night, and no one was in a hurry to finish anything. Everyone at the table behaved like family toward Anton, as if they had known him forever, and they welcomed Lillian into the fold with questions about her life in America, her family, and her husband.

"You must bring him for dinner tomorrow," Caterina said. "It's never any trouble to set out an extra plate or two. He would be most welcome."

"Thank you. I'll tell him."

As Lillian sipped her wine and devoured the flavorful pasta, she was astonished by the hospitality of everyone she had met at the winery so far. There was a delightful sense of joy in the daily routine of waking in the morning, working in the vineyards, then taking time at lunch to enjoy a delicious meal with a small amount of wine followed by espresso. Everyone seemed especially happy to go back to work after their long and leisurely *riposo*, and she was completely, unequivocally enchanted.

~

It was nearly eleven when Matteo pushed back his chair to say good night. Caterina began to clear the table, and Lillian stood to help. She and Caterina spent some time in the kitchen tidying up, until Caterina ushered her out because she had an early-morning shift at the hotel reception desk.

When Lillian returned to the candlelit arbor, Anton was standing and saying good night to Francesco, who turned and said good night to Lillian before entering the villa.

"Does he live here?" she asked.

"He has an apartment on the ground floor."

"And the Guardinis?" she asked, curious.

"They live in a smaller villa on the property." He turned and pointed in a southerly direction. "It's just down the hill, about a five-minute walk. It's surrounded by wild roses and fig trees."

"That sounds charming," Lillian replied.

"It is. And they have three very friendly cats."

His description made her wish she could see the place for herself, but it was long past time for her to say good night, so she looked away. "I should probably be going."

Anton removed his hands from his pockets. "I'll walk you back."

"Thank you, but it's not necessary. I can find my way."

"I'm sure you can, but it's a beautiful night, and I could use a bit of exercise after two helpings of Caterina's chocolate dessert. Indulge me, if you will."

She laughed. "All right."

Lillian waited while he went into the kitchen to fetch a flashlight, then followed him down the stone path and around the side of the villa to the driveway and main gate. He opened it with the keypad, and they passed through. It closed automatically behind them.

"Thank you so much for dinner," she said. "The food was incredible."

"It's the least I could do after being so heavy handed in the tasting room. Do you feel better now?"

"Much better. Although I didn't feel *bad* before. I felt quite good, actually. I was just hungry."

He smiled and looked down at the ground as he walked. "I hope your husband won't feel left out when you get home. He'd be welcome to join us tomorrow or any other night."

"I appreciate that. But it's not as if we didn't try to invite him. I let the phone ring forever."

They walked at a leisurely pace down the dirt lane between two rows of Italian cypresses. Not a single breath of wind moved the humid summer air, and Lillian marveled at the pine-scented tranquility of the Tuscan countryside.

"Earlier today," she said, "when I asked why you preferred Italy to London, you told me it was a long story, and you suggested we open a few bottles of wine before we talked about it. But at dinner, you brushed it off. You said you liked it here because Tuscans have more fun." She glanced up at him. "But I feel like there must be more to it than that."

His footsteps were steady as they walked along the lane, guided by the long beam of the flashlight he held in his hand.

"Yes, there's more. You're very intuitive. How much time do we have?" His voice held a touch of humor, and a twinkle of moonlight caught his eye.

"As much as we need."

As soon as the words passed her lips, she felt a little apprehensive. What would Freddie think if he knew she was walking in the moonlight with her handsome, wealthy boss after drinking wine with him for hours, and that she was asking him questions about his private life? Telling him they had all night to talk?

A soft breeze whispered through the cypresses. Lillian looked up at the starlit sky and pushed thoughts of Freddie from her mind. That's what he did when he was working. He pushed her from the room and from his mind. *Go away*, he said, without ever actually speaking the words.

"It's a rather sordid tale," Anton said. "The truth is . . . I only go back to London to visit my mother and sister, and I plan it when my brother's not there."

"Oh dear," Lillian said. "What happened between you and your brother?"

"Where do I even begin?" Anton exhaled heavily. "At the beginning, I suppose. My brother and I built a company together. We were equal partners, but when it became more profitable than either of us ever imagined it would, he took advantage of a situation when I had to step back from the daily operations. I was sick for a while."

"Oh. What was wrong?"

"Non-Hodgkin's lymphoma."

"I'm so sorry. That must have been awful. Are you okay now?"

"Yes, I'm a lucky survivor, fully recovered. But during that year, my brother pretended to be looking out for my best interests. I couldn't work, so he offered to buy out my half of the business so that I could focus on my recovery and pay medical bills. It seemed like a fair offer. It was a lot of money, more than I ever dreamed the company could be worth, and I honestly thought he was being overly generous, propping me up when I was at my lowest, so I took the money. As soon as the contract was signed and I no longer had any ownership or authority, he sold the company for ten times the amount he paid me. I found out later that he had been brokering the deal for months while I was sick. He knew what it was really worth when he made the offer to get me out of the picture."

Lillian slowly shook her head. "That was a terrible thing to do. You must have felt very betrayed."

"Yes. It was my sister, Mabel, who found out the truth. She learned it from my brother's wife, who spilled the beans about how he had been keeping me in the dark the whole time, quite intentionally."

"Do you ever speak to him now?"

"No. He divorced his wife and moved to New York with his millions. Now, he does nothing but live the high life in a penthouse apartment and sails on his yacht with a bunch of Wall Street types. It's not my idea of a good time, but it was what he always aspired to. I think he knew that I would have turned down the offer to sell the company if I was still involved, and he just wanted the fast cash."

"What sort of business was it?" Lillian asked.

"Computer technology. He was the business manager, while I was the math geek. He sold the software I developed to IBM, which cut me out of the industry with a noncompete clause. I didn't even realize that that was buried in the contract when we dissolved the partnership, so it was my own fault. I should have had my own lawyer looking out for my interests, but I trusted my brother and the lawyer who handled our business affairs. He told me it was a good deal and that I should take it, but he knew all along about the offer from IBM."

"Couldn't you have fought that?" she asked. "It sounds almost like fraud."

"I probably could have," he replied, "but at that point, I just wanted to leave all that greed for the green stuff behind me and get back to . . ." He paused, as if he wasn't quite sure how to explain it.

"Back to the land," Lillian said, matter-of-factly.

"Exactly."

They reached the end of Cypress Row, where the chapel came into view. The bell tower was silhouetted against the moon.

"Look at that," she said. "It's so magical. I don't blame you for wanting to live here."

He nodded. "I was here on holiday with my wife and spotted an advert in an estate agent's window in Montepulciano. I'll never forget that day. After what my brother did to me, I had ten million pounds burning a hole in my pocket, and the Maurizio family was desperate not to sell to one of their corporate competitors, so I thought . . . why not?"

Ten million pounds?

"Your wife was keen to buy a winery?" Lillian asked, fighting to recover from her astonishment.

He gave her a sheepish look. "Not exactly. But she knew how badly I wanted it, so she was willing to compromise, as long as I promised not to spend every last farthing we had. I also had to promise that she'd be able to fly home anytime she wanted, so that's where we stand. I stay here, and she comes and goes as she pleases."

"Does she always take the children?" Lillian asked. "Or do they stay with you sometimes?"

"So far, she's been taking them," he replied, "but she never stays away for too long."

"That's good. You must miss them."

"I do."

Lillian wanted to ask more about that, but they reached the bottom of the hill and arrived at the little cluster of stone buildings where the shed was located. All the guest suites were occupied. The windows were lit up, but Lillian's apartment was dark.

"Looks like Freddie isn't home yet," she said.

Anton stopped as well. "Where was he today?"

"I'm not sure. He's been going to Florence to do research, and sometimes he stops at coffee shops to write on his way home, but this seems late."

"Are you worried?"

"I'm not sure. He could just be on a roll."

"Do you want me to come in? Maybe he left a note."

She thought about it for a moment and decided that it might not be a good idea to invite Anton inside. If Freddie came home, how would that look?

"I'm sure he's fine," she said. "And I should get some sleep. But thank you for walking me back."

Anton hesitated a moment, shining the flashlight on the ground, studying her expression in the moonlight. "I enjoyed our conversations."

"So did I." There was a note of intimacy in her voice, and something about that made her feel guilty, as if she were on the verge of stepping over a line she shouldn't cross. On the other side of that line was a deeper friendship with a man she found fascinating and very attractive. It was dangerous territory, to be sure.

"Call me at the villa if you need anything," Anton said. "If you're worried about your husband."

"I will. But I'm sure everything's fine. He's just late. Like me."

"All right." Anton paused a moment, then turned to go.

Lillian stood on the gravel driveway, watching him walk up the forested lane with the flashlight illuminating his way through the darkness. There was a sudden chill in the night. Hugging her arms about herself, she continued to watch him until he disappeared over the crest of the hill, and then she dug into her purse for her key.

A moment later, she was switching on all the lights in the empty apartment, wondering where Freddie was. What if he'd gotten into another car accident? The roads in Tuscany were full of unfamiliar twists and turns, up and down the sides of mountains. It was worse after dark, when other cars came speeding around bends with their headlights blinding your eyes.

Not sure what she would do if Freddie didn't come home soon, Lillian washed her face and put on her nightgown. She slipped into bed and tried to read but couldn't concentrate. She was worried about Freddie.

She didn't want to fall asleep until he came home, so she rose from the bed and sat down at the kitchen table with a bottle of nail polish. As she dipped the brush into the bottle and painted a light-pink color on her nails, her thoughts wandered to a memory of the dinner table under the grape arbor. She recalled the sound of everyone's laughter when Domenico told a story about his dog, Nacho, who had once lapped up a puddle of red wine that had leaked out of a fermentation barrel in the winery. Nacho—just a puppy at the time—had staggered outside and fallen into a bunch of empty flowerpots. Poor Nacho had to be carried up to the villa to sleep it off.

Lillian had just finished a second coat of nail polish when car headlights shone through the window and swept across the wall. She stood and hurried to the door, letting out a breath of relief when Freddie got out of the car that Anton had loaned to them. He ran up the steps with his backpack slung over his shoulder and walked in.

"You're still up," he said, brushing past her. "I had an amazing day. I wrote seven pages after exploring a neighborhood where my characters get into some trouble."

It was obvious that he was pleased and excited. Lillian was happy for him, of course, but for the first time in their relationship, she was excited by something of her own: a fulfilling day, both professionally and personally. She had received high praise from her employer, learned all sorts of new things about wine, met the most amazing group of people, and tasted food that was surely sent from heaven.

"Is there anything to eat?" Freddie asked. "I'm starving."

He opened the fridge while Lillian shut the door behind him and locked it. "I'm sorry, I didn't cook anything. I just got back myself."

"Really?" He found canned soup in a small pot, left over from the night before. "I'll just have this." He passed it to her, and she placed it on the stove to reheat it.

"Did you have to work late?" he asked, removing his coiled notebook from his backpack and opening it to look at something he had written. He became instantly distracted.

"Yes, I did. The boss came to watch my tour, and I did really well, even though I was nervous. I felt like I was on a stage, performing a soliloquy."

Freddie sat down at the kitchen table and flipped the page. "Yeah?"

She poured him a glass of milk. "Yes, and then I had a private wine tasting lesson with Mr. Clark himself, and he invited me to dinner at the villa. He invited us both, actually. I called you, but you weren't here."

"I was writing," Freddie said.

"I figured." Lillian put the milk back in the fridge. "I wish you could have seen it. It was a gorgeous table outside under an arbor of grapevines and mini lights, and they eat like that every night, with wine and good conversation. The food was incredible."

Lillian stirred the soup on the stove, then served it up and placed the bowl in front of Freddie, but he ignored it. His attention was focused on something in the notebook.

When he didn't ask her anything more about the dinner, she picked up her bottle of nail polish and went to the bathroom to put it back in the medicine cabinet. When she returned to the kitchen, he had closed the notebook and was eating his soup.

"They invited both of us to dinner again tomorrow night," Lillian said. "Do you want to come? They usually eat around eight."

Freddie grimaced apologetically. "Ah, Lil, I wish I could. It sounds amazing, but I hit a roadblock today, and I need to do some extra research. That's what I want to talk to you about, actually." He paused and sat back. "This might sound crazy, but I'd like to go to Paris."

Lillian blinked a few times in astonishment. "Paris?"

"Yeah. I know, it's not what we planned, but I'm on a roll, and I really think the rest of the story needs to happen there. We could leave first thing in the morning."

She drew back, as if he had just thrown a glass of cold water in her face. "Tomorrow."

"I know, it's short notice. But my characters are going to take the train there to follow the killer, but I don't want to tell you anything else about what happens when they get there. I just want to write it, and then I want you to read it without knowing what's coming so that you can give me good feedback. I think you're going to like it."

She sat down at the table. "Wow. Paris."

"It's really not that far from here," he said. "So could you come? I hate the idea of traveling alone, trying to figure out the trains on my own. You're so much better at that than I am."

She frowned a little and spoke gently. "Freddie, I don't think I can. I only just started here. It wouldn't feel right to ask for time off so soon after my first day, and besides that, we can't really afford for me not to be working. I need to keep making the minimum payments on the credit card, and if you need extra money for travel . . ."

He chewed on his bottom lip and looked away. "Yeah, I get it. I shouldn't have asked."

"No, it's fine."

Neither of them spoke for a few seconds.

"Can you at least help me figure out the train?" he asked, looking up again.

"Of course. How long will you be gone?"

"Just a few days," he replied. "A week at the most. What I need to do is soak up the atmosphere and visit a few of the locations I have in mind." He thought about it for a moment. "I'm going to have to find a hostel to stay in, something that won't cost too much."

"Okay."

He reached for her hand and squeezed it. "I was so afraid you were going to say no."

"I wouldn't say no," she replied. "Your dreams are my dreams, remember? And that's why we came here, so that you could finish your novel. I can't wait to read it."

"I can't wait for you to read it either," he replied, sitting back. "But I have to polish it first. I should be able to do that when I get back here." He finished his soup and carried the empty bowl and spoon to the sink. "So let's just keep doing what we're doing. It was a brilliant idea to come here, Lil. I owe you for talking me into it. If it weren't for you, I'd probably be back at my desk in Tallahassee, stuck on chapter ten."

"I'm glad it's been helpful," she replied.

His gaze was riveted on her face, and he spoke softly. "I'm a very lucky man."

Standing on opposite sides of the kitchen, they watched each other for a heated moment. Lillian felt a tingling in the pit of her belly. Fine wine was still coursing through her blood, left over from her evening at the villa.

Freddie pushed away from the sink. "Coming to bed?"

It had been a long time since they'd made love. She couldn't even remember the last time. She was usually asleep when Freddie came to bed after a late-night writing session. He was a night owl and she was an early riser, but tonight, each of them, for reasons of their own, felt impassioned.

She followed him to bed, got under the covers, and slipped out of her nightgown.

Afterward, when Freddie rolled onto his back and fell into a deep slumber, Lillian listened to the sound of his breathing and was surprised by a feeling of emptiness she had never experienced with her husband before. It left her frustrated, both sexually and emotionally, and resulted in a sense of foreboding that kept her awake until dawn.

CHAPTER 12
FIONA

Tuscany, 2017

It was walking distance from the main hotel facilities to Maria Guardini's honey-colored Tuscan villa, nestled cozily between a grove of chestnut trees on one side and a straight row of towering green cypresses on the other. The sun was just setting as I made my way along the gravel drive and up a narrow set of stone steps. Twilight cast a golden glow on the house, and I stopped to smell the pink roses outside the front door before I knocked.

No one answered, but when I smelled the delicious aroma of meat cooking, I remembered that Maria had told me to come around to the back of the house. I made my way there and found her spreading a white linen cloth on an outdoor table beneath an ivy-covered trellis.

"There you are," she said, smiling warmly. "Welcome." She kissed me on both cheeks.

"I didn't want to arrive empty handed," I said, "so I picked some wildflowers along the way." I held them out.

"Perfect for the table," Maria replied. "Come inside."

Maria led me into the kitchen, where Marco stood at the stove, stirring a pot of something. "*Ciao*, Fiona."

"Hi, Marco."

An older Italian man in a well-worn corduroy blazer entered the kitchen from the back terrace. He stomped the soil off his boots and held up a wicker basket. "Success!"

Maria greeted him with a firm kiss on the mouth. "Fiona, this is my husband, Vincent. Vincent, this is Fiona Bell, Anton's daughter from America." She gave him a look and raised an eyebrow.

Vincent set the basket on a wooden chair. He strode toward me, took hold of my face with his big calloused hands, and kissed me hard on both cheeks. "*Benvenuta*. Welcome."

Joy bubbled up inside me, and I laughed. "It's nice to meet you."

Vincent returned to the wicker basket and handed it to Maria. "Porcini mushrooms were everywhere."

"I've never loved you more," she replied.

"The best mushrooms of the year," Marco explained.

"I take it you didn't get them at the store?" I asked, amused.

Vincent laughed, as if I had just told a hilarious joke. "I found them in the woods, not far from here. A prime location every year. Maria will cook them up for you, nice and fresh." He passed by Marco at the stove and gave him a playful rub on the head. "Soup smells delicious. What a feast we will have. Now, if you'll excuse me, I will go and change into something more comfortable."

Maria smirked at him before he disappeared up a narrow staircase at the back of the kitchen.

"He's in a very good mood tonight," Maria explained as she set the basket on the worktable.

"Why is that?"

"Do you have to ask? Neither of us expected Anton to be so generous this morning. It feels like we won the lottery."

"I've been feeling that way myself," I replied. "Thank you for having me for dinner. Is there anything I can do to help?"

"*Sì*. We need to wash these beautiful mushrooms, then slice them very thin, like paper. Here's a good knife. You wash and I'll cut. Then we will cook and eat the most delicious pasta you've ever tasted in your life."

I exhaled with laughter. "Pinch me, Maria. I think I've died and gone to heaven."

CHAPTER 13
SLOANE

Sloane dressed for dinner, then unscrewed the cap of her mascara and leaned forward over the sink, closer to the mirror. She was about to touch the brush to her lashes when Chloe screamed from the bedroom. Sloane jumped and nearly gouged out her eyeball with the mascara brush.

"Chloe, don't scream like that!" She leaned forward again and whispered under her breath, "That child is going to put me in an early grave."

Chloe howled and sobbed. *"Mom!"*

Taking her daughter's cries more seriously the second time around, Sloane dropped the mascara brush into the sink and ran out of the bathroom. "What's wrong?"

Chloe scrambled off the bed and held out her phone. "Why did Daddy send me this?"

Evan walked in with his hand buried in a bag of potato chips. "What's going on?"

"I don't know yet." Sloane snatched the phone from her daughter. She looked at the picture on the screen and sucked in a breath. "Oh my God. What is this?"

"I don't know!" Chloe sobbed and wrapped her arms around Sloane's waist.

Focusing closely on the image, Sloane recognized her husband's private parts along with a text message. Hey baby, are you in the mood for this tonight?

Sloane's heart dropped like a stone with stomach-churning speed. Almost immediately, her cell phone vibrated in her pocket. It startled her, but she knew who was calling. She pulled it out and checked the display.

"It's your father," she explained to Chloe, fighting to remain calm and in control when her heart was pounding like a sledgehammer and she had no idea how she was going to manage her temper over the next few minutes. "I'm sure there's a reasonable explanation for this, sweetheart," she said, stroking Chloe's shiny blonde hair. "I'm going to keep your phone for a minute and go talk to Daddy." Sloane pointed at Evan and snapped her fingers. "Put on a movie for her, will you? Hurry up."

While Evan dashed to the television, Sloane went into the bathroom, shut the door, and answered her husband's call.

"Alan, what the hell?"

He spoke in a panic. "Are you with Chloe? Is she on her phone right now?"

"Not anymore," Sloane replied.

"Shit. Did the text come through? Did she see it?"

Sloane cupped her forehead in a hand and sat down on the edge of the bathtub. Always, with Alan and his many indiscretions, she felt heartbreak, sadness, emptiness, and most of all humiliation. She had become rather adept at keeping her chin up and pasting on a happy smile while hiding her anguish and turning a blind eye. Today, however, she felt something entirely different. Something new.

"Yes, she saw it, you idiot. What is wrong with you? I feel like I'm going to throw up right now."

"It was an accident," he insisted. "I swear I didn't mean to send it to her."

"No?" Sloane's blood began to boil hard and bubble over. "Well then, that makes it totally fine. Who *did* you mean to send it to? Never mind, I don't want to know the answer to that question."

Sloane pressed a hand to her belly. She felt completely emptied out of patience and tolerance toward her husband. Those feelings had been replaced by a mother's rage that her daughter had been exposed to such a horrible image. At the same time, she was furious with herself for giving her heart to a man like Alan and believing that he could make her happy and be a good father.

Glancing at the bathroom door, where Chloe's pink bathrobe hung on a hook, Sloane felt a muscle twitch at her jaw. "Wait a second. Yes, I do want to know. Is it the nanny?"

"Come on, Sloane. Of course not."

She hated it when he used that tone—as if she were being irrational and unreasonable. Whenever he spoke to her like that, she backed down—rather pathetically, she now realized—but tonight she didn't care what he thought. She was fit to be tied.

"Excuse me for asking," she replied, sarcastically. "So if it's not the nanny, who is it?"

"No one you know." He spoke with impatience.

His sense of entitlement was unimaginable.

When Sloane didn't respond, the silence gained weight, and eventually he spoke in a more appeasing tone, almost as if he were trying to charm her or flirt with her. "Relax, will you?" he added. "It's nothing."

"Nothing? You're telling me it's nothing." She looked at Chloe's pink bathrobe again. "If that's the way you're going to play it, fine. I need to hang up now."

"Wait a second. Listen . . ."

"No, *you* listen, Alan. Right now, I need to figure out how I'm going to explain to my seven-year-old daughter that her father didn't mean to send her a dick pic. That he meant to send it to someone else. Think about that."

Alan was quiet for a moment. "Wait, Sloane. Look . . . I'm sorry. I was rushed. It was stupid of me."

"And there we have it," she said. "Now I know for sure that you're a moron. I don't even know what to say to you right now."

"Sloane, stop."

"No, Alan. *You* stop. I can't do this anymore."

"You can't do what?"

For the first time in their marriage, he sounded worried.

"All of it. I'm hanging up now. Don't call me back. Good-bye."

She ended the call and sat on the edge of the tub for a few seconds, heart racing, stomach churning with anger, heartache, and fear for whatever was about to come next in her life. How was she going to deal with this? She felt paralyzed and couldn't move.

After a moment, she took a few deep breaths, counted to ten, and left the bathroom to check on Chloe and somehow try to explain to her children what just happened.

~

"Priceless!" Connor threw his head back and laughed.

"It's not funny." Sloane seethed as she glanced around the crowded restaurant. "She's seven years old. Something like this could scar her for life." She reached for her wine. "I wish Mom hadn't gone home."

Connor waved a hand through the air dismissively. "Relax. Chloe will be fine." Growing bored with Sloane's motherly concerns, he signaled for the waiter to bring him another scotch on the rocks.

"I'm telling you," Sloane said, "it was the last straw. I can't take it anymore."

Connor made a talking gesture with his fingers. "You've been saying that for two years. No one believes you. Least of all Alan."

"I mean it this time," she replied. "I'm going to call my lawyer first thing in the morning."

"Sure you will." The waiter arrived with Connor's second scotch on the rocks. He swirled the liquid around in the glass and watched the ice cubes clink together. "Yum."

"I'm serious, Connor," Sloane said, running out of patience for his apathetic sarcasm. "It's not just because it's completely humiliating, which it is. And it's not because I'm hurt. I have to think about Evan and Chloe. What is this teaching them about life? Chloe's going to grow up thinking women are just playthings and that men can't be trusted."

"How is divorcing Alan going to fix *that*?" Connor asked, dispassionately.

"I don't know. But I feel like I need to get them out of LA."

"LA's not the problem."

She glared at him. "What are you saying? Are you suggesting that *I'm* the problem? Don't roll your eyes at me. I hate it when you do that."

He slumped back in his chair. "I'm just saying that a change in your geographic location won't suddenly make you a happier, more fulfilled person or a better mother."

She reached for her wine again. "Maybe it will."

"Or maybe it won't. Wherever you go, there you are. And your kids won't have a father. They'll come from a broken home. Is that what you want? What we had? Look at us now, cut out of Daddy's will. Your kids deserve better."

Sloane finished her wine and refilled her glass with the bottle they'd ordered—one of their father's most expensive vintages.

"Something has to change," she said. "And don't act like you're the poster boy for being happy and fulfilled. You're as miserable as I am."

"Only because Dad ditched me in his will," he replied morosely.

"He ditched me too."

Connor pointed a finger at her. "Which is why you shouldn't be thinking about divorcing Alan right now."

Sloane slouched back in her chair. "I can't let that be the reason I stay with him. Money isn't everything."

Connor let out a dramatic belly laugh. "You are an absolute scream."

She looked around the restaurant. "Seriously, Connor. Look at these people. They don't look rich to me, but they're all smiling and enjoying themselves."

"That's your problem. You always think the grass is greener on the other side of the fence. But trust me. None of these people are happy. They're just faking it, like everyone else."

The waiter brought the first course. Sloane ate it but couldn't really taste anything. It was difficult to make use of her senses when her entire world was collapsing all around her.

"What I think I want to do," she finally said, "is move the kids to London. We could start fresh, and I won't need Alan's money. Even if Dad's will isn't overturned, I can get by with what he left me."

Connor's expression grew strained, his eyes level under drawn brows.

"Slow down there, Sparky. We need to talk about that."

"Why?"

"Because he left the London house to me too."

"But you never go to London," she replied. "Why should it matter if the kids and I live there?"

"That's exactly why it matters—because I never go. Dad screwed us over with the winery, so I need to cash in on what, to me, is a useless piece of real estate. We need to sell it."

Sloane's lips fell open. "No, we can't do that. It's not useless."

Slowly, silently sipping his scotch, Connor stared at her from across the table. "Then you're going to have to buy me out, sis, because fifty percent of it belongs to me, and I want my money, not a money pit."

Sloane exhaled sharply with disbelief. "Are you serious? You know how much I love that house, Connor. And I'm close to Ruth. She's like a sister to me, and she's good for Evan and Chloe."

The mention of their cousin Ruth did nothing to soften the look of determination in Connor's eyes. "Then buy me out, and the house will be all yours."

He sipped his drink and watched her with narrowed eyes over the rim of his glass.

"I can't," Sloane replied. "If I do that, I'll have no savings."

Connor rolled his eyes, as if he couldn't believe how daft she was. "Come on. Just because you were dumb enough to sign a prenup doesn't mean Alan won't have to pay child support. If we sell the house, you'll have the proceeds on top of what Dad left you. Think of how much money that will be. Alan might give you the LA house in the divorce—if you actually go through with it—and you'll be sitting pretty. Stay in LA, for pity's sake. Bloom where you're planted."

Sloane sat back and thought about it. It was true. The house in Belgravia would bring in a tidy sum, but Alan had always been very clear about never giving up the LA house, not even for the sake of the kids, because he'd designed it himself. He'd want to buy them another. Maybe she could ask Alan to buy out Connor's ownership in the Belgravia house. But would Alan agree to that? Knowing him, probably not. He wouldn't want her to move his kids to another country. He'd try to control where she went by getting them a house in LA.

The waiter arrived with a serving of pasta, but Sloane sighed with defeat because all she saw in front of her was a plate full of carbs. It wasn't a large portion, but still . . . this would require her to drag herself out of bed an extra hour early to do cardio in the morning.

Feeling dejected, she glanced around at the other people in the restaurant. They were all laughing and talking and enjoying their food, along with each other's company. They were twirling fettuccine around their forks without the slightest concern.

Sloane turned her attention to her brother across the table. He was holding his phone up with one hand, using his thumb to scroll through messages, while mindlessly shoveling some kind of chicken penne into his mouth.

Sloane picked up her fork, bent forward, and breathed in the intoxicating aroma of the white truffle cream sauce. A memory of the woods outside their father's villa flashed through her mind. She remembered running and laughing, chasing the dog as he sniffed and dug at the ground.

All at once, something inside her dissolved into a puddle of nostalgic longing. She wasn't sure what she longed for exactly and wished she possessed a keener, deeper self-awareness. Twirling the pasta around her fork, she closed her eyes, then tasted the rich, al dente noodles. Flavors of mushroom, butter, and thyme came alive on her tongue, and the texture of the fettuccine caused a swift rush of sensory pleasure to course through her body.

"This is delicious," she said softly.

"Uh-huh," Connor replied, still scrolling through his Instagram feed.

All Sloane wanted to do in that moment was go straight home to her children and hug them.

CHAPTER 14
FIONA

It was, hands down, the best dinner of my life. I raised my glass of Brunello after the final course was enjoyed. "Please allow me to say something, and I mean this from the bottom of my heart. You Italians sure do know how to cook."

Maria raised her glass.

"*Grazie*, Fiona," Vincent said. "To wonderful food and good friendships."

"Cheers to that," I replied.

We sipped our wine as a cool evening breeze blew lightly through the trellis greenery.

"Tell us, Fiona. Will you be moving into the villa?" Vincent asked.

I set down my glass and thought about how best to answer the question. A part of me wanted to say yes—because that's what they wanted to hear, and I liked them all tremendously—but the situation was complicated. I couldn't lie to them.

"I'm not sure. I haven't really figured everything out yet. I'm still in shock, and I'm barely over my jet lag."

"She's staying at the inn," Marco explained.

"The inn," Vincent replied with a frown. "You should be at the villa." He turned to Maria. "Is Sofia still occupying Anton's room?"

Maria let out a groan. "*Mamma mia.* Clothes strewn everywhere. Shoes far and wide." She turned to Marco. "What happened when you went to pick her up in town? Can we dare to dream that she found somewhere else to live?"

Marco rested his arms on the table. "Not today. She had lunch with friends and got into the car with a pile of shopping bags."

Maria shook her head. "Someone's going to have to speak to her. She can't stay here forever, not now that Anton's gone. I'm certainly not going to clean up after her, and Nora is getting tired of making that same avocado toast she insists on every morning."

"I could speak with her tomorrow," I said, sipping my wine. "I'm curious to talk to her, actually."

Maria and Vincent exchanged a look. "She was the last person with your father at the end," Maria said, "so I understand your desire, Fiona, but be firm with her. Don't be taken in by tears. She can get emotional."

"I'll be careful."

A hush fell over the table, and the break in conversation helped me to remember something.

"Vincent, I almost forgot." I picked up my purse. "I went to the bank in Montepulciano today to collect something from Anton's safety-deposit box." I pulled the iron key from my purse and handed it to him. "Do you recognize this?"

He held it aloft against the flickering candlelight. "This looks quite old. Was there a note to go along with it, explaining where it belongs?"

"No, there was nothing else in the box."

He turned it over and laid it across his open palm, staring for a long moment. "I think I might know."

"Really?"

"I can't be certain, but this is probably the key to a room in the wine cellars. It's been locked for decades, and Anton wouldn't let anyone set foot in there. My father told me the key had disappeared years ago, but this is probably it. Anton had it all along, naturally. What a devil he was."

I sat forward. "What's in the room?"

"Wine, I presume," Vincent replied, "but I can't say for sure. I've never been inside." He handed the key back to me. "Maria has asked me to show you around the vineyards tomorrow. Meet me first thing in the morning, in the gift shop, and we'll go down to the cellars and try that key in the lock. We'll see if it fits."

I slipped the key back into my purse. "Thank you, Vincent. You're a gem."

"And now for dessert," Maria said, rising from her chair. "I hope you like chocolate, Fiona."

"Who doesn't?" I replied as I marveled at how the joy of spending time with such good people could outweigh the jet lag I still felt from my long journey across the Atlantic.

CHAPTER 15
LILLIAN

Tuscany, 1986

Lillian drove Freddie to the station to catch an early train to Paris, then spent half a day manning the hotel reception desk before she moved to the wine shop to begin a tour. Afterward, she led the group back to the shop to make purchases and was surprised to find Anton waiting there. Hands in his trouser pockets, one shoulder leaning against the doorjamb, he stood casually, smiling.

"How was the tour?" he asked the guests in a friendly fashion as they filed into the shop, one by one.

"Wonderful!" a woman said.

"Very educational."

"Fascinating."

Lillian brought up the rear. "Everyone," she said, "this is Anton Clark. He's the owner of Maurizio Wines."

"Marvelous!" an older man said, pumping Anton's hand. "You, sir, are living the dream."

Anton gave him an easy smile. "I can't argue there."

He remained to socialize with the group until they made their purchases and headed to their cars. When the last vehicle honked a good-bye as it pulled away from the gravel parking lot, Lillian waved. Then she looked up at Anton, who was standing at her side.

"That went well, I think," she said.

"It went more than well. You must have set a sales record, Lillian. Twelve cases to be shipped to America. What in the world did you say to them?"

She shrugged. "I don't know. I just expressed the things I felt last night when we were tasting the older vintages."

They walked slowly to the stone wall at the edge of the lot that overlooked the vineyards. Angry gray clouds shifted and rolled beyond the mountainous horizon.

"I hope it's all right," she said, "but I told them about Signor Maurizio's special private collections for his children and grandchildren. We stood outside the locked door, and they found it very moving. Then, in the tasting room, I showed them which vintages age particularly well, and I encouraged them to store a bottle or two at home, to put it somewhere special and wait five to ten years for a special occasion, like a daughter's wedding or the birth of a grandchild. I think that's what they were all planning to do with the cases they bought. And I think it goes without saying that they'll talk about those special bottles with their friends. It'll be good for word of mouth."

He turned to her. "That's brilliant, Lillian. Maybe there's hope for us in America after all, with all these cases shipping out across the ocean."

They stood side by side, looking across the green landscape. The tall cypresses swayed in a fresh, cool wind, and the leaves on the grapevines fluttered and whispered.

Lillian pointed. "Look at the rain over there. It's blotting out that mountain completely." She sighed. "Oh, to be holding a paintbrush right now . . ."

His head turned, and he looked at her raptly. "Do you paint?"

She chuckled at the idea. "No, but I admire those who can. I understand the desire."

They faced the horizon and watched the dramatic weather unfold.

"It's coming this way," he said. "It'll be good for the soil, but we'll have to eat indoors tonight. Will you come? Bring Freddie, of course."

She kept her eyes on the horizon. "I'd love to come, but I'll be on my own tonight. Freddie left for Paris this morning."

"Whatever for?"

"To research the ending of his book."

Anton looked up at a bird hovering lightly on the wind. "How long will he be gone?"

She shrugged. "Your guess is as good as mine. Last night he said it would just be for a few days, but I suspect he'll stay until he's finished it, however long that takes."

They started to walk back toward the gift shop.

"Well then," Anton said. "You must come for dinner this evening—and every night this week. I'd hate to think of you eating alone."

The idea of him thinking of her at all caused a strange stirring in her. "That's very generous. I accept your invitation."

Thunder rumbled, soft and low, in the distance.

"Do you have an umbrella?" he asked. "You might need one to walk to the villa later." Without waiting for her to reply, he waved at her to follow him into the gift shop and through the back door into the administrative offices. "Take this one," he said, retrieving a sturdy black umbrella from a large terra-cotta urn full of them. "You can keep it. As you can see, we have plenty of them, all monogrammed with the Maurizio logo. I had them made up specially for the employees."

"Genius," she replied, looking it over. "Why aren't we selling these in the gift shop?"

He turned to the accounting clerk, who was busy at his desk. "Paolo, why didn't we think of that?"

The clerk raised his hands in surrender. "Don't look at me. I'm just a bean counter."

Anton returned his attention to Lillian. "You, my dear, have a very good head for business."

They smiled at each other in earnest, and she felt a rush of excitement, then had to look away.

"I should get back to work," she said, sensing a sudden awkwardness. "I'll see you later."

Outside, the wind had picked up, and the clouds were shifting wildly as they moved across the sky. A fresh fragrance with the promise of rain filled the air. As Lillian inhaled deeply, her body seemed to vibrate with exhilaration. Was it just Tuscany that thrilled her? Or was it something else inside her that had changed since she'd arrived? She felt as if she had been splayed wide open, and it felt good, because she wanted, for the first time, without fear, to let down her guard and experience everything life had to offer. At the same time, that openness came with a noticeably daunting awareness of her own vulnerability.

~

The rain came, just as Anton said it would. Lillian walked briskly with the big black umbrella, her feet skipping over puddles, up the hill to the villa. She was drenched because of the wind when she arrived, and Francesco made a fuss over her. "My poor signorina! You should have called. I would have picked you up in the car."

"I'll remember that for next time," Lillian replied with laughter, feeling joyful as she removed her jacket, shook away the raindrops, and hung it on the coat-tree.

"Come, come. Follow me." Francesco led her into a large reception room with a hot fire blazing in the hearth, cozy lamplight throughout, and ancient family portraits on the walls. Domenico and Anton were standing in front of the fire, engaged in a conversation, Domenico gesturing with his hands as he spoke.

As soon as Lillian walked in, Anton's eyes met hers, and he smiled. From clear across the room, she felt strangely disembodied, yet connected to him somehow—as if they shared a secret no one else knew.

"You made it," he said as she approached. "I was afraid you might change your mind, for fear of drowning."

She laughed. "I almost did. It was coming down in buckets. It was refreshing, though."

"Come, my dear," Francesco said, taking hold of her arm. "Move closer to the fire. We'll dry you out."

"Thank you." The warmth was like a balm to her senses, heating her blood.

The men talked about the vineyards and how the rain would affect plans for the next day, because a crew was coming to remove suckers and trim the vines.

"It'll be muddy," Domenico said, "but the shoots will be dry as soon as the sun comes over the mountain."

"What are suckers?" Lillian asked.

Anton explained that they were smaller shoots that robbed nutrients from the larger ones where the grape clusters hung. "It's enjoyable work," he said. "They snap off easily, so it's a good day in the fields."

She thought about that. "Where will you be at eleven o'clock? Because the tour guests love to see the actual work happening. It makes them feel like they're getting a peek behind the curtain."

Anton turned to Domenico. "Where will we be late morning?"

"With the Syrah," he replied and described the location of the field.

Caterina walked in and greeted Lillian with kisses on both cheeks. "How wonderful that you came."

They chatted briefly about the weather, then Caterina suggested it was time to eat.

They dined indoors with wax candles on the table and platters of antipasti to begin. Caterina brought hot tomato-and-basil soup, followed by squash-filled ravioli that melted in Lillian's mouth.

A sizzling roasted peppercorn steak followed with fresh green beans, and finally, there was peach gelato with thin, buttery sugar cookies for dessert.

All this was accompanied by the perfect pairing of wine for each course.

Domenico raised his glass. "To my lovely wife, who brings a grown man to tears with her squash ravioli."

"To Caterina," Anton said, raising his glass as well, then leaning in his chair to kiss her on the cheek. "Thank you for another splendid dinner."

At the end of the evening, Lillian helped in the kitchen, and Caterina shared her secret recipe for the squash ravioli, which wasn't really a secret at all because Caterina loved sharing anything and everything when it came to food.

She rinsed a plate and handed it to Lillian to dry. "Tell me about your husband. Anton said he left for Paris this morning. Why does he leave you?"

Lillian bristled at the underlying suggestion that Freddie had "left" her. "He has work to do," she explained. "He's writing a book, and he needs to do some research."

"Is he published?"

"Not yet, but we're hopeful that this will be his debut novel. When he gets an agent, everything will be easier, financially. Then we can start a family."

Caterina considered this for a moment. "So you are the breadwinner?"

Lillian cleared her throat. "Yes, I suppose, for now, but I don't mind. I enjoy working. Especially here." She smiled.

"But you want to have a family, *si?*"

"Yes, very much so."

Caterina dipped a large ceramic bowl into the hot, soapy water. "You must tell us the name of your husband's book so that we can buy it when it's published."

"Fingers crossed," she replied.

Caterina passed the bowl to Lillian, and she set it on the worktable behind her. "Your husband must be very creative," Caterina continued, as she scoured an iron skillet in the sink. "There is something about artistic men that is very appealing, don't you agree?"

"*Sì*," Lillian replied.

"Anton is an artist," Caterina casually mentioned. "Did you know?"

Lillian remembered how enraptured he had seemed when she mentioned that she wished she had a paintbrush to capture the clouds. "No, I didn't. What sort of artist is he?"

"He paints with oils. He's very good."

Lillian chuckled softly. "I'm both surprised and not surprised."

"Why is that?"

"Because he seems to have an artistic soul." It was there in the way he spoke about wine and pleasure and a deeper meaning to everything.

Later, Lillian and Caterina returned to the dinner table to drink some grappa with the men. As soon as there was a break in the conversation, Caterina pounced on the opportunity to change the subject.

"Anton, I told Lillian about your art."

Everyone fell silent. Anton sat back in his chair and inclined his head, scolding her a little with his tone. "Cat . . ."

"I couldn't help myself!" she replied defensively. "It just slipped out."

"Is it supposed to be a secret?" Lillian asked, innocently.

Domenico slapped the table with his hand. "That has been my question since the day I met this man. Why won't you show anyone your paintings, Anton? They're very good. They deserve to be seen and enjoyed."

"I don't paint for other people," he replied. "I just do it for myself."

"What do you paint?" Lillian asked, sipping her grappa.

"Nothing, really," Anton replied.

"He paints Tuscany," Domenico told her, flat out. "This man sees everything with fresh eyes. He has a very unique style. Maybe it's because he's British . . . I don't know."

Lillian sat forward and rested her chin on her hand. An enchanted smile came to her lips. "I should have guessed."

He sat forward as well. "Why do you say that?"

"Because I've noticed how you study the clouds and the mountains and the trees. It's as if you can't wait to put it all on canvas. I didn't understand it before, but now I do. And today, when I said that I wished I had a paintbrush . . ."

"Yes."

A breeze through the open window caused the candle flames to dance on the table. No one spoke, and Lillian felt the heat of the grappa moving pleasurably through her bloodstream.

Domenico spoke in a deep, commanding voice. "Take her to your studio, Anton. Otherwise, she'll lie awake all night wondering if we're just humoring you, overselling your talent because you're the boss." He turned to Lillian. "For all you know, maybe he paints like a three-year-old."

Lillian sat back and laughed. "I doubt that."

Domenico waved a hand through the air. "Take her, Anton."

Francesco agreed. "Yes, Anton. Take her upstairs. Show her a picture or two. What harm could come from it?"

Anton's gaze never veered from hers. "All right, Lillian. Let's go. But promise you'll be kind."

She smiled at him. "I always am."

They stood up from the table. Anton said, "You might as well all come. I know you're dying to see what she thinks."

"I am, actually," Domenico said as he rose and followed them out of the room while Caterina blew out the candles.

Anton led the way through the house and across an outdoor stone courtyard that resembled a monks' cloister. They reentered the villa on the opposite side and climbed to the second floor, where they came to an oak door. Anton pushed it open and switched on a chandelier.

"The light is terrible in here," he said. "I never paint at night, and I rarely paint here in the day either. It's just for storage, really."

Lillian walked in. She was immediately fascinated.

"Where do you work if not here?" Moving slowly along the back wall, she looked down at dozens of oil paintings stacked vertically on the floor, leaning into one another.

"Outdoors," he replied.

She noticed three easels folded and standing against the opposite wall and a steel case full of well-used paint tubes lying open on a small table.

Domenico, Caterina, and Francesco had followed them into the studio as well, but they remained quiet, looking around.

Anton stood by the door with his hands in his pockets, and Lillian sensed that this was torture for him—as if they were all intruding noisily upon his private life. Her heart ached a little, and she wished the others hadn't joined them. She wished they were alone. He would have been more comfortable, she believed, if it were just the two of them.

"May I?" she asked, indicating a collection of canvases on the floor under a window.

He nodded.

Lillian crouched down and flipped through a batch of medium-size paintings. The colors were vibrant yet tempered. There was a mellowness to everything. A sense of calm.

She was no expert or scholar when it came to art, but she knew enough to recognize an impressionist style, not unlike Monet. Anton had painted Tuscany with a gentle hand while celebrating its movement—the wind in the cypresses, the mist creeping through the valleys, the sunset disappearing behind the mountainous horizon. Fields of yellow sunflowers pointing their faces to the sky. A meadow of poppies fluttering in a fresh breeze. Tuscan architecture in the changing light of dawn. Steep, narrow, twisting cobblestone lanes. Romanesque churches. Piazzas alive with Italians.

"These are incredible," she said. "You should show them to people."

"Sometimes he'll give one away," Domenico explained, "if it's a friend who can pry something out of his greedy grasp."

Greedy probably wasn't the right word, Lillian thought, but she let it go.

"I'm amazed by all this, Anton. You're very talented." She rose to her feet and turned to him. "Is there anything you *can't* do?"

Attractive laugh lines crinkled around his eyes. "Plenty. But isn't that what life is about? Trying new things? Finding out what you love doing? Then taking a deep dive into it?"

She wondered how many paintings were stored in this studio. One hundred? How long had it taken him to paint all of them?

She strode slowly toward him. "Thank you for showing them to me. I feel honored."

An awkward silence ensued as she and Anton watched each other under the stark light from the chandelier—although it was only awkward for the others, who turned away and pretended to be looking at the paintings.

"I should probably get going," Lillian said. "Thank you for dinner and for showing me this."

The air around her felt electrified, but then she noticed a look pass between Domenico and Caterina. She remembered that Anton was a married man, and everyone in the house must be acquainted with his wife and children.

"I can drive you," Francesco said.

Domenico frowned at him. "Don't be ridiculous, Francesco. You've had too much grappa. Anton will walk with you, Lillian. Lord knows he needs the exercise."

"That's true," Caterina agreed.

"Speak for yourself, Domenico," Anton replied with laughter as he turned and headed for the door.

A short while later, Anton and Lillian were making their way down Cypress Row, where the air smelled of sweet pine and damp earth. Fireflies sparkled in the greenery.

"I'm still thinking about your paintings," Lillian said. "Would you let me look at them again sometime?"

"If you like."

Their footsteps tapped lightly in unison. Wispy clouds passed in front of the moon.

"You know . . . ," she put forward, carefully. "I have a thought, but I don't want to step over the line. When I say it out loud, you might regret hiring me."

He chuckled at that. "Never."

Lillian inhaled a slow, deep breath. "All right, then. I'll just throw this out there. Anton, have you ever considered putting some of your artwork on the wine labels?"

Anton said nothing for several seconds, and she worried that she had indeed crossed the line and he was trying to decide how to respond tactfully. When he finally spoke, his voice was quiet. "That's very interesting."

She put one foot in front of the other, glancing up at him as she walked, trying to gauge what he was thinking.

"But the Maurizio family name is a national treasure here in Italy," he finally said. "This winery has had the same image on its label for over a hundred years."

"I know. And it's a sketch of the villa, like every other old-world wine label out there in circulation. Don't misunderstand. I wouldn't change that, not for the vintage wines. But the new ones that you're developing . . . I can't imagine a better way to put your own stamp on those bottles. The Maurizio family name is the foundation, of course, but from what I've gathered about you, Anton, you're very passionate about this place. A hundred years from now, your wines and your contribution to the collections will have equal historical value. Perhaps you could try the new labels out with the Americans. Do a test batch. See how it plays."

He turned his eyes to meet hers. "That's interesting as well."

They reached the little cluster of stone buildings where her guest suite was located. All the windows were brightly lit, except for hers.

"Here we are," she said, stopping on the gravel driveway. The wet grass in the surrounding yard glistened in the light from the lampposts.

Anton looked at her door, shrouded in darkness. "You've got me thinking," he said. "It's quite an innovative idea. It feels risky, though."

"I don't think so at all," she replied. "Would you like to come inside for a bit? We could talk about it. Brainstorm a little."

As soon as the words tumbled out of her mouth, she regretted the suggestion. There was an obvious attraction between them. She'd be a fool to deny it. If anything was risky, it was this.

"Sure," he said, but there was a hint of unease in his tone. Nevertheless, he followed her up the stone steps, then held the flashlight steadily to illuminate the keyhole as she unlocked the door.

They entered the kitchen and sitting room. Everything was tidy and smelled clean after a visit from the maid that day. Lillian switched on a lamp and hung her purse on the back of a chair.

"Have a seat." She gestured toward the armchair. "Would you like a drink? We have rum and cola."

It was Freddie's rum. He would notice if she had some. He wouldn't mind, but he would mention it.

"That sounds exotic."

"Allow me to indulge you." She smiled as she withdrew the bottle from the top shelf in the cupboard and mixed two drinks over ice.

"So tell me," Anton said, sitting back in his chair and crossing one long leg over the other, "how do you see it working for the Americans? Changing the labels, I mean. Don't they come here wanting to experience the Old World? Isn't that what they're looking for? Ancient buildings and all that?"

"Yes, most definitely," she said, taking a seat on the sofa across from him. "That's what brings them here, but from what I've seen, they're most interested in purchasing the wines that have some sentimental story attached to them. Even if they're young wines, when I talk about something personal in regards to the harvest of a particular year—like the difficulty you had with days of rain which held you back and had you all in a mad panic last year—they love hearing about it. Every group buys a number of bottles because there's a story attached."

"But how do you see new labels playing into that?"

"Because they'll be *yours*. They're a testament to your passion for Tuscany. And just between us, I think they like the fact that you're an outsider, like them. I can see it in their eyes when I talk about you. You had a dream, and you followed that dream. And now you're finding a way to marry the Old World with the New. North Americans connect with that idea." She sipped her drink and sat back. "Or maybe I'm wrong, Anton. I don't know. This is why I think you should try a small test batch from the first harvest of your own signature wine to see how it does. If it sells, you can expand on that strategy."

She took another sip of her drink and thought about it further. "I think something new and modern and unique might do very well in America. People seem to like extravagance these days. Price the bottles high and make them feel like they're buying the winemaker's work of art—that they're drinking his passion. Literally."

Realizing she'd been carried away by her own passion for the ideas she was putting forth, Lillian shook her head at herself. "I'm so sorry. I'm going overboard, aren't I? It's too much. I'll blame it on the rum."

He frowned at her sudden need to backpedal and sat forward, resting his elbows on his knees. "Not at all. I'm devouring every word you're saying. I think it's brilliant. I love it."

Her whole being seemed to grow light. She floated on the air like a feather. But then the telephone rang, and she hit the ground, hard. She leaped off the sofa to answer it.

"Hello?" It was Freddie. "Yes, I'm here. I just got back. I was at dinner at the villa. How are you?"

She faced Anton and stared at him while she spoke to Freddie, who told her about his travels that morning and his first impressions of Paris. His voice was animated, and he hardly took a breath as he described the city's architecture, the beauty of the Seine, and the thrill he'd experienced when he saw the Eiffel Tower for the first time.

"That's wonderful." In that moment, Lillian felt guilty looking at Anton while she spoke to her husband, so she turned and faced the wall.

Freddie continued to talk. He confessed that he had spent the entire day walking around and hadn't written a single word. "But it was time well spent," he explained. "I need more of this before I can sit down to write. I don't want to force it or try to finish the story when I'm not ready. It has to feel right. You know?"

Lillian didn't say anything right away, and he was quiet for a few seconds.

"Lil? You there?"

"Yes, I'm here. Of course, that makes sense," she replied, because she'd always been supportive of his creativity, and she couldn't imagine behaving otherwise. "It has to feel right. When it comes to your setting, you need to feel confident in your descriptions."

"It's not just the *descriptions*," he said with a note of frustration. "The setting is going to affect what happens with the plot. It could change everything. I might need to take it in a whole new direction."

With a sudden sinking feeling, Lillian bit down hard on her lower lip. "Really? Is that going to take you more time? I mean . . . you thought you'd get it finished this summer."

Silence.

"I know, Lil," he finally said. "And you've been so patient. I love you for that, and I'm going to do my best. I'll write like crazy while I'm here."

Lillian continued to stand with her back to Anton and spoke softly into the phone. "Do you plan on staying in Paris for a while? Or will you come back here to write?"

You should come back, Freddie. You should come back right away.

Silence again. "I'm not sure. I found a cheap room near that old bookstore, Shakespeare and Company. It has a desk, and I feel like I'll get more done here. If I go back to Tuscany to work, I'll want to spend time with you. Besides, it's just not the right atmosphere there. Can you understand?"

Lillian began to feel a little sick to her stomach. "Of course, I understand."

There was a clicking sound and some static in the phone. "You've been so supportive," Freddie said, "and I promise there's a light at the end of the tunnel. As soon as I sell this book, you can do whatever you want—quit your job and eat bonbons all day. And we'll get pregnant. I promise."

If only she had a nickel for every time he said, "I promise."

"You're the best wife in the world," he added. "What would I do without you?"

She inhaled deeply and turned around. Anton was watching her with concern.

"You should put that on a plaque," she suggested.

Freddie chuckled into the phone. "I will. Better yet, I'll make you the star of the acknowledgments page."

Anton lowered his gaze, sipped his drink, and set it on the little table beside his chair.

"I should get going," Freddie said. "This is long distance, and I don't have any more change for the phone. I don't know when I can call next. I need to stay focused. Don't worry if you don't hear from me, okay? I'll be fine here."

But what about me? she wanted to ask. *Don't you want to know if I'll be fine?*

The line went dead, and Lillian hung up the phone. A knot formed in the pit of her belly, and she realized her heart was pounding because of the conversation. Why? It wasn't the first time Freddie had disappeared, mentally and emotionally, into another world when he was suddenly feeling inspired. But he had never left her for days on end to go and write somewhere else.

It wasn't that she didn't trust him. She knew he wasn't cheating on her, unless she considered his manuscript to be his metaphorical mistress. It was something else that troubled her in that moment—the fact that she was feeling an intimate, emotional connection to a man who was sitting in her kitchen at midnight, drinking her husband's rum. A man she respected and admired. A man who inspired her passions about her work, which, for the first time in her life, didn't feel like work at all.

Now her husband had no intention of returning to her anytime soon. She was on her own in beautiful Tuscany, making new friends, finding out who she was, looking at the world with a newfound sense of wonder and awe.

It felt hot in the apartment suddenly, and Lillian lifted her hair off the back of her neck as she returned to the sofa. She picked up her drink, swirled the ice cubes around in the glass, and listened to them clink together.

"That was Freddie," she said.

Anton sat very still, watching her.

"He's loving Paris." She raised the glass to her lips and took a sip.

Anton cleared his throat but said nothing.

"I'm not sure when he'll be back. He wants to stay there to write until he finally types 'The End.'" She fanned herself with her open hand.

"Are you all right?" Anton asked.

"Yes, just a little warm. Don't worry. I'm used to this," she explained. "Freddie's been working on this book since the day we got married. It's very important to him. It's just . . ." She paused. "It's taking an awfully long time."

When Anton said nothing, she looked away, closed her eyes, and pinched the bridge of her nose. "I'm sorry. I apologize."

"For what?"

"I'm not sure. Maybe for sounding like an unhappy housewife. But I'm not unhappy. I swear."

He sat forward slightly. "But something's wrong."

She thought about that for a moment. "Maybe. I suppose I always thought I would do something amazing with my life. I thought it would be motherhood, but it's starting to feel like all I ever do is support my husband's dreams."

"There's nothing wrong with supporting your husband's dreams," Anton replied. "It's a good thing, if you ask me, but it has to go both ways. He needs to support your dreams too. That's where most couples run into trouble, I think. I speak from experience."

She leaned back on the sofa and looked up at the ceiling. "I realize that marriage takes work, but lately I've been feeling very alone, even when we're in the same room together. I'm not sure if we're on the same page about things, and I'm starting to wonder if I might have made a mistake when I married him."

God . . . oh God. Had she really just said that? She'd never said anything like that to anyone before. She'd never even admitted it to herself.

"I was pregnant," she confessed. "But then I lost the baby, not long after we were married."

Anton sat forward and rested his elbows on his knees. "I'm sorry to hear that."

Lillian sat forward as well. "Thank you. It took me a while to get over it and feel ready to try again, but now I'm starting to wonder if Freddie will ever be ready. He keeps saying he wants to finish his book first, but I have a feeling what he really wants is the freedom to write, and he doesn't want the distraction of having a child to look after, while that's all I've ever wanted."

"Have you talked to him about it?"

"Yes, but it's not easy. I can't force him to make a baby with me if he's not ready or doesn't want it." She shook her head at herself. "I think losing the baby was hard for him. Harder than he realizes. He doesn't handle loss well because his mother walked out on him when he was little. Maybe there's a part of him that's afraid he'll lose me to the child . . . that my focus won't be on him anymore."

"It's not your job to be a mother figure to him," Anton said.

Lillian lowered her gaze. "I know." Then she covered her face with her hands. "What is wrong with me? I can't believe I'm telling you all this. You're my boss."

"It's fine," he replied, nonplussed. "Maybe I can help somehow."

She lowered her hands to her lap and found herself laughing. "Anton. How could you possibly help?"

He chuckled as well and sat back. "I don't know. That was a ridiculous thing to say."

There was something about the tone of his response that caused a fluttering in her belly. "Actually, no, it wasn't ridiculous. It helps that you're listening. Thank you." For a long, easy moment, they sat in silence, while she continued to reflect upon her relationship with Freddie. "I think part of the problem is that I've always been inclined to put his needs before my own. I have this inherent compulsion to do everything in my power to make sure that he's happy. So I'm the one who supports us financially so that he can pursue his dream. I don't turn off the light at night until *he's* ready to go to sleep. And I'm the one who waits for *him* to want to have a baby. My being ready isn't part of the equation."

"You're very generous," Anton said. "Is he generous as well? Does he ever put your needs first?"

She met Anton's gaze directly. "I honestly can't remember a time when that happened."

Anton stood up and crossed the room to sit beside her on the sofa. "I've often thought that a marriage is like a covered wagon, full of the stuff of life. The man and the woman are the two workhorses who pull it. Eventually, it gets heavy. There are children in the wagon, a home that needs to be maintained, feelings that need to be protected and nurtured when life throws curveballs. It works when both partners pull together, but the journey can't continue for long if one partner unbuckles the straps and decides to ride in the wagon, because it's easier, and because he knows his partner will keep pulling no matter what. Sometimes it can't be helped. If someone gets sick or is suffering in some other way . . . physically or emotionally or financially . . . when that happens, the other person needs to bear more of the load, but generally, when both partners are capable, husband and wife should be a team, pulling together, or at least taking equal turns."

Lillian reclined on the sofa and closed her eyes. "That's exactly what it's been like. In five years, I've never once gotten out of the harness."

"What about Freddie?"

"He's been riding in the wagon the whole time, and quite frankly, I'm getting a little tired." She glanced upward. "He's always consumed by his book, or so he says, and promising he'll do his part later. But later never comes. It's always tomorrow, tomorrow, tomorrow."

Anton reached for her hand and gently squeezed it. "Are you afraid to push for what you want?"

She stared down at their clasped hands. "Afraid? Of Freddie? Goodness, no. I was attracted to him because he was the opposite of my father, and I'd never been involved with someone who didn't punch things when he got angry."

"Not all men are like that," Anton told her.

"I know. At least, I think I know. Do you ever punch things?"

He smiled to himself as he spoke. "I can't pretend that I haven't kicked a flat tire. Lord knows I curse. But I've never hit another person. Not even in the schoolyard when I was a kid."

Her eyebrows rose in amazement. "That must be some kind of record."

He chuckled. "Maybe. I was a math nerd."

"I still find that so surprising," she replied. "Math and art . . . it's usually one or the other, or so I thought."

A dog barked somewhere outside. The air was hot and humid, and they were still holding hands, perspiring in the heat.

"I enjoy talking to you," Lillian said, her eyes downcast.

Anton sat back and stared at her with wonder. "I enjoy talking to you too. And that's why . . . I should probably go."

A part of her wanted to beg him to stay, but she knew what would happen if she did. The attraction she felt was palpable. If they sat there much longer, they would fall into each other's arms. They would kiss, and desires would escalate.

He stood up, and she was glad. She followed to see him out.

"Thank you again for dinner," she said.

He reached out and pushed a lock of her hair behind her ear, and his touch upset her balance. "Good night."

"Good night."

As soon as she closed the door behind him, she pressed both her hands to her flushed cheeks. Closing her eyes, she let her head fall back against the door.

"This can't be happening," she whispered with a rush of euphoria and a sense of excitement over what the future might hold. It was quickly followed by despair.

CHAPTER 16
FIONA

Tuscany, 2017

I opened my eyes, discovered that it was morning, and marveled at the fact that I had slept soundly the entire night. I often had trouble sleeping. I'd wake in the predawn darkness and fret about all sorts of things—my father's health, issues at work, debts that couldn't be repaid. Anton had been inexplicably generous in his will, but I wasn't entirely confident that all my money troubles were over. For one thing, Connor was not going to surrender without a fight, and even if he did, I still didn't feel right about keeping everything for myself. It was too much. That alone should have been enough to make me toss and turn for hours, but for some reason, it hadn't disrupted a single dream the night before. It must have been the jet lag.

After rolling over to check the clock, I yawned, stretched, and sighed at the pleasant notion that it was only half past six. I had time for a leisurely shower and an extra cappuccino at breakfast before I met Vincent for my vineyard tour at nine.

An hour later, dressed in black cargo shorts and a white T-shirt, I was wandering past the front desk on my way to the breakfast room when Anna called out to me. "Ms. Bell, someone just called for you!"

I stopped and approached, accepted the slip of paper she held out, and read a name and phone number. "I don't know this person."

"He's an *agente immobiliare*," Anna told me. "A real estate agent from Florence."

"Why is he calling me?"

"He wouldn't say, but he made me promise to ask you to call him. He used the word *urgente*."

"Urgent?"

"*Sì.*"

I backed away from the desk. "Thank you, Anna. I'll call, but I need coffee first. And please call me Fiona." I tucked the message into the pocket of my shorts and went for breakfast.

~

A half hour later, after I finished my second cappuccino and found myself sitting alone in the breakfast room, I keyed in the real estate agent's number on my cell phone. "Hello, is this Roberto? This is Fiona Bell. I received a message that you called?"

"*Sì!* I am happy you returned my call. I understand that you are the new owner of Maurizio Wines."

"That's correct," I replied with some curiosity. "News travels fast. Where did you hear that?"

"I have spies everywhere," he said mischievously.

I sat back and crossed one leg over the other. "That sounds rather alarming."

He laughed. "I am only joking, signora. Do forgive me. I am sorry for your loss. Your father was a great man."

I wasn't about to tell him that I'd never even met this so-called great man to whom he referred. "Thank you, I appreciate that. Can I help you with something?"

He paused. "I hope so. I am calling to ask if you have any interest in selling Maurizio Wines."

With a sudden rush of butterflies in my belly, I rose to my feet and walked out of the breakfast room to the flagstone terrace. The morning sun was shining brightly. I closed my eyes and lifted my face to feel its warmth on my cheeks. "I don't really know what my interests are at the moment. I only just arrived, and I'm getting to know the place."

"You're American, am I correct?"

"Yes, that's right."

"Do you have any experience running a winery?"

I opened my eyes and strolled leisurely across the terrace. "Not yet, but the staff here seems very knowledgeable."

He was quiet for a few seconds. "No doubt. Maurizio Wines is an exceptionally well-managed company. But I do have a buyer who is willing to make a generous offer."

"Really." I couldn't resist. I had to ask. "How much are we talking about?"

Roberto made a few grumbling noises. "My client would require that his accountant examine the books first, of course, before we begin any official negotiations. But he has given me permission to offer you ninety million euros today, to close the deal without an audit."

I halted in my tracks and strove to remain calm. "That is an attractive offer."

"*Sì*, it is, signora. You could be on a flight home to America in less than a week. A very rich woman!"

My eyes followed the horizon from west to east. A heavy pink haze was hanging over the distant rolling fields. A butterfly fluttered across the rosebushes at the edge of the terrace. "I'll need to think about that."

"The offer will hold until midnight tomorrow," Roberto pronounced. "May I inform my client that you are considering it?"

I raked my fingers through my hair. "Of course. But you should know that the family may be contesting the will, so I can't guarantee

I'll even be in a position to sell to anyone. Can I ask who's making the offer?"

"My client prefers to remain anonymous."

I strolled slowly back across the terrace, taking extra long strides, then hopped across some flagstones, three at a time. "I understand, but I *will* need to know who I'm selling to, if I decide to sell."

"I will pass that along," he said.

"Please do. And give me time to think about it. I'll call you tomorrow if I'm interested."

"Very good, signora. Enjoy your day."

"I will, and same to you, Roberto."

I ended the call and stood immobile for a moment, completely unable to move. I felt a little dizzy and faint at the amount of money Roberto was waving in front of my face. Crouching low to the ground, I hugged my phone in a prayer position and squeezed my eyes shut.

"Holy moly," I whispered.

CHAPTER 17
LILLIAN

Tuscany, 1986

A flat tire outside Siena caused a bus tour group to cancel a morning visit to the winery, which left Lillian with nothing to do.

"Take the morning off," Matteo suggested. "Your next group doesn't arrive until two. Go for a swim in the pool."

"Are you sure?" Lillian asked. "I could help out in the shop."

"For what purpose? There are no customers." He waved her away. "Trust me, this place will be crawling with tourists in July. You should take advantage while you can. That's an order, soldier."

"Aye, aye, Captain."

A half hour later, Lillian was stretched out on a lounge chair in her blue bikini, reading a novel and sweating under the hot Tuscan sun. All the hotel guests were elsewhere, wandering around the shops in Montepulciano or driving to Florence in their air-conditioned rental cars, so it was blissfully quiet on the estate.

When it grew stiflingly hot, Lillian got up and dived into the deep end of the pool. She swam laps while she thought about Freddie in

Paris. What was he doing at that moment? Writing? Walking around the city? Did he miss her? Or was she out of sight, out of mind?

Moving through the cool water, she reached the far end of the pool, turned, and pushed with her feet to propel herself back in the other direction.

Her thoughts changed direction as well. An image of Anton sitting on her sofa the night before—drinking rum and talking about covered wagons full of the "stuff of life"—materialized in her mind.

She had never known a man who spoke that way about relationships. After he had gone, she'd slipped into bed and opened the window to look out at the clouds passing in front of the moon. The rain-scented air refreshed her body and soul, but she couldn't sleep, so she had spent the next hour comparing Anton to Freddie.

It wasn't a fair comparison. Anton was ten years older, more worldly and experienced in life, wealthier, and devastatingly handsome and sophisticated. Freddie wasn't *un*handsome, but he was thin and lanky, neither wealthy nor sophisticated. He was her husband, however, and Anton was someone *else's* husband, not to mention a father to two children. That was where Freddie won the day—because they were lawfully wed—and Lillian worked hard to remember her wedding vows as she struggled to fall asleep.

Now, out of breath from swimming fast and hard, she climbed out of the pool and padded across the deck to her chair, where she twisted her long hair to squeeze out the water. It dripped heavily onto her toes, splatting onto the hot cement.

The temperature was scorching hot, so she didn't bother to towel off and decided instead that it would be best to remain wet. Sitting down and inching back on the blue seat cushion, she put on her sunglasses and reached for her novel.

Moments of hot, sticky stillness elapsed. A bumblebee flew by. Church bells rang somewhere in Montepulciano, high on the hilltop.

Lillian tried to focus on her book in the sweltering heat, but she was distracted constantly by thoughts of Anton. He came into her mind like a cool breeze.

Lowering her book to her lap, she allowed herself to daydream. She found herself recalling the first time she had set eyes on him, moments after the crash, when he wrenched the car door open and peered in at her. *Is everyone all right?*

A movement caught her eye just then. She sat forward on the lounge chair, her heart lurching in her chest, because it was him walking casually toward her, down the grassy slope to the pool, smiling the entire way. Lillian swallowed hard and raised her sunglasses to the top of her head. Heaven help her, he was the most attractive man she'd ever seen in real life. On that morning, he wore a baby-blue T-shirt and navy shorts, his jaw unshaven. He was covered in sweat. The T-shirt stuck to his chest and shoulders. All her senses began to hum, and her pulse quickened.

As he drew near, Lillian noticed he was wearing work boots.

"Hello there," he said, opening the wooden gate to step onto the sunny pool deck. "I didn't expect to see you here."

"My morning tour got canceled," she explained, quickly reaching for her cover-up and slipping her arms into the short sleeves. He was her boss, after all. She shouldn't be parading around the workplace in her bikini. "The bus had a flat tire outside Siena."

"That was bad luck." He flicked the iron latch on the gate to close it behind him and walked toward her. "Bloody hot, isn't it?"

"Yes. The water's nice, though."

He arrived at the lounge chair beside her, sat down with his back to her, and began to unlace his boots. She couldn't resist looking at the firm muscles across his back and the way his broad shoulders narrowed to a slim waist.

"Were you working in the vineyard?" she asked.

"Yes. We've been there since daybreak, but now it's siesta time. Too hot to work in the sun."

He removed his boots and socks, stood up, and stripped off his T-shirt.

Lillian took one look at his bare chest, and her breath caught in her lungs, for he was fit, tanned, and muscular, with dark chest hair.

After tossing the shirt onto the lounge chair, he strode to the outdoor shower, rinsed off, then dived straight into the pool with a big splash. She watched him swim below the surface like a torpedo from the deep end to the shallow before breaking the surface and flicking his hair out of his eyes.

"Feels great!" he shouted. "You should come in. It's too hot to be sitting in the sun."

She couldn't resist. Standing up, she shrugged out of the cover-up, let it fall, then strode quickly to the edge of the pool and dived in. When she emerged, Anton was treading water a few feet away.

"I can't believe how hot it is," she said, "and I live in Florida." She ran her hand down her face to whisk away the water.

They swam around each other for a moment or two.

"How is the sucker removal going?" she asked with a grin.

"Very well." He ducked beneath the surface and swam to the shallow end. Lillian did the same but swam in the opposite direction.

Before long, it grew awkward, perhaps because they both recognized a mutual attraction and knew it was dangerous. Perhaps, in the water, under the hot Italian sun, with their bodies bare, it was best to put some distance between them.

Eventually, Lillian got out of the pool and returned to her lounge chair, where she toweled off, sat down, and reached for her book again.

Anton continued to swim laps.

She opened to the page where she had inserted the bookmark but only pretended to be reading. How could she possibly concentrate when she couldn't take her eyes off Anton and her entire being was humming with awareness?

After a time, he relaxed in the water. He closed his eyes and floated on his back.

Cicadas buzzed like electric currents in the olive trees. A butterfly flitted lightly across the surface of the water.

Eventually Anton opened his eyes and swam to the side of the pool. "Are you coming for dinner tonight?"

Lillian laid her book down on her lap. Lifting her sunglasses off her nose to look down at him, she asked, "Am I invited?"

"Of course. You're invited every night. Everyone expects you."

Their gazes locked and held. She felt her shoulders burning under the hot sun. "Then I'll be there."

He pushed away and swam backward, keeping his eyes on her the entire time. "What are you reading?"

She held up the book. "*Clan of the Cave Bear.*"

"Is it good?"

"I'm not sure yet. I only just started it, and I'm having a hard time staying focused. I can't seem to concentrate."

He swam to the ladder and climbed out of the pool. Water glistened on his torso and dripped from his shorts. Lillian watched his every move as he stalked toward her. The muscles in his upper arms tensed and flexed as he used his T-shirt to dry himself.

"It must be contagious," he said. "I can't seem to concentrate lately either."

Her lips parted slightly while her heart thudded against her rib cage. His nearness was overwhelming.

"I'll see you at dinner," he said.

"Okay."

He gave her a brief glance before he picked up his boots and walked toward the gate.

Lillian couldn't tear her eyes away from his shirtless body as he sauntered up the grassy hill. If she were sensible, she would come up with some sort of excuse to get out of dinner at the villa that night. But the way Anton made her feel inside eradicated any possibility of acting sensibly. She was overcome. Mostly, it was a sexual desire—she couldn't deny it—but that wasn't everything. Something about Anton Clark felt like home, and all she wanted to do was run toward that place and curl up in it.

~

They dined outdoors that night, by the light of a dozen thick white wax candles. It was a larger crowd than usual and included a few vineyard workers and a new Italian tour guide—a university student who lived in town. Her name was Teresa, and she was tall, slender, and very pretty. Before dinner, Lillian had watched Anton speak to her for a while at the edge of the lawn, swirling his red wine around in his glass, holding it up to the light of the sunset and showing her how to identify the legs and articulate the aromas. Lillian began to wonder if it was his habit to be kind and attentive to all his tour guides, and perhaps she was making too much of the attraction between them. Life would certainly be easier if that were the case, if she could sweep her infatuation aside and recognize it as nothing more than a foolish crush on her handsome, charismatic boss.

When they sat down to eat, Caterina served a mouthwatering lamb stew with warm biscuits and salty butter, while Domenico presented a special vintage of Brunello to go along with the stew. The mixture of flavors exploded deliciously on Lillian's tongue. For dessert, they enjoyed a dark-chocolate-and-cherry cake with whipped cream and coffee.

Lillian noticed that Anton was more reserved than usual. He didn't seem quite himself. She was also conscious of how Teresa and Matteo seemed to be hitting it off at the far end of the table. Anton hardly looked at Teresa, but he met Lillian's gaze frequently. He watched her while others were talking and while she was simply enjoying her meal. Whenever she felt his eyes on her, she looked up and shared a private communiqué with him, which she recognized as a desire to be alone together. She wanted it, and she knew he felt the same. It was real. She had imagined nothing.

Afterward, no one batted an eye when Anton announced that he was walking Lillian back to her guest suite. It was a gorgeous summer evening under a three-quarter moon. Teresa said good night and was picked up by her father in front of the villa. Mr. and Mrs. Guardini wandered off hand in hand, laughing as they talked, and Matteo remained at the table with Francesco, discussing petrol prices and American cars and dipping into a bottle of scotch.

As soon as Anton and Lillian were beyond the gate and alone on Cypress Row, with nothing but the beam of the flashlight illuminating their way, Anton said, "I'm glad you came tonight."

"Me too," she replied. "But you were quiet. Is everything all right?"

The air was humid, and it caused her sundress to stick to her skin.

Anton looked down at the ground. "I'm sorry about that. Something happened this afternoon."

"Can you tell me about it?"

He paused, then took a breath. "After I left you at the pool and went back to the villa, there was a message that my wife had called, so I called her back." He hesitated again, and Lillian waited for him to continue. "She told me that she didn't want to come here anymore, that the children were better off in LA, near her family. She wants a divorce."

Lillian's heart ached for him. "Oh, Anton. I'm so sorry."

"I asked her to reconsider," he continued. "I suggested that we get a house here for her parents to come and stay whenever they want. Maybe a flat in Montepulciano or even Florence if they prefer the city. But she didn't like that idea. She made it clear that she preferred America over Italy and that she wanted her children to grow up there. Not here."

"But they're your children too."

"I did remind her of that, but she's going to put up a fight."

Lillian lifted her gaze. "How could anyone not want to raise children in a place like this?"

"I wish she shared your feelings. Now I'm looking at another legal battle. I suspect she's going to bleed me dry, financially."

Lillian looked up at the sky. "I'm so sorry. I can't even imagine. I wish there was something I could do to help, but I don't know what that would be."

"You're doing it."

She wasn't entirely sure what he was referring to and was afraid to ask.

They reached the quiet corner of the estate where her guest suite was located and paused in the gravel parking lot. Lillian dug into her purse for her key.

She wondered if she should invite Anton inside to continue the conversation. Uncertainty abounded as she allowed him to shine the flashlight on the dark stairs while she climbed to the top and inserted the key into the lock. When she pushed the door open, she turned to him.

He looked very forlorn. And handsome. She didn't want to say good night. She wanted to talk some more.

"Would you like to come in?" she asked.

He nodded and started up the stairs.

~

Lillian switched on the overhead light. They both squinted, so she moved to the small lamp by the sofa and lit the room more gently.

It was stiflingly hot in the apartment. While Anton stood at the door, Lillian went from room to room, opening all the windows. She returned to the kitchen to switch off the main overhead light, and the room took on a cozy golden glow.

Anton had not moved from his spot at the door. "Lillian . . ." The timbre of his voice held a note of apology.

Did he not want to stay?

He wet his lips. "I'd understand if you would prefer that I go."

"Why do you say that?"

"Because you're married, and your husband is away, and I'm . . . well, I'm still married. And you work for me. I don't want there to be any questions about—"

"Please stay," she implored. "We'll just talk."

He hesitated briefly, then shut the door behind him.

Lillian removed her sandals and padded into the kitchen. "Would you like some coffee?"

"That would be nice. Thank you."

She set to work, spooning grounds into the stainless steel percolator, knowing full well that it would keep her up all night, but she didn't care. Anton was here.

He moved to the sofa and sat down. "I can't help but wonder now, in light of what's happening, if my wife just married me for my money."

Lillian poured water into the coffeepot and flipped the switch. "I'm sure that's not true. You're an incredible man. A woman would have to be mad not to fall in love with you."

He chuckled softly. "That's very kind. For the record, I wasn't fishing for a compliment, but I do appreciate it. Nothing to get a man down on himself like a woman telling him she never wants to see him again."

Lillian sat down next to him on the sofa. "She didn't actually say that, did she?"

"Not in so many words, but the overall message was the same." He exhaled sharply. "The fact is—if she loved me, she wouldn't want to be apart, no matter where I lived. But I suppose you could say the same thing about me. Maybe I'm making my choice, too—this winery over everything else. But she never asked me to sell it and move to LA. I don't think that's what she wants."

Lillian laid her arm across the back of the sofa and rested her temple on her finger. "Do you love her?"

He thought about that for a moment, then lowered his eyes. "Not enough, I suppose. My children, though . . ."

Nodding with understanding, Lillian stood up to check on the gurgling coffeepot. "Tell me about how the two of you met."

He spoke while watching her retrieve two mugs from the cupboard and prepare a serving tray.

"It was just after I'd recovered from my illness and my brother bought me out of the company. I didn't really know what to do with myself at that point. I met Kate at a charity event for the homeless. She was working for the caterer, serving drinks and canapés. Later, she told me that for her, it was love at first sight, and maybe it was for me too. She was gorgeous, and I was taken with her American accent. We flirted, and before you knew it, we were heavily involved. A year later we got married, and everything seemed fine. She enjoyed living in London, and I thought we'd do anything for each other, go anywhere together. We came to Italy on a holiday, and we both fell in love with the place. When I spotted this winery for sale, she seemed in love with it, too, but maybe she was just caught up in the moment, or she was humoring me. Or maybe she thought I wouldn't actually go through with it—go so far as to buy a winery in a foreign country and move there permanently."

Lillian set the mugs on the tray and poured the coffee. "Go on," she said.

He sat back and stretched out. "The winery took up a lot of my attention that first year. I was busy, and she didn't show much inter-est in the business side of things, much less the work in the fields. Harvesttime is backbreaking work. Long hours. That's when she started to get homesick for LA. So her solution was to get pregnant and start a family. I wanted children from the beginning, so I was game. Our first child—my daughter, Sloane—kept her happy for a while, until another harvest season rolled around, and she complained constantly about me being gone all the time. We fought about that, but we got through it, and she got pregnant again. Everything was fine for a while, but Kate never had any interest in the workings of the winery."

"Which is your passion." Lillian brought the tray of coffee to the sofa and handed Anton his cup.

"Yes. Whenever I talked about it, she was bored to tears and made no secret of it. She saw it as something that took up my time and attention. Maybe she was jealous of it, in a way."

"It's strange to be talking about this," Lillian said as she sat down, "because sometimes that's how I feel about Freddie's manuscript. I know I can't compete with his passion for his book, and it's disheartening." She paused. "But let's not talk about that."

Anton spooned sugar into his cup.

"Tell me more about Kate," Lillian said.

He sat back again and sipped his coffee. "Well . . . she was always a city girl. She preferred shopping malls, while I preferred the outdoors. Although, in my defense, I do believe she misrepresented herself when we were dating. She was always keen to go camping and cycling with me. That stopped as soon as we tied the knot. She might have gone with me to a beach on a Saturday afternoon, but otherwise it was dinner out, movies, dance clubs. Maybe the willingness to go camping was all just an elaborate scheme to lure me in, and I fell for it."

He leaned forward and set his cup down. "I'm sorry, Lillian. I've gone on and on. Tell me to stop, will you?"

"No. I want to hear it. I want to hear everything."

He was quiet for a moment and looked away. "Maybe I should be grateful that we're calling it quits now, rather than dragging things out for years when neither of us is happy because we don't have anything in common. Truthfully, I can live without Kate, but I can't accept being away from my children. That's what's killing me right now. I don't know how I'm going to survive this."

Lillian reached for his hand and squeezed it. "You'll get through it, and you'll get a good lawyer who will make sure that you'll stay a part of their lives."

He shook his head. "Los Angeles is halfway across the world."

"You can go there and visit. And they can come here. They must love it here, Anton. What child wouldn't?"

He finished his coffee and set the empty cup on the tray. "Can I use the bathroom?"

"Be my guest."

He stood up and left the room. While he was gone, Lillian carried the tray to the sink and rinsed out the cups, then stacked everything to wash in the morning.

She heard the water running in the bathroom. Then the door opened, and Anton emerged.

Lillian wiped her hands on a tea towel and faced him. His brow was furrowed. He leaned his shoulder against the doorjamb between the hall and the kitchen and pressed the heels of both hands to his eyes.

"Oh, Anton . . ." She approached him. "Don't worry. Everything's going to be fine."

He shook his head. "I'm afraid I'm going to lose them."

She took his face in her hands. "No, you won't. You're their father, and you'll always be a part of their lives. You have this beautiful piece of paradise to share with them. They're going to love coming here. And one day, they'll bring their own children here."

His eyes glistened with dampness, and she pulled him into her arms, where he drew comfort from her soothing words and gentle touch. His shoulders heaved with emotion, and he whispered into her hair, "Thank you."

"For what?"

"For being here."

Lillian drew back. "I'm grateful that you hired me. I know it might sound strange, but I feel completely transformed by this place. For the better. And you've been in my thoughts, Anton. Quite a bit."

"You've been in my thoughts too. Ever since the first moment I saw you."

His words filled her with exhilaration, and she couldn't think about Freddie. He didn't even exist for her in that moment. All she could do was tremble with the hope that all her powerful bottled-up longings would finally be fulfilled. Anton stroked her hair. The next thing she knew, she was pressing her cheek into the firm muscles of his chest. He held her close, tight against him, his big hand cupping the back of her head, and she felt as if she were dissolving into him somehow, that everything in her life had brought her to this moment. For the first time in her trifling existence, all seemed right with the world.

She had never been the type of woman to romanticize anything. She had always been overly practical, sometimes to a fault, but on that night, in Anton's arms, she felt as if she were being swept away on a powerful current of soulfulness. Her desire for him was unfathomable, and it wasn't just physical passion. It felt, unbelievably, like love. The kind of love that people wait for and dream about all their lives. The kind of love people died for. It hardly seemed possible that she'd only known him a few weeks. It seemed like he had been inside her heart forever, just waiting to step out of it, into her world.

The apartment was sweltering. Lillian felt almost dizzy. Her flesh was damp with perspiration. She lifted her gaze and looked up at Anton with a sense of wonder, and he smiled. His happiness moved her to tears.

"I've been smitten," he said, "since you climbed out of that mangled car, fell to your knees, and seemed to worship the ground beneath your feet. Then I took you to the hospital . . . and your husband was in the back seat . . . but it was as if he didn't exist. I told myself it was the shock of seeing your car go off the road. That it was adrenaline or something. But every day since, each time I saw you, I've loved you more."

Lillian felt weightless. "It's been the same for me. Freddie picked a bad time to leave me."

She wished she hadn't mentioned Freddie. She didn't want to think of him. She didn't want to face the dread of an inevitable pain that would come when she woke from this beautiful dream and had to face reality. Being in Anton's arms was the only reality that mattered to her now.

His hands at the small of her back invited her closer, pulling her snug against him. "If you were mine, I'd never leave you, and I would do anything to make you happy."

He stared at her for a few heart-stopping seconds, gauging her expression, seeking permission to move things a step further.

She did not discourage him.

Anton lowered his mouth to hers. His lips were soft and searching, hungry with passion. Her arms slid up and around his neck, and she returned the kiss with reckless abandon. She wanted to take hold of him and never let go, for this moment to go on and on.

This time, she didn't think of Freddie. It was as if he had ceased to exist because Anton had taken up all the space in her world. She hadn't known emotions like this were possible.

Finally, she drew back and took Anton by the hand. She led him to her bedroom, dark except for the moonlight streaming in through the open window. Her heart raced as he gathered her into his arms and eased her onto the bed. He moved over her like a shadow, filling her with rapture and joy.

They made love through the night, pausing only to sleep for brief spells until one of them woke and reached for the other. Breathlessly, Lillian whispered in his ear, "Is this even real?"

"I don't know. It feels like a dream."

They shared Lillian's bed until the sky brightened at dawn. Then they rose and got dressed, walked hand in hand across the dewy grass to sit on a stone wall overlooking a vineyard on a sloping field below. The sunrise bathed the Tuscan hills in a soft pink mist. Anton and Lillian marveled at the beauty of it, and in that perfect moment, there was no knowledge of pain or unhappiness anywhere in the world. They were together in their own private version of heaven.

CHAPTER 18
FIONA

Tuscany, 2017

It wasn't easy to keep a secret that made your heart want to burst out of your chest. Ninety million euros. Cash in hand. A done deal without an audit. I could board a plane back to Florida in a week, and this secret of mine—and my mother's—would be swept under the rug forever.

But how would I explain the money to Dad? And what would I do with it? Split it with Connor and Sloane? How would I divide it?

Walking briskly across the parking lot toward the gift shop, I looked down at my feet and listened to the sound of my sneakers crunching over the clean white gravel. The movement grounded me and reminded me that none of this was set in stone. Connor still wanted to fight the new will, so I would be wise not to let any dreams of financial freedom get too out of hand.

I entered the gift shop and found a dark-haired woman on a step-ladder, filling a top shelf with bottles of wine. She wore navy trousers and a red golf shirt with the Maurizio Wines logo on the breast pocket.

"*Buongiorno*," she said, climbing down. "You must be Ms. Bell?"

"Yes. I'm here to meet Vincent Guardini. But please call me Fiona."

She approached and held out her hand. "I'm Mia, the gift shop manager. It's nice to meet you." We shook hands. "Vin's already here. He's in the office. Vin! Fiona's here!"

He walked into the shop through an open door at the back and smiled warmly at me. "What a beautiful morning for a walk in the vineyards, *sì?*" He kissed me on both cheeks. "You've met Mia?"

"Yes."

"Wonderful. Let's get started, then. First, let me show you the office. Come, come." He beckoned for me to follow him through the back into a large room with half a dozen cubicles and large windows that let in plenty of light. "Everyone, this is Fiona Bell, Anton's daughter from America. Our new owner."

People stood up from their desks, and Vincent introduced me to each person individually. Then he took me into a separate office to meet the sales-and-marketing manager.

Afterward, we walked outside to the parking lot, where Vincent led me to his car—a cute little blue Fiat with a dent in the side.

"Are we going somewhere?" I asked.

"Many hectares to see," he explained. "Quicker to drive."

I slowed my pace. "Vincent . . . I wonder if you wouldn't mind taking me to the wine cellars first. Remember that key I showed you last night?"

"*Sì.*"

"I have it in my purse, and the suspense is killing me."

He stopped and regarded me with understanding. "We can't have that. We will go. The cellars are this way."

He led me up the gravel road past the chapel to the little hamlet of medieval buildings. We climbed a set of stone steps to a terrace that took us to a large door with a keypad lock.

As soon as we entered the building, we descended a steep set of stairs to a large underground room with high cathedral ceilings of stone. I was struck by the fragrance of wine, oak, and a cool, earthy dampness.

Vincent led me past long rows of giant oak barrels on their sides, and he explained that the wine would age there for two years before it would be bottled and aged further in many modern, state-of-the-art cellars all over Tuscany.

"This place is like a labyrinth," I mentioned as he led me through more rooms lined with wine racks full of dusty bottles and down dimly lit, narrow corridors. At last we came to an ancient-looking door with iron fittings, set into a stone arch.

"This is it," Vincent said. "The dead end where no one ever comes. Do you have the key?"

I dug into my purse, pulled it out, and gave it to him.

"Let's give it a try." He inserted it into the keyhole and turned it. The mechanism clicked, and Vincent pushed the heavy door open on creaking hinges. "It works. After you."

I sucked in a breath of anticipation as I stepped across the threshold into a small, dark wine cellar with low ceilings. Vincent pulled the chain on a hanging light bulb, but it was burned out. We had to rely on the dim light reaching in from the corridor and the glow from our cell phones.

"You were right," I said. "It's just wine in here. But why would he keep it locked?"

There were no racks, just dusty bottles stacked on wooden slabs. I bent to look more closely at a rough-hewn wooden plaque above one of the batches. "This one says 'Lorenzo, 1920.'"

Vincent moved to a smaller batch. "This says 'Bianca, 1926.'"

"Who were they?" I asked.

"I'm not sure." He continued along the wall and shone his light on the other batches. "Ah . . . here's something . . ."

I joined him. "This plaque says 'Connor, 1984.'" I moved to the next one. "And this one says 'Sloane, 1982.' These bottles must be from the years his children were born. But who are the others?"

"Judging by the dates," Vincent replied, "and the Italian names, they must have been the Maurizio children. They all died years ago."

A chill rippled down my spine. I backed into the center of the room and rubbed at my arms. "It's kind of morbid, don't you think? Except for Connor and Sloane, all these people are dead. These plaques are like grave markers."

"Not everyone's passed on," Vincent mentioned, aiming the light from his cell phone at another batch of wine in the back corner. "Come and see this." He removed the plaque from a hook on the wall and passed it to me.

FIONA, 1987

"My goodness. That's the year I was born."

Vincent picked up one of the bottles and wiped it clean with the palm of his hand. "The label says '87, but I don't recognize it. Anton must have made a special blend in your name. It's definitely one of his paintings."

My heart skipped a beat. "It is? Let me see." Surprised by the realization that Anton had put his own artwork on the bottles, I examined the image. It was a field of sunflowers with an impressionistic style, and there was a blonde woman standing at the edge of the field. I wondered if it was supposed to be my mother.

"It's very beautiful," I said. Then I turned to the next batch and blinked a few times with astonishment. "This one says Lillian. That's my mom. Nineteen eighty-six. That's the summer she spent in Tuscany." I moved to check the label on one of the bottles, and sure enough, it was another of Anton's paintings—a sunrise over the Tuscan hills.

I checked Connor's and Sloane's bottles, and they also had Anton's paintings for labels, unlike all the others with traditional Maurizio labels—a sketch of the villa. "This is such a surprise," I said, looking around the room.

It was the first time I had considered the possibility that Anton might have truly loved my mother.

"Do Connor and Sloane know about this cellar?" I asked.

"I couldn't tell you," Vincent replied.

I thought of the rolled canvases in Anton's studio and was desperate to go and look at them. Only then did I recall what I had been hoping to find in this secret cellar. "The letters aren't here."

"Apparently not. You'll have to keep searching." He moved to the door, and I followed him out. "We should keep this door locked," he said, "and guard the key well, Fiona. Those are precious vintages. There's a small fortune in there."

"I understand."

He locked the door, gave me the key, and escorted me out.

~

After my morning tour of the vineyards, I decided to take a swim in the pool before heading up to the main villa. I was halfway down the grassy hill when I spotted Sloane stretched out on a lounge chair, wearing a red one-piece bathing suit and a wide-brimmed straw hat. Two children were in the pool, splashing around.

I was half-tempted to turn around and go elsewhere, but it was scorching hot outside, and I had been looking forward to a swim all morning, so I pressed on and opened the wooden gate.

At the sound of the gate closing, Sloane slid her sunglasses down her nose to see who was approaching.

"Hi," I said without shyness, walking toward the lounge chair beside her and dumping my towel there. I kicked off my flip-flops and pulled my T-shirt off over my head. "What a scorcher."

Holding her sunglasses low on the tip of her tiny nose, Sloane inspected my red polka-dot bikini and plastic shoes. "Yes, it's very hot today."

"Are those your children?" I asked, bending forward to pull my shorts down to my ankles.

Sloane pointed a well-manicured finger at them. "Yes, that's Evan, and the younger one is Chloe."

I rested my hands on my hips and watched them frolic. "They're cute. I guess I'm their new aunt. Or half aunt. Is that the right word?"

"I've no idea," Sloane replied, turning her face in the other direction.

I decided to ignore Sloane's frosty tone. "I'm going in for a swim. Have you explained the situation to them? Do they know who I am?"

With a touch of panic, Sloane inched upward on the chair. "No. I haven't told them anything yet. I suppose I'm still getting over the shock of it myself."

"You and me both." I shaded my eyes in the bright sunshine. "Well, I'll just go in for a quick dip. Don't worry—I won't say anything. It wouldn't be my place to do that."

I took a quick outdoor shower on the pool deck. Then Sloane watched me move to the deep end, where I paused to check the depth before I dived in. The water was wonderfully refreshing. I swam laps for a few minutes, then stopped for a break at the shallow end, where I floated on my back.

The children batted a small beach ball back and forth.

Closing my eyes, I listened to the sound of their laughter.

After a time, I climbed out of the pool and returned to the lounge chair for my towel. Sloane sat up and removed her sunglasses. "Thank you for not saying anything."

I bent to dry my legs. "No problem. It's a complicated situation, and we don't know how it's going to turn out. Things might work out in your favor, and I'll just end up going home, and you'll never see me again."

Sloane watched me curiously. "You seem pretty relaxed about the whole thing."

Squeezing the water out of my hair, I shrugged. "I wouldn't exactly say I'm relaxed, but I came here with nothing, so if I leave with nothing, at least I will have had a pretty cool trip to Italy and met some nice people."

"But the *money* . . . ," Sloane said with disbelief.

I finished drying off and stretched out on the chair beside Sloane. "Honestly? I'm trying not to think about that too much. If I get too excited about the idea of being rich, it'll be a hard row to hoe, for sure."

"Now you know how Connor and I feel," she replied.

I sat up and turned to look at her.

"We've been expecting this inheritance all our lives," she continued. "There was no reason to ever doubt it."

I regarded Sloane intently. "I'm sorry. I do get that, and I swear I didn't do anything to tip the scales in my favor."

The children splashed each other with gusto until Chloe began to cry and complain. "Mom! Tell him to stop!"

"She started it!" Evan replied.

Sloane sat forward. *"Evan, stop splashing your sister!"*

That ended the skirmish immediately, and the children swam to chase after the beach ball, which was floating away from them.

"I had dinner with Connor last night," Sloane mentioned, surprising me with her desire to initiate a conversation. "He told me that your father's in a wheelchair."

"That's a simple way of putting it," I replied. "But yes. He's a quadriplegic. If I'm not with him, we need home care, pretty much around the clock."

Sloane adjusted the angle of her hat. "That must be difficult. You could use a financial windfall, no doubt."

"A little extra money wouldn't be unwelcome," I replied. "We just bought a new van with a chair lift, and the loan payments are taking a serious bite out of our savings."

Sloane kept her eyes fixed on her children in the pool. "Well, now. That makes me feel very self-absorbed."

"Why?"

"Because all I can think about is the fact that I need money, too, and I don't want you to have it because I want it, quite desperately at the moment."

"Why is that?"

She exhaled heavily. "Because I've been thinking about asking my husband for a divorce, but if I do, I won't get anything in the settlement, except maybe some child support."

"But you *did* get money," I reminded her, sitting forward slightly on the lounge chair. "A few million British pounds, if I remember correctly."

Sloane waved away a butterfly. "I know that, and I feel like a spoiled brat for saying this, but it doesn't feel like very much money when you're used to a certain standard of living. I have two children to raise, and . . ." She paused. "Oh, don't look at me like that. It might sound laughable to you, but I have no doubt you'll understand what I mean soon enough."

I chuckled. "I doubt that. I'm sorry—I don't mean to be judgmental, but I'm having a hard time feeling sorry for you. You've been rich your entire life." I waved an arm about. "Look at this place! This was your summer camp."

Sloane shook her head. "I don't feel very rich right now. All I feel is alone and stuck in a bad marriage because I signed a prenup where I'd get nothing if I left my husband. And I'm terrified about how I would raise my children without a father. On top of that, I'm convinced that my own father hated me because I never came to visit him, and that's why he cut me out of his will. So I suppose it depends on your definition of the word *rich*. And Fiona . . ." Sloane turned to me. "As far as money goes, it's all relative. I don't know what your situation is, but if you have a roof over your head and a brand-new van, a homeless person might consider you to be rich as Croesus."

I drew back slightly. "Wow. Okay, you win that round."

We sat in silence, each of us watching the children.

"I didn't mean to suggest," I said, after a time, "that having money means you've lost your right to be unhappy. Life sucks sometimes, whether you're rich or poor. And I'm sorry about your marriage. It's always sad when a relationship doesn't work out. I wouldn't actually know about that from experience. I've never been married, but—"

"My husband sent a dick pic to our daughter last night," Sloane bluntly announced.

I regarded her with surprise. "He did what?"

"Not on purpose," Sloane explained. "Apparently, he meant to send it to a woman he's been screwing behind my back. No idea who she is."

I tamped down my surprise. "I'm sorry. Truly."

"Thank you." She swallowed hard, and I had the sense that she was fighting to hold back tears. "Obviously, I'm angry with him, but I'm angry with myself, too, because it's not like I didn't see this coming. My husband was always a flirt. Even on my wedding day, I knew deep down that he wasn't capable of being faithful to me for the rest of our lives, but he was so handsome and successful, and I was completely infatuated with him, so I went through with it anyway. I just stuck my head in the sand, telling myself everything would be different once we were married. That he would change and settle down. Become a family man."

"That's gotta be rough."

"It is. Especially when I look at those beautiful kids, who don't deserve to grow up in a house where their mother is an emotional wreck all the time, completely insecure and heartbroken and trying to hide it. How am I supposed to be real with them when I'm faking everything? I'm trying to pretend that our life is perfect and beautiful so that all my friends will envy me. But honestly, who cares what they think? Wouldn't it be more fun to just let my natural hair color grow out and eat pasta without worrying about looking bloated the next day?"

"I do love pasta," I said. "What color is your hair?"

She removed her sun hat and showed me her roots. "It's brown, not black."

I bent to look closely and nodded without judgment.

Sloane put her hat back on and sighed heavily. "You know what they say. Women often marry some version of their fathers, and according to Mom, our father was a lady-killer of the highest order." She shook her head. "Sometimes I wonder if handsome, wealthy men are even capable of being faithful to one woman for the rest of their lives when younger women are always throwing themselves at them."

I struggled to find the right words. "I wouldn't know anything about that either. I've never really known any handsome, wealthy men. My ex was a regular Joe. He had his faults, but at least he was faithful. And I never met our father, so I have no idea what he was like."

Sloane sat forward and pulled off her hat. *"Evan! Don't hold your sister's head under the water! Do you want her to drown?"* She sat back and let out a breath of frustration. "How am I going to do this on my own? I'm doomed."

"That's not true," I assured her. "I think you're going to be just fine. Obviously, you're good at keeping a watchful eye on things. I mean, look . . . Chloe's not drowning."

"Maybe not, but her parents might be splitting up, and she's going to have to live in two different homes and probably always blame herself for what's about to happen to her family because she screamed her head off when the dick pic came in." Sloane tipped her head back to rest on the lounge chair and watched a cloud float across the sky. "Call me a pessimist, but I have a feeling the traditional institution of marriage is a dying pipe dream."

"Let's not lose hope," I replied. "Lots of couples spend their entire lives together and are very happy. My parents, for example. Even though my dad came with a lot of challenges, my mom was devoted. She would have done anything for him. I'm sure they'd still be together today if she hadn't passed away."

Sloane gave me a look. "I don't want to be insensitive, but aren't you forgetting the fact that you were only born because your mother cheated on your dad?"

I thought about that for a moment and couldn't deny that Sloane had touched on something. Maybe I did look at my parents' marriage with rose-colored glasses.

But how could I not? All I remember is how my mom doted on my father every day of her life, until she passed that baton to me.

"Yes," I said, "but I don't think it was quite like *that*. I mean, it wasn't an actual *affair*. I don't know what it was exactly, but . . ." I thought of the special wine collections that Anton had created for my mother and me—which he'd kept hidden and locked away for thirty years—and shook my head. "What am I saying? I don't know anything anymore. I have no idea what happened between them."

I'd always thought I had it all figured out—that my mother's relationship to my biological father was a one-night stand, at best, or possibly nonconsensual. But after seeing the secret wine cellar, I had to consider the possibility that I might have been wrong about their relationship and wrong about Anton Clark as a whole.

An oncoming train of regret was picking up speed.

With more questions than ever knocking around inside my head, I sat up, swung my feet to the ground, and donned my T-shirt. "I should get going. I'm sure your brother is up at the villa at this very moment, searching through boxes and files for those mysterious letters from my mother."

I pulled on my shorts, slid my feet into my flip-flops, and started off, but I turned back to say one more thing.

"Sloane, no matter what happens with the will, you shouldn't worry. At the very least, you'll have a house of your own in London with family nearby and quite a bit of money in the bank. You can raise your children with a clean slate."

"Connor wants to sell it," she told me. "He wants the fast cash."

I stepped a little closer, wanting sincerely to help. "I see. Well, you could always take your half of the proceeds and start fresh somewhere new."

"But I love that house," she argued, "and so do the kids. It's the only place we have left that actually feels like home." She glanced around and looked up at the hilltop town of Montepulciano in the distance. "I never brought them here. I wish now that I had, because it's very special. You're lucky, Fiona. Don't take this for granted."

"I'll try not to," I replied, thinking of the sales agent named Roberto who had offered me €90 million for the winery. He was still waiting for me to return his call. "And as for that house you love in London . . . if it feels like home, then you should buy Connor out, take ownership, and live the life you want to live. Don't accept defeat just yet. Remember, your husband sent a dick pic to your daughter. That's not okay. Did you get a screenshot?"

"Yes."

"Then trust me. He's not going to leave you in the lurch. He'll probably buy Connor out for you and maybe even rethink whatever's written in the prenup, as long as you agree to keep quiet about what he did. So get yourself a good lawyer. Okay . . . I gotta go." I turned to jog off the pool deck just as Evan knocked the beach ball out of the water, sending it bouncing toward the fence.

"I'll get it!" I shouted, running to fetch it. I picked it up and served it back like a volleyball.

"*Grazie!*" Evan said, jumping to catch it.

"*Prego!*" I replied gregariously, then hurried to the gate.

"Mom, who was that?" I heard Chloe ask.

187

Sloane watched me close the gate, then waved for her children to come out of the pool. "Come and sit next to me, both of you, so I can explain who she is."

I turned to look back as I walked up the grassy hill and saw Sloane holding Chloe on her lap. Suddenly, both children turned and looked at me. They waved.

I smiled and waved back.

As I continued up the hill, I felt more determined than ever to find those letters.

CHAPTER 19
LILLIAN

Tuscany, 1986

Another week went by, and Freddie didn't bother to call. At least that's what Lillian told herself. Maybe he had called. There was no answering machine in the guest suite, and she wasn't often at home. She was either working at the front desk, conducting tours, or helping in the fields during her off hours—for no other reason than the pure pleasure of it. There was something addictive about pruning vines and snapping off suckers. It was incredibly satisfying. And of course, it was an excuse to work alongside Anton during the day, though there were others around as well.

He and Domenico taught her all sorts of things about planting and growing grapes. She was a keen student, absorbing information like a sponge.

"I love it here," she said to Anton one night after dinner at the villa, as they walked back to her suite. "I love everything—the food and the wine and the olive groves and the grapevines and the musty smell of the cellars. I can't blame you for wanting to buy this place. It takes hold of your soul."

He reached for her hand and kissed the back of it.

"And I was thinking," she continued. "If you really wanted to make this place your own, to create your own history here, you could set aside some special collections for your two children and add them to the private cellar, like Mr. Maurizio did. You could put your own special labels on them to set them apart."

Anton stopped on the road and regarded Lillian with wonder. "You amaze me. It's a marvelous idea. We're about to start bottling the wine from the year Connor was born, and bottles from Sloane's birth year are aging in the cellars. I know which is the very best blend from that harvest. That's what I will choose for her. Thank you."

"I can help with labels, if you like," Lillian offered.

He nodded, and she saw, in the bluish light of the moon, a look of admiration on his face. "You're leaving your mark on this place too," he said. "You're creating your own history here, and I'm glad."

They walked in silence for a moment until he asked, "Have you heard from Freddie?"

Lillian stiffened at the mere mention of her husband's name. How easy it had become to let herself forget that she was married. She was not without guilt over what was happening—flashes of shame and remorse sneaked up on her quite frequently—but it was a two-way street. Freddie had made it clear many times over the years that her happiness was not his primary concern. Her value to him was in the many ways she supported him, financially, creatively, and emotionally.

"No," she said. "I suspect he's gone deep into the writing cave. When he gets inspired, he has a tendency to forget about the world. The real world, I mean. Me included."

Their footsteps tapped lightly over the dirt road as they followed the glow from the flashlight.

"What will you say to him when he finally does call?" Anton asked. "Or if he simply shows up without warning."

"He won't do that," she replied. "He'll want me to pick him up at the train station, and the last train from Paris gets in at eight forty every night."

"What if he takes a taxi to surprise you?"

"He wouldn't do that either," she replied. "He's not romantic like that. Although . . . I suppose . . . you never know. Maybe he'll be sitting on the sofa holding a bouquet of flowers for me when we walk through the door. That would be awkward." She shook her head at herself. "I'm sorry. That wasn't funny. I don't know why I said that. I'm not being cavalier about this, and I don't know what I would do if he showed up unexpectedly."

The windows were dark when they arrived at her apartment, so they went inside, confident that Freddie had not returned.

Later, they lay together in her bed beneath a light cotton sheet, facing each other.

"He's not going to stay away forever," Anton gently mentioned.

Lillian closed her eyes. "I know. But I don't want to think about that right now."

"We have to eventually. What will you do, Lillian?"

She rolled onto her back and watched the ceiling fan spin slowly. "I don't know. I'm so happy here. I've never felt this happy. It's you, of course. I'm crazy in love with you, and every day I wake up in a state of total bliss. But I also love the work I'm doing here. I love giving the tours, watching the grapes grow, pruning the vines, learning about wine making. I can hardly wait for the harvest." She turned her head on the pillow to look him in the eye. "This is going to sound corny when I say it, but I feel like this is my calling."

Anton wove his fingers through hers and kissed her hand. "I feel the same."

She rolled onto her side again, facing him. "But I'm married. And so are you."

"Not for long," he replied. "I'll be free soon."

Her heart trembled with uncertainty. She was afraid to hope, afraid to dream.

Anton inched closer to her. "I believe this is the reason why we're both here, in Tuscany, at this moment. It's not a coincidence. It's why you met Freddie when you did, because he was writing a book set in Italy. It's why your timing was off with him—that he didn't want to start a family when you did. That's why you convinced him to come here to finish his book. And it's why I was driving behind you when your car went off the road. All of it happened so that we could find each other in extraordinary circumstances . . . so that we would understand the importance of it."

Lillian squeezed his hands. "Are you saying this is fate?"

He rose up on an elbow and laid soft kisses on her forehead, eyelids, and cheeks. "Call it whatever you like. All I know is that we were meant to find each other, and now that you're here, I can't let you go. Stay with me, Lillian. We'll have as many children as you want."

"Stay . . . ?"

"Yes." His eyes shone brightly in the glow of the moonlight from the window. "When Freddie comes back, tell him that we love each other and that you want a divorce. You can move into the villa with me."

The weight of those words shook Lillian to her core. "Move in with you? Anton, it's barely been half a summer."

"It doesn't matter. I'm certain about this. You're the woman I was born to love." He kissed her fiercely, passionately, leaving her burning with desire.

Lillian began to weep softly, her tears staining the pillow.

"You're the only woman I want," he said, "for the rest of my life."

Her heart broke wide open, and she wept with a strange mixture of joy and misery.

"It's not that simple," she said. "Freddie has no idea what's been happening since he left. I can't just ask him for a divorce out of the blue.

He'll be completely blindsided. It would devastate him, and despite his faults, he doesn't deserve that."

Anton wiped away her tears and gave her a moment to collect herself.

"I love you," she said, "but I do care for him, and I can't be heartless."

They lay quietly in the darkness, holding each other while Lillian felt the weight of the world on her shoulders. She buried her face in her hands. "I don't know what to do."

~

In August, the grapes grew plump and sweet and began to change color from bright green to deep purple. Lillian accompanied Anton and Domenico into a vineyard one afternoon to assess the mildew situation.

"Look here," Domenico said. "The leaves are lush and beautiful, but they're creating too much shade and trapping moisture on the grapes. That's a recipe for rot, so we must do more pruning here. And it's time to cover these vines with bird nets." He pointed at the sky. "We must prevent those hungry flocks from helping themselves to the Syrah."

He spoke more about how they must keep a close eye on the grapes each day to determine the best time to begin the harvest.

When they finished their inspection of the field, the sun was high in the sky, and it was time for a rest. Domenico headed back to his little villa to enjoy lunch and a nap with Caterina.

"How about a swim?" Anton suggested as soon as they were alone behind a tractor at the edge of the vineyard. He backed her up against the big rubber tire and slid his arms around her waist.

"That sounds wonderful. I have until the three o'clock tour. Let's meet at the pool in five minutes. I just need to change into my bathing suit."

There was a dreamy intimacy to his kiss, and she didn't want it to end.

Eventually, they parted and emerged discreetly from behind the big tractor to walk away in opposite directions.

Strolling along the shady, forested lane toward her guest suite, Lillian touched her fingertips to her lips and felt her cheeks flush at the memory of Anton's kiss. She couldn't believe her life. She had never felt so happy and alive yet so conflicted at the same time. She didn't want to hurt Freddie, but she wanted desperately to leap into an unknown future and remain in Tuscany forever, with Anton. It seemed so sudden. It frightened her. What if this was just a mad, impulsive infatuation or temporary insanity brought on by nothing more than an intense sexual attraction?

She reached the apartment, flew up the stone steps, and inserted the key into the lock. Sunlight spilled across the terra-cotta tiled floor as she pushed the door open. She smiled and wondered where she'd put her bikini after her last swim. Was it hanging in the shower, or had she placed it in the drawer in her bedroom?

She stopped dead on the threshold, however, when she looked up and saw Freddie sitting at the kitchen table, eating a sandwich.

She stood there, blank, stunned, and shaken. "Freddie . . . you're back."

He gulped down a mouthful. "Hey!" He wiped his face with a napkin and stood. "I didn't expect you until later. I wanted to surprise you. Happy to see me?" he asked as he approached her.

Lillian stumbled forward slightly as he pulled her into his arms and hugged her. "Of course."

Freddie held her away from him, at arm's length, dipping briefly at the knees. He laughed uneasily. "You don't look happy. You look like a deer caught in the headlights."

Hastily, Lillian pasted on a smile. "I'm sorry. I'm just in shock, that's all. And maybe a little sunstroke. You didn't call. I would have picked you up at the train station. But this is wonderful. I'm so happy to see you."

He took a few steps back and held out both hands. "Look at *you*! You're so tanned! Have they got you working in the fields now?" There was humor in his voice.

"Well, yes, actually . . ." She was about to explain about the careful pruning she'd been doing lately and tell him how she'd been learning about soil content, hydration, and fermentation, but Freddie turned away and reached for his backpack on the floor.

"Guess what's in here." He picked it up and held it aloft.

Lillian wondered if it was a gift for her from Paris, but he answered his own question before she could guess.

"My manuscript." His eyes glimmered with pride. "I finished it, Lil."

His words hit her like a gust of wind, knocking her a step backward. "Seriously?"

"Yes," he replied. "I typed 'The End' yesterday. Then I made a copy, and I mailed it to the agent this morning, just before I got on the train."

His excitement bubbled up around him as he waited for her response, but she was dumbstruck.

"Lil . . . did you hear what I just said?"

She shook her head as if to clear it. "I did. I think the sun has melted my brain." She strode forward and set her hands on his shoulders. "That's amazing. I'm so proud of you."

"Proud of *us*," he replied. "We did this together. You and me both, because I never could have finished it without all your help. Coming here was the best thing ever. I know I wasn't keen at first, but I'm glad you pushed me, because it turned out to be the spark that lit a fire under me to actually get it done. So thank you."

She had never seen Freddie look so proud, which caused an ocean of guilt to wash over her, because she was about to flatten that happiness with a confession that she had been unfaithful to him. Worse . . . that she was in love with another man. Deeply, profoundly in love.

"You're welcome," she murmured, hesitantly.

Freddie unzipped the backpack and withdrew a thick wad of paper held together by elastic bands and plunked it on the table. "There it is. All four hundred and thirty-six pages. There's probably room to cut some stuff, but I'll let an editor take care of that." He gazed at her imploringly. "Will you read it, Lil?"

Baffled, she could do nothing but stare blankly at him. *Now* he was asking her to read it? They had been married for five years, and not once had he ever permitted her to read a single word, not even when she begged.

"Of course," she replied, robotically. "You know how curious I've been."

"I do, and I'm sorry for keeping so much of this hidden from you. I think . . . I was just afraid that you'd hate it, and if you did, it would have derailed me because I respect your opinion so much."

Another wave of guilt washed over her.

He sat down at the table, pushed his plate back, and smiled up at her. "Now, we can go home," he said. "I feel like celebrating. We should go out for dinner tonight in Montepulciano and order a bottle of wine."

She frowned. "What do you mean, go home?"

"I mean, I *did* it. I finished the book, and now I want to get home, because that's the address on my cover letter to the agent. I'll need to be checking the mailbox every day."

She gestured toward the telephone. "Couldn't you have given him the phone number here?"

"Well . . . no. That would be an overseas call. I didn't want to put any obstacles in front of him."

She stiffened with annoyance. "But Freddie, I've committed to the whole summer here. They spent time training me, and they expect me to stay until after the harvest in September. I can't just quit on them."

"Oh." He sat back, looking dumbfounded. "Are you worried about references? Because it won't matter after I sell this book. You'll be able to stop working."

She struggled to cling to her patience. "Do you realize that not once since you walked in the door have you asked what *I* wanted? You never do."

"I thought you wanted me to finish my book."

Frustrated, she spoke in a rush. "Maybe I like working. And you don't even know if a publisher will make an offer on your book. Even if the agent accepts it, it could take years to find a home for it and start earning royalties. And not all books get published. Most of them get rejected. I know this because I read your *Writer's Digest* magazine all the time."

Silence. All the color drained from Freddie's face. It was the first time Lillian had ever stuck a pin in his dream bubble.

"Don't say that. Not today, when I'm feeling on top of the world."

She put her hand over her eyes. "It's not my intention to bring you down. I'm sure your book is great and the agent's going to love it." She lowered her hand and looked at him directly. "But your dreams of publication aren't going to put food on the table while you wait to hear back from him, and that could take months, maybe even a year. Besides, I love working here. I've never enjoyed a job so much in my life. I'm passionate about all this, and I want to learn more about wine making. I'm even toying with the idea of taking a sommelier course."

"What?" Freddie frowned and scratched at his jaw. "A sommelier? You know you can't drink when you're pregnant, right? Does that mean you don't want to start trying?"

The look on his face left her frazzled. She wasn't sure if it was disappointment she saw or relief. She honestly had no idea.

A deep frown set into his features, and she waited for him to elaborate—to tell her that a career in the wine-making industry was a pipe dream, that a sommelier course would cost too much, or that he was happy with a career plan for her because he didn't want to have children after all—he'd never wanted that—and he had been stringing her along all this time. She almost *wanted* him to say those things so that they could fight and shout at each other. Someone might even throw something. It would be a first for them, but maybe it might feel good, for once, to vent her frustrations about their marriage. After five years, she felt like a pressure cooker.

Freddie stood up and walked toward her. He pulled her into his arms.

"I'm sorry," he said, rubbing her back. "You've been supporting my dreams ever since the day we met, so if you want to stay here and finish out the season, we can do that. And if you want to take a class about wine tasting, we can do that too. I'm just so happy that I finished my book. Now that it's done, we can start living. We'll do whatever you want."

She should have been relieved. Finally, her husband was thinking of their life together, not just his own personal dreams and goals. More importantly, he had proven yet again that he was not the sort of man who shouted or smashed things, which was why she had chosen him as a husband in the first place. In that way, he had never disappointed her.

Why, then, was her stomach churning with exasperation?

Just when she'd grown tired of waiting for Freddie to put her happiness first and had finally come to a decision about a future without him, he decided to return with a completed manuscript and the fulfillment of all his promises.

Had she been wrong to lose faith in him? Had she given up too soon?

God, oh God . . . Anton was waiting for her at the swimming pool. She wanted desperately to go to him and tell him about Freddie's return, to talk everything over. He would understand what she was feeling because he understood her better than anyone, including Freddie. He would help her make sense of it.

At the same time, she couldn't deny that her physical attraction to Anton was still overpowering, and her desires were waging a battle against the loyalty she felt toward Freddie. Was that all it was, where

Anton was concerned? Physical attraction? Had she lost touch with what really mattered?

Stepping back, Lillian spoke without making direct eye contact with Freddie. "Dinner in Montepulciano sounds perfect." She couldn't possibly take him to the villa. "But right now, I have to get back to work. I just came back to put on a different pair of shoes."

How appallingly easy it was to lie to him. Poor Freddie believed her without question.

"All right," he said. "I'll make reservations somewhere. You got paid yesterday, right? We can afford it?"

"Yes." She went to the bedroom to change her shoes but stopped in the doorway when her gaze fell upon the bed. Thankfully, the maid had visited that morning. The sheets were freshly laundered, and the whole apartment had been vacuumed and mopped.

Lillian entered the room, opened the wardrobe, and put on her deck shoes.

"I'll see you later," she said, hurrying for the door.

Freddie set his plate in the sink with a clatter. "Okay. Love you."

His words hit her like a gut punch. She paused for a few seconds, sinking into a sea of doubt, but quickly gathered her wits about her and flew down the steps.

~

Anton was swimming below the surface, shooting across the turquoise bottom of the pool. When he surfaced at the shallow end, Lillian was pacing back and forth on the cement deck. She couldn't catch her breath.

He took one look at her and said, "Is everything okay?"

Two guests were sunning themselves on lounge chairs at the far end of the pool.

"He's back," she whispered heatedly, pacing like a caged tiger.

"Who's back? Freddie?"

"Yes. It was exactly like you said. He wanted to surprise me. He was sitting at the kitchen table when I walked into the apartment just now."

Anton wasted no time climbing out of the pool. He padded to a deck chair, dried off, and pulled on his shirt.

"Come with me," he said, leading her to the gate.

She followed, and they climbed a sloping gravel path to a nearby building that housed the game room. They entered, and there were no guests inside.

Anton closed the door and locked it behind them. While he switched on the overhead lights, Lillian crossed to the Ping-Pong table in the center of the room.

"I don't know what to do," she said. "This changes everything."

"No, it doesn't. You knew Freddie would come back eventually. Nothing has changed. It's the same as it was last night."

She felt as if she were hyperventilating. Unable to look Anton in the eye, she paced around, chewing her thumbnail. Anton watched her with concern.

"He finished his book," she told him. "He mailed it to a New York agent this morning. Then he suggested that we go home."

"Home to America?" Anton strode forward. "What did you say?"

"I told him that I liked it here, that I'd made a commitment to work until the end of the summer, and I didn't want to leave. He seemed to accept that. He said we could stay."

There was a steely edge to Anton's voice. "It's not up to him. It's up to you."

She glanced at him. "I know that. If he had pushed me to quit, I swear I would have fought him about it. But he didn't do that. He was unreasonably agreeable."

Anton studied her expression, then moved slowly around the Ping-Pong table, approaching her as if she were a fawn in the forest that might spook and run. "Lillian . . ."

She held out a hand. "Please, don't come any closer. Just give me a minute to digest this. I need to figure things out."

"I thought we had it figured out last night."

"We did," she replied, "but now I'm not so sure anymore." She laid her hand on her belly. "He's my husband, Anton."

Anton tried to reach out to her, but she backed away from him.

"Don't worry," he said. "Everything's going to be fine."

"Is it? I'm about to tell my husband that I've been having an affair—that I've been sleeping with another man in our very own bed. Poor Freddie. He has no idea."

Anton gestured toward a sofa. "Let's talk about this. Come and sit down."

"No." She started pacing again. "If I sit down with you, you'll touch me or kiss me, and I'll forget about everything—my life back in Tallahassee, my wedding vows . . ."

"Then tell me what to do," he said. "Do you want *me* to talk to Freddie?"

Her eyes flashed to meet his, and she scoffed bitterly. "Are you joking? No, Anton! You've done enough."

Her voice was cold and exact, and she felt the pointed cruelty of her words like a dagger to his heart.

Part of her regretted it. She didn't want to hurt Anton, because he was right. Nothing had changed. She was still madly, passionately in love with him. She could feel the energy from his body, just a few feet away, and all she wanted to do was dash into his arms.

An excruciating longing rose up inside her like a hot fire, clouding her judgment. She didn't dare look at Anton. If she did, she would crumble. She would fall into him, apologizing, telling him that she didn't mean it.

Instead, she reminded herself that she was a married woman who had become infatuated with a handsome, older man who was also her wealthy boss. It happened because her husband had been neglecting her and because this place was like something out of a fairy tale.

She had indeed lost touch with reality. She had been seduced by beauty. But it wasn't real. This wasn't her life. Freddie was her husband and she loved him, and he loved her.

Lillian stopped pacing and met Anton's frantic gaze. "This was a mistake."

The space between them crackled with electricity. Lillian was horrified by the sound of those words on her lips, but she couldn't take them back. She told herself that she had done the right thing to have spoken them.

"We have to end it," she added, in case he didn't understand.

"No."

"Yes. We shouldn't have let this happen. We took it too far, Anton. You must realize that. I don't know what we were thinking. You're my boss, and I'm married, and you have a wife and children. This was wrong."

"Please don't say that."

"It's true." Panic flooded into all her nerve endings. "I have to go."

She bolted for the door, but he blocked her path. Their eyes met with feverish intensity. He took hold of her arm, and she melted instantly. All her resistance fell away.

"Leave him, Lillian." Anton pulled her close and touched his forehead to hers. His jaw was unshaven and rough. She felt the heat of his breath on her lips.

"It's not that easy."

"I know it's not, but you have to do it."

She couldn't pull away. Tears streamed down her cheeks. *One last time,* she told herself. *One last kiss . . .*

Her hands slid up to his shoulders, and she couldn't hold back. Desire eclipsed everything. Anton backed her up against the wall and kissed her fiercely until she let out a sob.

"Please, Anton. I have to go."

He dragged his mouth from hers and stepped back, his chest heaving.

Somehow, she found the strength to turn and walk to the door.

Outside, the sun was blinding in her eyes. The heat made her feel dizzy. Or maybe it was the aftershocks of Anton's kiss and the chaos of her emotions.

She tried to tell herself that she had done the right thing—that she was a married woman. What she felt for Anton was just a temporary sexual attraction.

Freddie was her husband of five years. He was a good, kind man, and he didn't deserve to be betrayed. She couldn't leave him.

CHAPTER 20
SLOANE

Tuscany, 2017

While Connor made off for the garage behind the villa in search of Lillian Bell's mysterious lost letters, Sloane took her children to the winery gift shop. The sun was high in the sky when they left the villa, and beyond the iron gate, tall cypresses swayed in the wind. The path down Cypress Row was as familiar to Sloane as the back of her hand, and she recalled a pink bicycle she rode when she was young, back and forth from the villa to the wine cellars. It boasted a shiny silver bell and blue foil tassels, like a cheerleader's pom-poms, that dangled from the grips of the handlebars. How she loved to pedal fast down the hill, racing with her cousin Ruth while Connor followed on his three-wheeler.

She was pleased to see Evan running ahead, shouting "I'll race you!" and encouraging Chloe to keep up. Sloane jogged as well, and soon they circled around the bend and arrived at the main parking lot, out of breath and laughing. Sloane recovered and led them to the large stone building that housed the main inn, dining room, and gift shop.

"Let's see if we can find some souvenirs to take home for your friends," she suggested, not entirely sure they could find age-appropriate gifts in a winery gift shop, but it was worth investigating.

Inside, a college-aged young woman was manning the desk. Sloane let Evan and Chloe browse through the displays of cookbooks, key chains, magnets, and coffee mugs. Most of the tall shelves displayed bottles of wine and grappa in special gift boxes.

A family of tourists walked in and said they were there for the guided tour. The girl behind the desk checked the list and told them it began outside on the stone patio.

Sloane thought of Fiona Bell's mother, who had been a summertime tour guide thirty-one years earlier and had somehow managed to upend all their lives. Sloane found herself making enquiries at the desk.

"What exactly does the tour entail?"

The young woman didn't seem to realize that Sloane was the daughter of the late owner and these were his grandchildren. Why would she when Sloane was totally clueless about her father's business operations?

"It starts with a guided walk through the vineyards," the young woman explained. "Then you'll visit the cellars, and it ends with a wine tasting. Are you interested in the English or Italian tour?"

"English," Sloane replied.

"Then you're just in time. It starts in five minutes."

Sloane wanted to go but didn't think a wine tour would be an appropriate activity for her young children. "Maybe another time," she said, "when I can come back on my own."

A few minutes later, after purchasing some pens and a couple of umbrellas with the Maurizio logo printed on them, Sloane left the gift shop with Evan and Chloe.

Out on the stone patio that overlooked the sloping vineyards below, a young American guide in a red T-shirt and black golf skirt was just beginning the tour. She was an attractive, dynamic speaker with honey-colored hair and a natural beauty, most likely a summer student, and was explaining the types of grapes that were grown on the estate.

Sloane found herself growing curious about the looks and charms of Fiona Bell's mother thirty-one years ago. She supposed if the woman was anything like her daughter, who seemed to possess a rather endearing and relaxed personality, their father might have indeed become genuinely infatuated. It was certainly plausible.

~

When Connor returned to the villa after a fruitless search for the mysterious letters, Sloane convinced him to take a step back, regroup, and eat some gelato. He finally agreed to take Evan and Chloe into town for a few scoops.

As soon as they were gone, Sloane took advantage of some rare private time and collapsed onto an upholstered chair in her bedroom. For a while she sat there, alone, noticing the silence as she looked around at the familiar furniture, window coverings, and light fixtures, none of which had been changed since she was a child. A memory came to her then, of Maria playing cards with her on the bed while it poured buckets of rain outside the open windows. Connor was nearby, on the floor playing with his Hot Wheels racetrack, taking great pleasure in crashing Dinky cars together.

Once again, Sloane found herself longing for the happiness she'd known as a child, when life was simple and she felt no pressure to be perfect. A card game with the housekeeper. The smell of rain outside the window. And a father who would scoop her up, hug her tight, and tell her how much he missed her after she stepped off a plane from America.

When the memories began to melt and dissolve into regrets for all the lost years with her father, who finally, in the end, gave up on her, Sloane rose from the chair and ventured downstairs to the kitchen, where she found Mrs. Dellucci kneading dough on the worktable.

"Is Maria around?" Sloane asked, wishing now that she had been more friendly and attentive toward Maria over the past few days, especially during her father's funeral. At the time, Sloane had felt like a stranger in a foreign country among people who didn't approve of her, and she and Connor didn't help matters by keeping to themselves because they didn't want to discuss their plans for the winery—which was to sell it to the highest bidder. Sloane had avoided Maria because she couldn't bear to have that conversation with her. She didn't want to disappoint her, so Sloane kept her head down and pretended she needed to wallow privately in her grief. But now, after the reading of her father's will, what she and Connor had planned to do with their father's winery was a moot point. Sadly, she couldn't go back to the day of the funeral for a do-over.

"She went home for lunch," Mrs. Dellucci replied, still kneading.

Recognizing a well-defined cold shoulder from the woman, Sloane felt like a heel because she knew she deserved it, so she decided to take a walk, pick some wildflowers, and visit Maria at the cozy little villa where she lived. How long had it been since Sloane had seen it? She hoped it wasn't too late. She hoped that Maria would be willing to visit with her, one last time before she left.

Twenty minutes later, she caught a whiff of roses just before the villa came into view. Cicadas were buzzing in the forest, and the sun was warm on Sloane's cheeks as she emerged from the path to the gravel lane, then made her way across the garden and up the stone steps to the front door.

Suddenly nervous and wondering if this was a fool's errand, she hesitated before rapping the brass door knocker. Perhaps Maria would give her the cold shoulder as well, and Sloane would be forced to skulk away in shame and embarrassment, onward to a life full of even more regrets.

The door opened, and Sloane shook herself out of her doldrums. She threw on a bright smile for Maria, who stared at her with surprise.

"Hi, Maria. I hope I'm not catching you at an awkward time. I had a few minutes to myself this afternoon and thought I'd pop by and bring you some fresh flowers."

Maria regarded her suspiciously for a few seconds, then reached out to take hold of the bouquet. "What a surprise. They're beautiful, Sloane. How thoughtful of you. Would you like to come in?"

Sloane smiled gratefully and entered the foyer, which brought on yet another rushing cascade of nostalgia. How many times had Sloane run up and down those stairs when her father had something to do in the office? Her mother often said that Maria was a dutiful babysitter who never refused an opportunity to look after them. Comments like that, however, always came on the heels of a criticism about their father.

Sloane followed Maria into the kitchen, where Maria found a vase for the flowers, filled it with water, and set it on the antique hutch where she displayed her dishes.

"How are your children getting along?" Maria asked as she arranged the flowers just so. "I suppose they're missing their friends."

"Not as much as you would think," Sloane replied as she wandered around the kitchen, looking at everything. "I think they're secretly enjoying this time away from all the social activity that doesn't seem to let up, even for a ten-year-old. You'd be surprised at the daily dramas."

"These are different times," Maria replied with understanding. "I don't envy parents today. Would you like an espresso?"

"That would be nice. Thank you."

Maria set about preparing it, and Sloane took a seat at the table.

"I suppose you're wondering why I'm here," Sloane said.

"You came to bring me flowers," Maria cheerfully replied.

"Yes, but I came for another reason as well." Sloane took a deep breath to try and get this right, to say the things she needed to say for her own emotional well-being in the future. "The kids and I will be leaving in the next few days, and I feel badly that you and I didn't get a chance to catch up."

Maria said nothing as she prepared the coffee. Sloane soldiered on.

"I wanted to tell you, Maria, that I have very fond memories of you. You made a difference in my life back then, when my parents weren't exactly what I would call happy to be together. But you kept Connor and me busy with fun things to do, and I enjoyed the time we spent together. I just wanted you to know that."

Maria carried two small espresso cups on saucers to the table. "I enjoyed spending time with you too. I missed you when you stayed away. So did your father."

Sloane spooned some sugar into her cup. "Yes, that's obvious to me now, and I feel badly about that too. I think when you're young, you believe your parents will always be there, and well . . ." She paused. "I think Connor and I were more selfish than most children, and Mom didn't try to steer us another way. I think she preferred that we weren't close to Dad. She was bitter toward him, and she encouraged us to do what we wanted, which was to stay in LA, because she knew it would hurt him." Sloane suddenly recognized her mother's motivations because she was paddling in those same waters herself, feeling angry toward Alan and wanting to cut him out of her life completely and take her children with her.

"It colored how we felt about Dad," Sloane continued, "and I don't think we had a fair perception of him."

"I'm sorry to hear that," Maria replied, "but I can't say I'm surprised. Your mother never liked it here. Maybe she worried that if you spent time here, you would eventually choose him and this place over her."

"I suspect that's true." Sloane was quiet for a moment, then looked up. "Did Dad know he had a heart condition? Did anyone know?"

Maria shook her head. "He seemed healthy as a horse. It caught us all by surprise. But that's life, I suppose. It's important to cherish every day, not take anything for granted." She sipped her espresso. "How are you holding up? You were very quiet at the funeral."

Sloane sighed. "Yes. Dad's passing was a shock to us. And I have to be honest, even though I hate to admit it—but Connor and I were distracted. All we could think about was what we were going to inherit in the will. I don't even remember much about the wake. It was like I slept through it all. I barely glanced at Dad in his coffin. I suppose I didn't want to face the fact that he had actually died. It didn't really hit me until the next day, when we were waiting for the lawyers to arrive and tell us what he'd left to us. Then suddenly I realized that he was gone, and I'd never see him again, and this part of my life was truly over, because Connor wanted to sell the winery."

Sloane realized she had been stirring her tiny cup of espresso the entire time she had been talking. She dropped the spoon into the saucer and buried her forehead in a hand. "I'm so sorry, Maria. I've been completely self-absorbed. For years. All I wanted was a life that was perfect, a life that everyone would envy. It was all Mom ever wanted for me, and she encouraged me to marry Alan, who I now realize was a total louse, even then. But he was rich, and she loved that about him." Sloane bowed her head and shook it. "You must think I'm a terrible, shallow person."

Maria said nothing for a moment, then reached across the table and touched Sloane's hand. "I don't think that."

Sloane tried to pull herself together. She took a few calming breaths.

"Did Dad ever talk to you about us?" she asked. "Did he say he was disappointed? Or that he hated us?"

"He didn't hate you," Maria replied. "He loved you very much, and he missed you. I know it because he used to cry about you sometimes if he'd had too much to drink."

Sloane bowed her head. "Oh God. That's not easy to hear." She sat for a moment, quietly reflecting. "I should have kept in touch with him. With all of you. I'm going to regret that for the rest of my life."

Maria shook her head. "No, don't do that to yourself," she said. "Just love your children and try to be happy. Be grateful for the time you did have with your father. Wherever he is now, I'm sure he's seeing what's in your heart today."

Sloane squeezed Maria's hand. "You're still an angel." Then she sat back and finished her espresso. "I don't know what happened between him and Fiona's mother. We might not ever know, but whatever it was, I think I'm going to have to learn to accept it."

She thought of Connor's reaction to the will and doubted he would ever accept it. He would keep fighting, or at the very least, he would be bitter about it forever. Sloane wondered if Connor had inherited more of their mother's genes than she had, because their mother never seemed to be able to move on after a divorce without a great deal of hostility.

"I don't want to turn out like my mom," Sloane quietly added, "believing that everyone is the enemy and life is a battlefield and whoever gets the most money in the end wins."

"Then don't," Maria said simply.

Sloane nodded and wished once again that she had gotten to know her father better.

~

During the walk back from her visit with Maria, Sloane called her cousin Ruth. "Did you get home okay? How was your mum on the flight?"

"She did fine, all things considered," Ruth replied. "She's pretty sad about your dad, though."

"I know. I'm sorry." Strolling back along the path that circled around one of the vineyards, Sloane looked down at the sun-warmed soil beneath her feet and was grateful to have her cousin to talk to. "I'm just walking back to the villa after a visit with Maria."

"How is she doing?"

"Good. Acted like a second mother. Makes me wish I had visited more when I had the chance."

"Life's not over yet. You can still visit her anytime."

"But the winery belongs to Fiona now. I'd feel awkward."

"I understand. That's going to be strange." Ruth paused. "But I have to say, it was shocking to see how much Fiona looked like a female version of your dad when he was younger. And I saw a resemblance to you too. You could be sisters. Wait a second. You already are."

Sloane chuckled.

"So what's she like?" Ruth asked. "We had to leave right after the meeting, so I didn't get a chance to talk to her. And Mum was in shock over what your dad did. She would have preferred that he leave the business to her and me, if not you and Connor. Then at least it would have remained in the family."

"Fiona is family, though," Sloane reminded her. "And I'd describe her as very down to earth. Not materialistic. I talked to her earlier today, and she was surprisingly relaxed about the situation with Connor. She was basically saying, *Whatever will be will be.*"

"Wow."

Sloane sighed. "I wish I could be more like her, considering what's going on with Alan. I didn't tell you about the picture he sent to Chloe last night."

Sloane relayed the story, and naturally, Ruth was shocked. "My God. And you signed a prenup. What are you going to do?"

Sloane reached the end of the path and approached the back of her father's villa. The sight of it caused an intense feeling of loss in her, as if everything familiar and steady in her world was falling away, like a giant sinkhole beneath her feet.

"I'm not sure yet," she replied. "But I do know one thing. I don't want to have any more regrets, so I guess I'm going to have to do some serious soul-searching."

CHAPTER 21
FIONA

I was on my way to Anton's studio when I passed his bedroom door and heard a woman crying from inside. The door was ajar, so I listened for a few seconds before I knocked gently. "Hello? Sofia, is that you? Is everything all right?"

She sniffled and said, "Go away."

I hesitated in the corridor. "Are you sure? Maybe you'd like to talk?"

She offered no response, so I pushed the door open a little and peered inside.

Wearing a clingy white dress and holding a balled-up tissue in her hand, she sat on the edge of the bed. Her eyes were smeared with black mascara, and the room was a disaster. It looked as if a high-fashion bomb had just exploded.

"Hey there," I gently said. "What's going on?"

Sofia shuddered as she inhaled and waved a hand in front of her face. "I don't want to talk about it. You would not understand."

I sauntered to an upholstered chair and sat down, elbows on knees. "Maybe I would."

She dabbed at the inky wetness under her eyes and gave me an icy stare. "I know why you're here. To tell me to leave."

I swallowed uneasily, because that was indeed at the top of my to-do list for the day.

Sofia blew her nose into the tissue. "You don't have to say it. I'll spare you the trouble. I've already started packing my things."

Glancing around at the clothes, shoes, and scarves strewn about the room, I thought *packing* wasn't quite the right word for whatever was happening there. "Do you need any help? I'd be happy to—"

"No. You should go, Fiona, because I know you hate me."

"I don't hate you."

"*Sì*, you do. Everyone in this family hates me. Kate . . . Connor and Sloane . . ."

I bowed my head. "I won't lie, Sofia. They probably do, but I'm pretty sure they hate me even more."

That caused her to lift her watery gaze. "Maybe that is true."

A hot afternoon breeze blew in through the open window, and I fanned myself with my hand. "Do you have somewhere to go after this?" I asked.

Sofia stood and lifted a suitcase onto the bed. "I have a friend in Florence. She's offered to let me stay with her until I find a place of my own. I'll be okay. Anton was very generous. He gave me presents and enough money to last a little while." She moved to the wardrobe, gathered up a bundle of clothes, and laid them into the suitcase with the hangers still attached.

"Do you mind if I ask you a question?" I said.

"I don't mind." She returned to the wardrobe to fetch another armload of clothes.

"Did Anton ever speak to you about my mother? Because I have no idea what happened between them all those years ago, and no one around here seems to know anything."

Sofia laid the clothes in the suitcase. "He never talked about other women with me. He always made me feel like I was the only woman in the world."

I thought about things Connor had said about his father—that Anton knew how to make a woman believe that he'd "never felt like this before."

"Did you love him, Sofia?" I asked. "For real?"

She stuffed some shoes into the corners of the suitcase and packed everything in tight. "*Sì*. Why else would I be crying?"

I sat back in the chair. "I never met Anton myself, but I keep hearing that he was mean and ornery and a tyrant. And a womanizer."

She shook her head. "He was never that way with me. He treated me like a princess. He was very good to me."

Feeling more perplexed than ever, I sat forward again. "Okay . . . I have another question for you. Did he ever mention any letters that might be important concerning his will? Or did he have a secret place where he kept private papers?"

Sofia fought to zip up the overstuffed suitcase. "You're not the first person to ask me that question today."

"No? Who else spoke to you?" I could most certainly guess.

"Connor," Sofia replied. "Anton's horrible son. And I will tell you the same thing I told him. I don't know anything about any letters, and I don't know where Anton kept his private papers, other than the winery office or his studio, which was where he stored things he didn't want to throw away."

Sofia seemed preoccupied with packing her bags, so I thought I should leave her alone. "Thank you," I said, rising to my feet. "I'll keep looking."

Deciding that I should hurry and resume my search for the letters before Connor got another lead on me, I turned to go but paused briefly at the door. Watching Sofia lift her heavy suitcase to the floor, I said, "Listen, Sofia . . . how about I give you my cell phone number in case you ever need anything. I know this has been a difficult time for you, but maybe we could get together sometime and chat. I'd like to hear more about my father's final days, and if you ever want to talk about anything else, or if you need a friend . . ."

She regarded me warily for a few seconds, then pulled out her phone. I walked back into the room, and we exchanged numbers.

"You're not like Anton's other children," Sofia mentioned as she slipped her phone back into her purse. "You're much kinder. You're like him. The very best part of him. I can see it in your eyes. I'm glad he left everything to you."

I felt strangely disoriented, as if I were floating upside down at the bottom of the ocean. What she was saying . . . the way she perceived my biological father . . . it was inconsistent with how others described him and how I'd always imagined him to be.

"Thank you," I managed to say and headed for the door.

"You could try asking Francesco," Sofia said at the last second. "He might know something."

I stopped and turned. "Who's Francesco?"

"The great-uncle of my friend in Florence. He was Anton's driver when he first bought the winery and a close friend. He retired many years ago, but they stayed in touch. That's how I met Anton, when I went with my friend to visit her aunt. Anton was there at dinner. He brought the best wine I'd ever tasted in my life." Sofia stared at the empty space in front of her, her thoughts filtering back to the day she'd first met Anton, while I stood gazing at her with astonishment. "He hasn't been well. He couldn't come to the funeral."

"Do you have Francesco's phone number?" I asked.

Wrenched back into the present, Sofia pulled her cell phone out again. "I don't, but I will ask my friend." Quickly, she sent a text, and almost immediately, a reply came in. "Here it is. His address and phone number. I forward to you."

As soon as I received the contact information, I began to feel the first traces of hope—that I would finally learn something about what really happened between Anton and my mother thirty-one years ago.

At the same time, I experienced a tremor of unease as I thought of my own father back home in Tallahassee, innocent of my whereabouts. Whatever truth I was about to uncover, I feared he would be devastated by it.

~

Francesco Bergamaschi lived with his wife in a stone villa in the coastal town of Piombino. When I spoke to his wife on the phone, I learned that he had just been discharged from the hospital after a serious bout of pneumonia. Marco was kind enough to drive me there the following morning.

"Thank you for agreeing to see me," I said to Francesco's wife, Elena, who answered the door with a friendly smile and invited me inside to a wide entrance hall with a rustic wrought iron chandelier overhead. "What a lovely home you have."

"*Grazie. Benvenuta.* Francesco is just outside, resting on the back terrace. Can I get you anything? Espresso? Wine?"

"Espresso would be very nice. Thank you."

Elena led me into the kitchen, where she stepped through a back door onto a white stone terrace overlooking the Tyrrhenian Sea. The sunlight sparkled blindingly upon the turquoise water.

Seated at a small bistro table, an old man with thick, wavy white hair swiped at the screen of a tablet on his lap.

Elena touched his shoulder. "Francesco."

He jumped and pulled out his earbuds. "*Cosa c'è?*"

"She's here."

With a bony, blue-veined hand that trembled, Francesco set the tablet on the table and slowly managed to rise to his feet.

"Please, you don't have to get up," I said, but he did so anyway.

He was tall and slender with a slightly hunching posture. At first, he appeared angry. His bushy eyebrows pulled together into an intense frown. But then he regarded me with wonder, and his eyes filled with warmth.

"*Miracolo*." He reached out and kissed me on both cheeks and gestured toward the other chair at the table. "Sit, *per favore*."

"*Grazie*."

He stared at me in awe, and I felt like a colorful fish in a glass bowl.

"You look so much like him," Francesco said. "In his younger days. Your eyes . . . like his. It's extraordinary."

My heart began to race, and I looked down at my lap. "You're not the first person to say that to me."

He sat back slightly, seeming out of breath from the exertion of getting up. "I never imagined I would meet you. If only Anton could see us now, God rest his soul."

Astounded by Francesco's familiarity with me—and feeling completely in the dark about the nature of my conception or the reason for my existence in the world—I set my purse on the terrace floor and forced myself to face Francesco directly. "I'm sorry to hear that you were ill."

He waved a hand dismissively. "That was nothing. I'm fine now, as you can see. But I was sorry to miss the funeral."

"Me too," I replied. "I didn't get here in time for that." We sat in silence for a moment or two, then Elena appeared with two small cups of espresso. "Thank you so much," I said to her and took a careful sip before setting the cup down in the tiny saucer. "So you've known about me?" I said to Francesco. "For how long?"

"Many years. I knew about you before you even came into the world."

I sat staring at him, stunned, staggered, and shaken by this newfound connection to the past. "I'm glad I found you," I said, "because no one in Anton's family or at the winery seemed to know I existed—at least not until this week. And no one has been able to answer questions about what happened between him and my mother. She wasn't able to tell me anything before she passed, so needless to say, I'm curious about that." I gazed out at the distant blue horizon. "And thank you for being so welcoming this morning. I haven't been very popular with certain family members back at the winery, so I appreciate this."

"Because of what was written in Anton's will," Francesco said perceptively, gazing out at the water as well. Seagulls screeched in a flock as they circled a fishing boat just off the coastline. "I confess," Francesco said with hearty laughter, "I would have liked to be a fly on the wall when Connor and Sloane learned what Anton had done."

I regarded him with surprise. "You didn't like his children?"

"It's not that. I loved them because they were Anton's, but they grew up to be very lazy and ungrateful. They expected to inherit the whole world without ever having to lift a finger and without ever giving anything to their father in return, and God knows he tried to be a part of their lives. They must have been flabbergasted."

"They were," I told him, "but they're not going down without a fight."

He looked at me curiously. "A fight? What sort of fight?"

"They want to prove that Anton was unduly influenced," I explained, "or pressured into changing his will. They can't understand why, after thirty-one years, he would leave the bulk of his estate to me— an illegitimate child he'd never met. I'm surprised too. Anton was never a part of my mother's life for as long as I was alive, and she only told me the truth because she was dying. She wouldn't share many details. She was hanging on by a thread at that point, so I always assumed it was something . . . I'm not sure how to say this, Francesco. I assumed it was something . . . unpleasant."

Francesco's head drew back as if I had swung a punch at him. "You thought Anton forced himself on her?"

I chewed my bottom lip. "I don't know. Maybe I thought that. I was only eighteen when she told me that my dad, who I adored, wasn't my real father. It was a shock, and I didn't know how to process it, and then she died within hours, so I didn't get a chance to have a proper conversation with her about what happened." I reflected upon my thoughts and feelings over the past twelve years. "I was too young for all of that. I was grief stricken and angry. It was a shock to hear it, and I felt betrayed—for myself and on my father's behalf. Maybe I still feel betrayed."

Francesco watched me with sympathy. "I was sorry to hear about your mother's passing."

I looked up. "Did you know her back then?"

"*Sì.* She was a very important person at the winery, and important to Anton."

"In what way?"

He regarded me with a frown of disbelief. "Do you really know nothing about what happened between them?"

I shook my head. "All I know is that she spent a summer in Tuscany so that my dad could research his first book and that she worked at the winery as a tour guide."

Francesco tapped his finger on his temple. "She was much more than a tour guide. She had a real head for business and a great nose for wine."

"Really," I replied, surprised. "I only ever knew my mother to be a caregiver to my father. She occasionally worked outside our home, but only part-time, temporary positions. She never revealed any personal goals or career aspirations."

"If it weren't for your mother," Francesco said, "Anton might never have gained a foothold on the American market for his wines. He was one of the first European winemakers to really understand how to sell effectively in North America."

I sat forward. "Are you telling me that he felt he owed my mother something for the success of his wine business? That she was responsible for it? Is that why he left it to me?"

Francesco closed his eyes, laughed softly, and shook his head. "No, that's not what I am saying at all."

"Then what are you saying?"

He scratched the back of his head. "I cannot believe you don't know. But it's Anton's fault for taking his promises so seriously, even beyond the grave."

"I beg your pardon?"

Francesco reached across the table and took hold of my hand. "Your mother was the great love of Anton's life. The only woman he ever truly loved, and that included his wife. He didn't want to let your mother go—it killed him to do it—but he did, because he loved her so much."

"I don't understand."

Francesco sat back. "Is your father still alive? The one who raised you, I mean."

"Yes, and he means more to me than anything, which is why this is all very upsetting to me. He never knew my mother was unfaithful. She begged me to protect him from the truth, and I've kept that promise all these years. He has enough to deal with in his life, every single day. I don't want him to learn about this and be hurt by it. He's been through enough. He doesn't deserve that."

Francesco's cheeks reddened, and my heart stilled.

"Why are you looking at me like that?" I asked. "Did you know my dad?"

He slowly shook his head. "No, I was never introduced to him. I never spoke to him, but I know what happened to him."

A strange numbness settled into the tips of my fingers and toes. "You're referring to his accident?"

"*Sì.* I was there that day. I know everything."

I stared at Francesco intently. "I hope you're going to tell me."

He slowly nodded. "Oh yes, Fiona. I'm going to tell you. I'm going to tell you everything, just as Anton told it to me."

CHAPTER 22
LILLIAN

Tuscany, 1986

"Why didn't you call me more often from Paris?" Lillian asked Freddie, after the waiter opened a bottle of wine at their table and poured two glasses. She wondered if things might have been different if he had called every night instead of only once a week, at best.

"It was long distance," Freddie explained. "And you know what my writing schedule is like. I always seem to be just getting started when you're getting off work." He wagged a finger at her. "But I did call a bunch of times when you didn't answer. You were probably up at the villa."

He watched her intently over the rim of his glass as he sipped, and she wondered uneasily if he suspected something.

Freddie narrowed his eyes. "You don't think I was cheating on you in Paris, do you? Because I was alone in the city of love? Or should I say the city of *amore*?"

He was just teasing her, but still, Lillian couldn't bring herself to look at him. On the one hand, she felt terrible for cheating on him, but on the other, she was devastated over the loss of Anton. That afternoon, her heart had broken into a thousand pieces.

She looked down at the place setting in front of her. "Of course I don't think that."

After a moment or two, Freddie grew pensive and serious. He reached for his glass and raised it. "We never made a toast. To our summer in Tuscany. And to me finishing my book. Here's to the next one."

Lillian raised her glass as well. "The next one?"

"Yes." He took a generous sip of his wine and set down his glass. "That's what I want to talk to you about, Lil. I already have an idea. It's not quite a sequel, but it'll be about one of the secondary characters. I don't have anything written down yet, but it's all up here." He tapped his forefinger on his temple. "And I promise this one won't take me as long to write, now that I know what I'm doing."

She stared at him with a niggling sense of dread, a troubling feeling of time slipping away, of waiting endlessly for the things she wanted out of life. Her lips parted slightly.

Freddie reached for her hand and squeezed it. "And I want to ask you about what you said today—about taking that sommelier course. I'm sorry if I didn't sound supportive. You just caught me off guard, that's all. But if you want to do that, you should. I want you to do what makes you happy, and we don't even have to *have* kids if you don't want to. I know how hard it was for you last time when it didn't work out, so if you just want us to pursue our passions and not be parents, that would be totally fine with me. Maybe it's how we're meant to live our life together. Either way, I've always wanted to support us financially with my writing, so I'm going to need to write another book and another one after that. It's what I want to do with my life. I know that for sure now. Coming here was the best thing we ever did."

Lillian swallowed uneasily. On some level, she had always known that Freddie wouldn't write just one book. He wanted to be a career novelist, which meant he would continue to write every day, forever and ever. He would disappear emotionally into the all-consuming cave where creation occurred, leaving her behind in the real world to live like a person who lived alone.

Maybe that's why she longed so desperately for a baby. She had wanted to fill up her world.

"Of course, you'll need a follow-up novel," she replied in the way she always did, supporting his dreams, hiding her own true desires.

But why? Was it because she knew, deep down, that he didn't care about her desires to begin with? That he only cared about his own dreams?

Did he even love her? Or was he just afraid of being alone? Of being abandoned, like his mother abandoned him years ago?

The first course arrived. It looked enticing, but Lillian had no appetite. She'd been on the verge of tears all afternoon and had to force herself to pick up her fork.

They ate in silence until Freddie sat back and inclined his head at her. "So . . . do you want to hear it?"

"Hear what?" she asked, feeling devastated in more ways than she could possibly comprehend.

"My story idea."

Lillian was often Freddie's sounding board. She had never minded in the past, and it was probably the most solid pillar of their relationship—the hours they spent brainstorming about his book.

"Fire away," she said, feeling numb and detached.

He launched into a description of the plot, but she found it difficult to follow. Not because it was convoluted. It was probably plotted more skillfully than his first book. But her emotions were in a tither. She couldn't get her mind off the heartbreak she felt over losing Anton, nor could she overlook the fact that Freddie had not the slightest understanding of what she truly wanted out of life.

She wanted to be a mother. It was what she'd always wanted, ever since she was a little girl. She wanted to build a happy home that was different from the one she had grown up in. To do that, she needed to love, respect, and understand her husband deeply, and she needed him to love, respect, and understand her equally in return.

It was clear to her now that Freddie was not that man. He didn't want to be a father. He only wanted Lillian to take care of him—and to never leave him.

~

That night, Lillian couldn't sleep. Freddie, on the other hand—due to the extra glass of Madeira port he'd ordered with dessert—had fallen into a deep, snoring slumber as soon as his head hit the pillow.

Before that, he had hinted at making love, but Lillian told him she didn't feel well. It wasn't a total fabrication. The day had been emotionally taxing, and she hadn't been able to finish her meal in the restaurant. They'd switched plates. Freddie had finished hers.

Rolling to her side, she rested her cheek on a hand and gazed out the open window. The night was dark, the moon a small sliver of light in the inky-black sky. A thin cover of wispy clouds blocked out the stars.

Lillian's mind teemed with stressful thoughts. After her dinner with Freddie, she couldn't imagine leaving Tuscany and returning to America, never to see Anton again—only to continue working at a job she didn't truly care about while waiting indefinitely for Freddie to want to have a child with her.

As she lay gazing up at the midnight sky, listening to him snore on the pillow beside her, her thoughts drifted to Anton. Her imagination came alive with excitement as she recalled all the moments they had shared, the conversations they'd had. There was no question that Anton aroused her passions more than Freddie ever had or ever could, in every sense of the word. She loved Freddie, but their relationship had never been passionate, not even in the beginning.

Her heart thudded and her emotions spun as she realized that she could not continue to lie in bed with anyone who wasn't Anton, so she slipped out, quietly pulled a dress from the wardrobe, and carried it to the bathroom. She changed out of her nightgown and stared at herself in the mirror.

What in the world are you doing?

She tried to convince herself to go back to bed with her sleeping husband, but there was no fighting what she felt.

Five minutes later, she was jogging up Cypress Row, through the darkness without a flashlight, but it wasn't a problem, because she knew every inch of the road by heart. She reached the main gate to the villa and keyed in the security code, then hurried up the wide stone steps to the front door.

It was locked. All the windows were dark. Anton slept on an upper floor, but Francesco's apartment was on the ground level, so she scurried around to the side of the house and rapped on his window.

The drapes flew open almost instantly, and he raised the sash. "Lillian. What are you doing?"

"I'm sorry to wake you," she replied, "but I need to speak with Anton. It can't wait until morning."

"*Sì*," he replied. "Go around to the front. I'll let you in."

He met her there a moment later and led her into the main reception room, where he switched on a lamp. "Wait here. I'll wake him."

She had no idea if Francesco knew what was going on between her and Anton. They had always tried to be discreet, but people weren't stupid. They had watched him walk her home every night while her husband was away, and he did not return for hours, sometimes not until dawn.

Still out of breath from her hasty scuttle up the hill, she sat down on the sofa in front of the fireplace and prayed that Anton would forgive her for ending things the way she had, earlier that day.

At last, he appeared in the doorway wearing plaid pajama bottoms. Shirtless. A thrill erupted inside her—a beautiful passion that made it impossible to imagine her future without him. He had done something to her. She was not the same woman who had married Freddie Bell five years ago. She understood that now. She had come into this world destined for something else—to be with someone else.

"Tell me you've changed your mind," Anton said in a deep, husky voice that burrowed into her soul in the most pleasurable way.

"Yes," she replied. "I'm so sorry. I was so stupid. Can you forgive me?"

He shut the door and locked it behind him, then crossed the room in a series of swift, sure-footed strides. Her question was answered when he pulled her into his arms and buried his face in her neck.

Pure, unadulterated euphoria exploded in the depths of her heart, and she whispered, "Thank God."

The next thing she knew, Anton was easing her onto her back on the sofa. His flesh was hot upon hers, and she disappeared into the pleasure of their deep, soulful connection. It delved into her bones— deeper still—as they made love passionately, with a mixture of both joy and anguish.

Afterward, Lillian closed her eyes and breathed in the intoxicating scent of Anton's body, his hair and neck damp with perspiration.

"Have you told him yet?" he asked.

"No," she replied. "I only just decided. He was asleep when I left."

"When will you tell him?"

"As soon as I go back. It won't be easy." She shook her head and covered her eyes with her hand. "He won't understand."

"I wish I could help you," Anton said. "I feel for him. Honestly, I do, because today, after you left, I felt like a part of me had died. I couldn't do anything except lie in bed and tell anyone who asked that I must be coming down with something."

A tear spilled from Lillian's eye. "I'm sorry." She touched her thumb to his lips. "But you know . . . I'm not sure that Freddie loves me the way you do. I don't think he ever has."

Anton touched his forehead to hers. "I'm glad you came back, because if I lost you, I don't think I would ever recover."

~

Lillian remained with Anton until dawn, then kissed him good-bye at the front door of the villa and hurried away, across the stone veranda and down the wide steps. Beyond the gate, she jogged through Cypress Row to the chapel and wine cellars and around the bend to the lower forest.

A thick mist floated through the valleys. The air smelled fresh, like ripening fruit. Crows cawed in the highest branches of the tall umbrella pines, and she regarded the majesty of the world with a renewed sense of wonder. She had never felt more alive, despite something dreadful that lay in her immediate future.

Instead of going straight back to the guest suite, where she would be forced to explain herself to Freddie and inflict terrible pain upon him, she decided to live a few minutes longer in a state of existence where he did not yet know the truth. Where he was sleeping soundly. Happy. The world would come crashing down on him soon enough. She might as well take this opportunity to linger in the status quo and prepare the right words.

Taking a left turn on the dirt road in the forest, she turned toward the swimming pool. It was a five-minute walk.

The water was tranquil in the early-morning light of dawn. She glanced around to ensure that she was alone, then slipped out of her dress, left it by the side of the pool, and dived naked into the cool depths.

Lillian swam laps, and the vigorous exercise strengthened her resolve. She had no regrets about her decision. To the contrary, she felt an invigorating sense of freedom and exultation, as if she had just been reborn. She believed that one day, after Freddie moved on and published his book, he would feel the same. His writing was what mattered to him most. Lillian's presence in his life was merely incidental. She was convenient in all things practical, like earning a steady paycheck and being there for him as a sounding board when it came to his book. She did not provide magic in his world. He found that in his stories while tapping away on the typewriter keys. Most importantly, he did not want children with her. He only pretended to—so that she would stay.

Later, after her swim, she slipped into her dress and strolled to the edge of the terrace to gaze across the rolling hills of Tuscany and the fiery pink sunrise. This was her magic. Her bliss. It was Anton's bliss too.

Lillian turned and walked back through the forest lane to the guest suite where Freddie was sleeping in their bed. She stared at the old stone building and took a deep breath to prepare herself, then removed her shoes and tiptoed barefoot up the steps. Quietly she opened the door, entered, and closed it behind her with a gentle click, so as not to wake him.

Their bedroom door was closed, so she went to the kitchen to brew a pot of coffee. When it finished gurgling, she poured herself a cup and sat at the table, where she sipped slowly in the early-morning silence, searching her mind for the right words—words that would deliver the truth to Freddie while sparing him as much pain as possible.

Lillian finally finished her coffee and gathered the courage to get up from the table and walk to the bedroom. She paused for a moment, closed her eyes, and took a breath, then opened the door.

She found herself dumbstruck.

The bed was empty. Freddie was not there.

CHAPTER 23
LILLIAN

The covers were tousled, but Freddie was gone. For several seconds, Lillian stood frozen in the doorway, her hand on the knob, her heart racing. Where was he?

She ran upstairs to the second bedroom and checked there, as well as the bathroom.

Good God. Did he know where she had gone during the night?

Lillian dashed out the door and down the steps to look for the car. It was parked under the overhang, which meant he hadn't driven anywhere.

Hurrying to the patio, she gazed about in all directions, across the vineyards and olive orchards, wondering if he had gone for a walk, but that was ridiculous. Freddie would never rise at dawn to go walking.

"Freddie!" she shouted, knowing she was causing a disturbance and waking guests in the other suites, but panic had taken over all propriety.

Heaven help her.

What if he knew?

~

Lillian called Anton at the villa, but according to Caterina, he had left early to work in the office. Lillian tried calling him there, but no one had seen him, so she hung up the phone and watched the road. With any luck, Freddie would saunter into the driveway with a smile on his face and a bag of pastries from the hotel dining room.

Ten minutes passed, and he didn't appear. Something was wrong. She could feel it.

In that moment, all hell broke loose. A siren blared in the distance, causing an ice-cold wave of terror to course through her veins. Then a car came speeding down the lane and skidded to a halt. It was Francesco.

He opened the door and got out. "Lillian! You must come! There's been an accident! Your husband is hurt!"

She called out to him from the patio at the top of the stairs. "What happened?"

"He was . . ." Francesco couldn't seem to answer the question. "Please, just come."

Lillian ran into the apartment to grab her purse, then hurried outside to Francesco's car. "I don't understand," she said, getting into the passenger seat. "Please tell me what happened."

Francesco was hesitant but finally managed to put a few words together. "He was hit by a car."

"What?" Lillian exclaimed. "Where?"

He pointed. "Up the hill, along the road to the wine cellars."

"Is he okay?"

Francesco glanced at her with unease. "I don't know. He wasn't conscious. They called an ambulance."

"But he's alive, isn't he?"

"*Sì.*"

By the time they arrived at the scene, the ambulance had already left for the hospital. Francesco turned the car around and followed in that direction.

~

By the time they reached the hospital, Freddie was in the ER. Lillian begged the nurse to let her see him.

"You must let the doctors work," the nurse said, escorting Lillian away from the doors and leading her into a private seating area, where Francesco and Anton were waiting.

Anton stood, and she went to him immediately. "Thank goodness you're here. I don't understand how this could have happened. What was he doing out on the road, walking at dawn?"

Anton offered no response, then turned and spoke in a low voice. "Francesco, will you excuse us?"

"*Sì*. I'll wait in the car."

With every second that passed, Lillian's heart pounded faster with fear. Anton led her to the chairs, urging her to sit down.

"There's something I need to tell you," he said. "The reason Freddie was on the road was because he saw you leave last night."

She frowned at him. "What do you mean?"

Anton paused and squeezed his eyes shut. "I'm sorry, Lillian. He followed you, then he saw you come inside the villa, and . . . he watched us through the window."

She stared dazedly at Anton for a moment while the words sank into her brain. She envisioned it all—Freddie following her in the darkness, creeping up to the window at the villa, watching the whole scene as she and Anton made love. A slow and heavy wave of horror began to roll in the pit of her belly. "No . . ." She buried her face in her hands. "Poor Freddie. This was my worst fear." She cried softly for a time, then turned to Anton. "What happened after that? Francesco said he was on the road to the wine cellars. Why would he go there?"

Anton spoke hesitantly. "Because he followed me."

With eyes still burning from her tears, Lillian waited uneasily for him to continue.

"After you left, I went to the cellars to check on something," Anton said. "I didn't know Freddie was there until I came out later and he was on the terrace, pacing, waiting for me."

She fought hard to understand exactly what had happened. "Did you talk to him?"

"Yes. He told me what he saw, and he was angry, obviously. I could hardly blame him. Then he came at me with his fists."

"That doesn't sound like Freddie," Lillian replied, shaking her head. "He's not the fighting type."

"Well, he was in a fighting mood this morning."

Lillian regarded Anton with shock and horror. "What happened after that?"

"He shoved me hard, up against the wall a few times." Anton lowered his gaze. "I took it because I figured I had it coming. I didn't fight back, but then he swung a punch at me, and . . ."

"What did you do?"

"I hit him."

A sickening bile began to spread through her insides. "And then?"

"We argued. He told me to stay away from you, but I told him I was in love with you and that you were going to stay here."

"You told him I was leaving him?" she asked with alarm.

Anton nodded. Lillian pressed the heels of her hands to her forehead and squeezed great clumps of hair in her fists.

This was not how it was supposed to happen. She had wanted to break the news to Freddie herself—to do it gently and help him understand. She couldn't bear to think how he must have suffered when he'd watched her through the window, making love to another man. What a devastating sight it must have been. Grief and despair tore at her insides.

She turned to Anton. "I still don't understand what happened to him. How was he hit by a car?"

Anton bowed his head. "After we fought, he turned and walked off. I went inside to calm down, to get my head on straight, but then

I worried that he would go back to your apartment and do something crazy, maybe hurt you, so I got in my car to make sure you were okay."

All at once, Lillian grasped what Anton was saying to her, and her stomach contracted violently with dread. "Wait. Are you telling me that you're the one who hit him?"

Anton said nothing for a moment, and then at long last, he nodded.

If Lillian hadn't been sitting down, her knees might have buckled. "Oh my God, Anton. You didn't do it on purpose, did you? It was an accident, right?"

"Of course it was," he quickly replied. "It was early. The sun was barely up, and there was a heavy mist. It seemed like he came out of nowhere."

"He didn't hear you coming?" she asked, struggling to understand.

"I don't know, but there's no shoulder on that road, and I was coming around a bend. Maybe I was going too fast."

Feeling sick enough to throw up, Lillian stood and walked to the window in the waiting room, where she stared at the glass, unable to see through it to the world beyond. The morning sun seemed to reveal a foggy film of dust and fingerprints that begged to be cleaned. She reached out and marked an X in the grime, then inspected her forefinger. The world seemed suddenly soiled and dirty, and she wiped her finger on her hip.

Anton's voice shook with anguish. "Do you believe me, Lillian? That it was an accident?"

"Of course," she replied, her voice heavy and listless. "I know you would never try to hurt anybody like that."

Or would he? How well did she really know him? They said love could be blind . . .

The nurse walked into the waiting area, and they both turned to her.

"Are you Mrs. Bell?" she asked.

"Yes," Lillian replied.

"Would you come with me, please? Dr. Santarossa would like to speak with you."

Without looking back at Anton, Lillian hurried to follow the nurse.

~

The doctor was just finishing up a phone call at the nurses' station when Lillian approached.

"This is Freddie Bell's wife," the nurse said to him.

He hung up the phone and turned to her. "You're from America?"

"Yes. How is he?"

"We're still working on stabilizing him," the doctor replied. "The good news is that he's regained consciousness."

She laid her hand over her heart. "Thank goodness."

"But he's had a very serious injury," the doctor continued. "He can't move his fingers or toes, and the x-ray has confirmed a C6-level fracture on his spinal cord."

Lillian frowned and shook her head at him. "You'll need to explain that to me. What does it mean?"

"It means . . ." He paused for a few seconds. "The bottom line is that this is a very serious situation, more than we can handle here. We're just a community hospital. He needs to be transferred to a trauma center in Turin. We've sent for a helicopter."

All the blood rushed to Lillian's head, and she felt sick and dizzy. "I'm sorry . . . what are you saying . . . exactly? Are you telling me that my husband is paralyzed? That he won't be able to walk?"

The doctor's expression was grim and serious. "All I can say is that right now he has no feeling in his legs or arms, which is not a good sign, but he has to get through the next few days before we can begin to determine a long-term prognosis."

Her head drew back. "What do you mean . . . 'get through the next few days'?"

The doctor reached for a clipboard on the nurses' station counter. "I'm sorry, Mrs. Bell, but your husband is very seriously injured. You'll need to prepare yourself for what might come. And we're going to need you to answer some questions. Do you have medical insurance?"

She was barely able to comprehend what he was asking her. "Yes, I have travel insurance for both of us."

"Good. The nurse will get that information from you. And as your husband's next of kin, you may need to make some decisions about consenting to treatments or surgery, so we'll need you to sign some papers right away."

Her heartbeat skyrocketed. "I thought you said he was conscious."

"He is, but he's drowsy from the medications, and he's not out of the woods yet."

"Do you mean he could die?"

The doctor paused. "I don't want to frighten you, but if you have close family members, you should call them." He turned to the nurse. "She can see him now, but keep it brief."

Everything seemed to be happening in a blur of sound and movement as the nurse began to lead her away. "Come with me," she said, and Lillian felt as if she were falling out of a dream and into a nightmare.

~

The nurse pushed a curtain aside to reveal Freddie on a hospital bed with a brace around his neck. He appeared to be sleeping, but as Lillian approached and bent over him, his eyes fluttered open. "Lil?"

She took hold of his hand. "Yes, I'm here, sweetheart."

He began to weep.

"No . . ." She pressed her cheek to his. "Everything's going to be fine. They're taking good care of you, and I'm here now." She drew back and cupped his cheek in her hand.

His brow furrowed with pain. "I saw you with him."

His words came at her like a knife. They lodged in her chest, and for a devastating moment, she couldn't breathe.

Freddie whimpered softly.

"Freddie, no, please, sweetheart . . ." She bent over him and tried to comfort him with soft kisses and soothing words.

"Do you love him?" he asked, his voice barely perceptible.

No matter the truth, she couldn't possibly answer that question in the affirmative. Not now, in this moment.

"I love *you*, Freddie. The only thing that matters is that I'm here with you now, and you need to get better. Don't think about anything else."

He spoke slowly, his words slurred. "I can't get it out of my head . . . what I saw."

She kissed his hand. "I'm so sorry. The last thing I ever wanted to do was hurt you. But please don't think about what you saw. I love you. You're my everything."

He lay quiet, unresponsive, eyes closed. For a long while, she sat next to him, never taking her eyes off him.

"I'm sorry," he said.

"For what, darling? You have nothing to be sorry for."

"I left you alone."

She swallowed uncomfortably. "You had your book to write. It was important to you. It was important to both of us."

He fell asleep, but after a moment, he opened his eyes and blinked up at the ceiling. "It was stupid of me. I didn't want this to happen."

She stood up and bent over him. "What was stupid, Freddie?" He didn't answer, so she whispered, "Freddie? Can you hear me?"

Panic shot through her veins, and she glanced up, wondering if she should call for the nurse.

The nurse yanked the curtain aside just then. "He needs to rest now," she said. "Come with me, please."

"Can't I stay?" Lillian asked.

"No, he's not stable, and the doctor needs to come in. You can wait outside. We'll let you know when the helicopter arrives."

Lillian stood. "Can I go with him in the helicopter?"

"No, that's not possible. You'll have to get to Turin on your own. Do you have someone to drive you there? If not, there's a train. It leaves often."

Surely Anton would allow Francesco to drive her. Or he would drive her himself.

"Come with me, please," the nurse said, growing impatient.

Lillian had no choice but to return to the waiting area.

Anton stood up when she walked in. "How is he?"

She sat down and explained Freddie's condition. "A helicopter is on its way to take him to a trauma center in Turin. Do you know where that is? I need to get there somehow. Can Francesco drive me?"

"Of course," Anton replied.

She wiped a tear from her cheek and fought to maintain her composure. "This is all my fault."

"No," he said, "it was an accident. If anyone is to blame, it's me." He tried to rub her back, but she pushed his arm away.

"Please don't, Anton. I just need to think of Freddie right now." Needing to put some distance between them, she stood up and looked around. "I could use some coffee."

"I'll get it for you." He left, and she sat down again.

While he was gone, she sat in a numb stupor. A siren wailed somewhere outside. A janitor dipped a mop into a bucket on wheels, then made his way down the wide hallway, swirling the mop in a series of figure eights, back and forth, cleaning the floor.

A short while later, Anton returned and handed Lillian a cup of coffee. She sipped it slowly until the nurse came in and asked for her insurance information. She dug into her purse, withdrew her wallet, and handed the nurse a card with a US telephone number to call. Then she followed the nurse to a phone that she could use to call Freddie's parents and her mother.

The hospital had a hazy, dreamlike quality to it. Nothing seemed quite real. She felt adrift and displaced as she relayed the news to the family.

Later, when she returned to the waiting area, time seemed to crawl, sluggish like a worm.

Before long, the distant din of a helicopter engine in the sky woke her from her trance. She stood when it landed, its blades beating against the air.

Lillian turned and met Anton's troubled gaze. "I need to follow it to Turin."

"Yes," he replied. "I'll tell Francesco. We'll drive you wherever you need to go."

"Thank you."

He walked out, and she felt as if all the air had been extracted from the room.

~

Lillian waited until Freddie was evacuated to the air ambulance, and then she exited the hospital through the main entrance, where the black Mercedes was waiting at the curb. Francesco sat behind the wheel. Anton got out of the passenger seat and held the door open for her.

"I'd prefer to ride in the back, if it's all the same to you," she said. "I think I'm in shock. I need to lie down and rest."

He helped her into the back, and they drove five hours to Turin in somber silence.

When they finally arrived, Anton got out of the car and opened the back door for Lillian. "Let me come inside with you," he said.

Squinting into the bright sunlight beyond the shaded overhang, she shook her head. "No, you should go home with Francesco."

Anton's eyes seemed almost frantic. "You shouldn't be alone right now."

"I won't be alone. I'll be with Freddie. He needs me, and his father is coming. He's trying to get here by tomorrow."

"Lillian . . ." Anton's voice was gruff and broken. "This is the last thing I wanted to happen. I need you to believe that it was an accident. I was worried about you. That's why I was going so fast."

Her nerves tightened to the point that she feared they might snap. "I know, and I believe you, Anton. I do."

Love had not made her blind. It had helped her to see further and more clearly than she had ever seen before.

"But it doesn't matter," she continued. "Either way, I can't be with you right now. I need to be with Freddie."

With a pained expression, Anton bowed his head. "I'll book a hotel room for you. Stay there as long as you need to. I'll make sure it's walking distance from the hospital."

"You don't need to do that," she said.

"Yes, I do. I need to do *something*, because I blame myself for this. I shouldn't have said the things I did. It wasn't my place to tell him you were leaving him. He was probably distracted when he was walking back and . . ." Anton bowed his head again.

Sadly, Lillian had no words of comfort to offer Anton—or to anyone else other than Freddie, because he needed all her support, and she felt completely emptied out. "I need to go inside." Bending slightly to peer into the car, she spoke to Francesco. "Thank you for the ride. You're a good man, Francesco."

"I will pray for you and your husband."

"*Grazie.*"

Anton was holding the top of the car door, his expression darkening with grief. "I'll call the hospital and leave a message for you with the hotel information," he said.

She recognized his pain and couldn't manage to look him in the eye. It was too much for her to bear. "Thank you. I appreciate it. I need to go now."

Without any further gesture of good-bye, Lillian turned and walked away from him. She did not permit herself to look back.

~

Six hours later, Lillian sat down at Freddie's bedside in the ICU, moments before he was taken into surgery.

His prognosis was the same. He had no sensation in his hands or feet, which meant the likelihood of him ever walking again was slim.

All was calm for a time while Freddie slept and Lillian sat next to him, her mind awash with regret. If only she had stayed in bed the night before and waited until morning to go and see Anton. If she hadn't sneaked out in the middle of the night, Freddie would be back at the winery, sitting by the pool perhaps, basking in the pride of his completed manuscript, plotting his next novel.

She would never get over the guilt of that decision, not as long as she lived.

Freddie groaned in the bed, and Lillian practically leaped out of her chair. "I'm here, darling. Are you all right? Can I get you anything?"

His brow furrowed with agony, and he mumbled unintelligibly. "I couldn't bear it." He was drifting in and out. "Please, don't leave me. I'll die if you leave me."

Lillian bent over him. "Freddie, darling, I'm not leaving you. I'm right here."

His face contorted with a look of intense pain. "I'm scared. What's going to happen to me?"

"Don't be scared. I'm here. I'll always be here, and I'll take care of you. Everything's going to be fine."

Her heart squeezed wretchedly as she grasped his terrible fear of what the future would hold for him and his fear of losing her. Overcome with sorrow, barely able to keep her balance, she looked him in the eye and spoke fiercely. "And do not ever say to me that you're going to die. You're going to get through this. We're going to get through it together, and if you give up, I swear to God, Freddie, I'll never forgive you." She squeezed her eyes shut, pushed through her grief, and braced herself for the tests and trials that lay ahead. "Whatever Anton said to you, it's not true. I'm not leaving you. You're my husband, and I love you. I'll never leave you, Freddie, I promise. In sickness and in health, till death do us part. Remember? Are you going to break that promise to me?"

He blinked sleepily, then drifted off. Numb with shock, stunned, and disoriented, Lillian stared at him for an agonizing moment. A medical team arrived to take him to the OR. After they wheeled him away, she sank onto the chair and wept inconsolably.

~

It was a short walk to the hotel after Freddie was taken into surgery, which she had been told could last five or six hours or more. In a horrendous daze, Lillian collected the room key from the front desk clerk, who cheerfully informed her that the room was already paid for.

Slipping the key into the lock, she surrendered to her exhaustion, aching for the soft bed that awaited her. The lock clicked, and she pushed the door open but stopped in the doorway when her gaze fell upon the bed, which was not empty.

"Anton . . . ," she uttered softly.

He was stretched out on top of the covers, asleep. At the sound of her voice, he sat up and quickly stood but did not approach her.

"You're back," he said. "How is he?"

Caught off guard by Anton's presence in the room, Lillian closed the door behind her, walked in, and set her purse on the TV cabinet.

"He's the same. No change. And he's in surgery now." They stared at each other uncertainly for a few seconds. "I didn't expect you to be here."

She didn't want him there. She wanted to be alone.

Anton took a step toward her, but she held up a hand. "Please, don't try to comfort me. I don't want that. I couldn't bear it."

If she fell apart now, there would be no coming back from it.

"I understand," he replied, watching her retreat into the bathroom.

She shut the door behind her and stared at herself in the mirror, then turned on the faucet and washed her hands. She didn't need to use the toilet—she had used the washroom at the hospital on her way out—but she didn't want to open the door either. She needed time to get over the shock of seeing Anton in her bed.

Heaven help her. Despite everything, his mere presence, without a word spoken, touched something deep inside her heart. And her body still yearned for him. One look into his eyes shook her to the core and made her want to melt into his arms for the comfort he would provide—but she couldn't do that. Everything was tainted now. Because of what they had done together, Freddie was in critical condition and might never walk again.

Searching for strength to get through this, Lillian reached for the door handle and walked out of the bathroom. Anton was still standing there, exactly where she had left him.

He gestured to a shopping bag on a table in the corner of the room. "I got you a toothbrush and some clean clothes for tomorrow."

She warmed at his kindness but fought to remain steady on her feet. When she moved to look inside the bag, she found socks and underwear, some toiletries, a pair of jeans, sweatpants, pajamas, and a few T-shirts.

"This is helpful. Thank you." She faced him, and they stared at each other in silence until she couldn't do it anymore. She couldn't keep from expressing her feelings. "I'm never going to forgive myself," she said.

"No," Anton firmly replied. "It's my fault, not yours. I shouldn't have told him you were leaving him. I should have left that to you. You would have handled it better. Now, I'm afraid you're going to hate me forever." He shook his head with remorse.

She moved to the bed and sat down. "I don't hate you."

Anton sat down beside her and took hold of her hand.

"You didn't know Freddie was going to be on the road where he was," Lillian said. "And he was throwing punches at you. I understand why you were concerned about me. At first, I wasn't sure, I didn't know what to think, but now I understand why you were driving fast. I know you would never wish to harm anyone. That's not who you are."

Anton spoke somberly. "What will happen now?"

Watching how his thumb gently stroked her knuckles, she found herself speaking matter-of-factly, as if she had tossed her heart into a deep grave and was now shoveling dirt upon it. "He'll be in surgery for the next few hours, but the doctors said it could be weeks before he'll be stable enough to go home. Then he'll need to go into a rehabilitation facility and learn how to live, probably as a quadriplegic. But it's not just the broken spinal cord that causes trouble. He's going to be vulnerable to all sorts of infections, and in his weakened state . . ."

Suddenly unable to go on, Lillian sobbed with grief onto Anton's shoulder, and he held her close.

When she finally recovered and wiped away her tears, she said, "Tonight, the doctor told me that statistically, most people who suffer an injury like this have an average life expectancy of only two years. It's not the spinal cord injury that takes them but some sort of other infection."

Tears filled her eyes again—hot, burning tears that streamed down her cheeks. Anton continued to hold her. He kissed the top of her head.

"I need to be there for him," she said. "I can't abandon him now."

Anton nodded.

For a long while, they sat together on the edge of the bed, dazed and traumatized, saying nothing. When Lillian yawned for the third time, Anton kissed the back of her hand. "You're tired. You need to get some rest."

"Yes."

He stood up, and she walked him to the door. Before he left, she took in the full force of his gaze.

"Where do we go from here, Lillian?" he asked.

"We don't go anywhere," she replied, almost instantly. "I can't see you again. Not while Freddie is fighting to survive. It would break his heart. I'm quite sure it would destroy his will to live."

Anton bowed his head with understanding and wept softly. She bowed her head, too, and they stood apart, afraid to touch each other.

After a moment, Anton stepped toward her for one last loving embrace. "I'm sorry. For everything."

"Me too. This isn't how I wanted this to end, for any of us." She drew back. "Please don't write to me or call me. Don't try to contact me. I don't think I could bear it."

"I'll do whatever you want me to do," he said, "but I won't stop loving you, and I'll wait for you. However long it takes. I'll wait forever."

She frowned and shook her head, her voice laced with sorrow. "Please don't say that. It sounds as if you'll be waiting for Freddie to die. I can't live with that."

He nodded and touched his forehead to hers, and she felt transported back to the vineyards and wine cellars of Tuscany, to the dinner table beneath the leafy trellis at the villa, where candle flames flickered in the warm evening breezes and laughter filled the night. To the conversations she'd had with tourists who were beguiled by the sights, scents, and flavors of Italy. It all felt like a fantasy with no connection to her current or future physical reality. From this moment on, those memories would become a part of her dreams.

She closed her eyes and worked hard to imprint the images in her mind. To never forget.

"I'll be here for you," Anton said. "If you ever need anything, you'll have it."

Her heart was aching, as if it were suffering a slow, painful death. She didn't want to drag this out. She wanted him to leave, to put a swift end to this unbearable torture.

Lillian lifted her face and kissed Anton softly on the lips, but he wouldn't let it go with that. He pulled her close and deepened the kiss for one final moment of passion.

When he drew back, a door swung shut over Lillian's heart, and she knew, from that day forward, it would be locked away forever, until she and Anton met again. In this life or in the next.

CHAPTER 24
FIONA

Tuscany, 2017

"I don't know how to feel right now," I said, wiping tears from my cheeks and squinting into the sunshine as a small sailboat passed by. "If what you're telling me is true, that means my father knew about my mother's affair all along and that it wasn't a secret at all. But I've been carrying the burden of that secrecy, hiding it from him, since I was eighteen years old."

There was something intense in Francesco's eyes as he watched me with scrutiny, and I wasn't sure what to make of it. He almost seemed to be enjoying this. I supposed he was relieved that the truth was finally out.

"But if my dad already knew," I said, "why did Mom make me promise to keep it secret from him?"

"Isn't it obvious?" Francesco replied. "Because she wanted Freddie to believe that you were his child. She asked Anton to keep the same secret, and he did. For the rest of his life, he never broke that promise."

"Because of the guilt he felt?"

"Partly, yes, but not entirely. The real reason Anton never revealed the truth was because he simply couldn't break a promise he had made to your mother. That's how much he loved her."

I pondered all of this as I twisted my signet ring around on my finger. "But my dad didn't even want children. Why did Mom feel she had to lie about it?"

"Because everything changed after the accident. She knew how afraid he was that she would leave him for Anton one day, and if he knew you were Anton's child, he might have simply given up wanting to live. She was very protective of him. She had to be, and I believe a part of her felt that, in the end, it was her purpose in this life."

"Her destiny," I said. "To care for someone who couldn't take care of himself." I looked across at Francesco. "She was always very good at being a mother—to both of us, I suppose. But when did Anton find out about me? Did Mom tell him when she found out she was pregnant, or did she tell him years later?"

Francesco shifted in his chair and crossed one long leg over the other. "She and Freddie spent four weeks at the trauma center in Turin, and when it was time for Freddie to leave the hospital and move into a rehab facility, her insurance company insisted that he be transferred back to America. By that time, she knew she was pregnant."

"Did she know that I was Anton's?" I asked. "For sure?"

"From what I understand, yes. She told Anton there could be no doubt. Women know these things, I gather."

"As long as we know how to use a calendar," I said with a sigh.

Seagulls soared above us, high against the blue sky, calling out to one another.

"Before your mother left the country," Francesco continued, "she saw Anton one more time in Turin. She asked him to come, and I drove him there. He spent an hour with her, on a park bench outside the hospital, and that was all." Francesco bowed his head. "He was devastated that day. It was a painful drive back to Montepulciano, let me tell you."

"What did she say to him?" I asked.

"She told him what I told you before—that she intended to pass their child off as Freddie's because she believed if he ever learned the truth, it would take away his will to live, and he was hanging on by a thread. Anton agreed to let her do whatever she felt she had to do."

My heart was breaking. I stood up and moved to the iron railing to look out at the sea. "Did they think it was just temporary? That my dad wouldn't survive for more than a few years? Is that why Anton agreed to keep quiet about it? Did they expect that they would be together again, eventually?"

"I believe that's what Anton expected," Francesco said. "And please don't think he was a bad person, wishing for your father to die. He never wished that. He felt guilty enough as it was, and he did everything he could to help your father."

I swung around to face him. "What do you mean?"

"Financially," Francesco explained with a shrug of his shoulder, as if I should know.

"Are you telling me that he supported us?"

"Yes, he sent money to your mother every month."

"But I thought we were living on medical insurance money and then the proceeds from my mother's life insurance policy."

He nodded. "You were. But Anton paid for your mother's insurance policy, just to be safe. It was his idea, not long after she left Italy. He wanted to make sure you'd be taken care of in the event of your mother's death. He was always a planner, very smart about money."

I bent over the railing and bowed my head. "I can't believe it," I said breathlessly. "All this time, I hated him. I thought he took advantage of my mother. If I'd only known."

A terrible regret came at me suddenly, knocking me off kilter. Anton, my real father, was dead, and I would never get the chance to meet him. It was too late now.

My heart squeezed agonizingly in my chest. What a fool I had been. I should have searched for the truth sooner. I shouldn't have buried my head in the sand, buried all my questions for the sake of my father's emotional stability.

Fighting to maintain my composure, I faced Francesco. "Why didn't Anton contact me and tell me what you just told me? I never knew he cared for me or for my mother. Why did he let me believe that he didn't?"

"Because he didn't know you knew the truth. Your mother's death was devastating for him, but it didn't change the promise he made to her—that he would wait until after Freddie was gone to approach you. All his life, he was waiting for that day."

"And no one expected my dad to live as long as he did," I replied with newfound understanding.

"Thirty-one years," Francesco said. "He certainly beat the odds."

"He outlived them both." I returned to my chair at the table and sat down. "Where do I go from here? How do I live with this?"

Francesco folded his hands across his lap and squinted into the bright sunshine. "It seems that your more immediate problem is making sure that Anton's final wishes are respected. He loved his children, and it's important for everyone to realize that he didn't disinherit them—although it might seem like that from their point of view. But I can tell you this, in no uncertain terms—he wasn't pressured into changing his will. He wanted his children to learn something, to learn how to be grateful and not take things for granted, and to be independent and budget their money, for pity's sake, and stop going through life thinking it grows on trees. Anton had a very strong work ethic, and I think this was his way of forcing Connor and Sloane to wake up to that. Heaven knows he tried to teach them that while he was alive, but their mother got in the way of it. Kate did love to spoil them."

I exhaled heavily. "I'm still shocked by it."

"Don't be. He knew it would bring you here, and I suspect he wanted his children to meet you and maybe learn a few things from you."

"But he didn't even know me," I argued. "What if I was as spoiled as they were?"

Francesco shook his head. "He knew your mother. He knew how she would raise you."

We sat together, listening to the gentle thunder of the surf on the rugged coastline below, breathing in the salty scent of the Tyrrhenian Sea.

"Thank you for all this," I said. "I don't know what I would have done if I hadn't been able to learn the truth. But I do have one more question."

"I'll try to answer if I can."

"I never got the chance to meet Anton. Marco described him as a tyrant, and Connor said he was ornery. Everything you've told me doesn't sound consistent with that. What was he really like?"

Francesco gazed out at the turquoise water. "When I first met him, and when your mother knew him, he was a joyful, passionate lover of life. As for him being a tyrant? I was loyal to him, right up until the very end, but I can't deny that he was difficult and bad tempered at times. There was a very specific moment when he lost his sense of joy, and he was never the same after that."

"When was that?"

"When your mother died. I believe all his hopes for future happiness died with her. Thunderclouds moved in, and they never left. And don't listen to what anyone says about him being a womanizer. He was faithful to your mother until the day she died. But then he just gave up. He was lonely. He wanted to fill the emptiness. Hence the women. But he was good to them." Francesco gazed up at the treetops. "I wonder if Anton and your mother are together now, at last. I like to think so.

I imagine them sitting together, watching the sunset. Enjoying a very good wine."

I couldn't help myself. I burst into tears as I pondered the many sorrows they had suffered after they parted, the guilt they both endured for their adultery, and the profound sacrifice they had made to pay for it—for the safety and well-being of my father in Tallahassee.

A strong breeze blew through the tall cypresses along the hillside, and through my tears, I watched the waves break against the rugged shoreline below.

When I finally collected myself, I reached for Francesco's hand across the table and squeezed it. "Thank you for everything. I'll never forget what you shared with me." I rose to my feet. "But I should probably go now."

"*Sì, sì*. But before you do . . ." He leaned over the side of his chair. "I have something for you. It might come in handy to push back the enemy."

"What do you mean?"

He picked up a shoebox from under his chair. "This is proof of what your mother meant to Anton and what she meant to him."

I accepted the box and opened the lid. To my surprise and profound relief, it was filled with letters from America, written in my mother's hand, addressed to Anton. "Oh my goodness."

"She wrote to him once a year," Francesco told me, "always on your birthday, until the day she died."

I let out a breath. "I've been looking for these. Everyone has been looking. How did you come into possession of them, Francesco?"

He shrugged again and spoke with humility. "Because I was Anton's good friend. After your mother died, he gave them to me for safekeeping in case anything ever happened to him. I was supposed to wait until after your father passed to deliver them to you."

"But he hasn't passed," I replied. "He's still very much alive."

Francesco gazed out at the sea. "True. But I'm not as good at keeping promises as Anton was. As far as I'm concerned, it was merely a suggestion that I wait. So there you are, Fiona. Those letters belong to you. Do whatever you wish with them, but may I suggest you use them to secure your inheritance? It's what Anton wanted. He knew how much your mother loved Tuscany and the winery. He always believed that her love for the place would be in your blood."

I closed the lid and hugged the shoebox to my chest. "Thank you, Francesco." I rose from the table, kissed him on both cheeks, and walked out.

CHAPTER 25
FIONA

The drive back to Montepulciano passed in silence while I read my mother's letters to Anton. Each one described my development and accomplishments since the previous year and included four or five photographs. Altogether, it was a detailed chronicle of the first eighteen years of my life, written with pride, love, and optimism.

But with each letter, what began in joy soon descended into sorrow when my mother surrendered to a candid, honest unloading of her burdens and hardships while caring for my father. She described nerve-racking trips to the hospital, frustrations with incompetent or uncaring home care workers, and a constant feeling of pressure to bolster my father's spirits whenever he grew maudlin, which was more often than I had ever realized. My mother wrote pages and pages of personal confessions that did not shy away from her loneliness, resentments, and regrets.

> Sometimes I think he enjoys seeing me suffer, but I suppose he has a right to take some pleasure in it . . . I would never complain to him. I confess these feelings only to you, Anton. You're the only one I can

> tell . . . Yesterday, I stayed home from work because
> the nurse canceled at the last minute. He didn't thank
> me. He never thanks me for anything . . . He knows
> I'll never leave him . . .

On numerous occasions, she apologized for complaining and assured Anton that she was at peace with her decision to remain at her post.

> I couldn't live with myself if I left him. I could
> never be truly happy, not even with you, my darling,
> in our beautiful Tuscan countryside. But the memory
> of it makes me happy in my dreams . . . It keeps me
> going . . .

She begged him, in every letter, not to come to her rescue, and she thanked him for the money he sent.

> It's just enough not to raise questions.

She ended every letter with *Yours, forever* . . .

I finished reading the last one, which my mother must have written shortly before her death. With tears in my eyes, I set it back in the box and turned to Marco, behind the wheel. "They really did love each other," I said. "I can't believe I thought the worst about him. I wish I had known."

"It's not your fault," Marco replied, reaching across the console to take hold of my hand. "Your mother didn't tell you everything."

"But why didn't she?" I asked, wiping at my cheek. "It would have made such a difference if I had known. I wouldn't have spent the past twelve years of my life hating a man who didn't deserve to be hated." Feeling torn—because I was still intensely loyal to my dad—I shut my eyes. "Or maybe he did deserve it, because he was the reason my mom was unfaithful in the first place. If not for him and his good looks and his delicious wine, my father probably wouldn't have spent most of his life confined to a wheelchair."

Marco squeezed my hand again. "I think all you can do is accept the past for what it was and be thankful for where you are today. Think of it, Fiona—if your mother hadn't fallen in love with Anton, you wouldn't be here right now."

I gazed out the car window. "That's true."

Two letters remained in the box, these not addressed in my mother's hand. I dug one of them out, bracing myself for the words it probably contained: news of my mother's passing. It was a business-size envelope with a typed address label. The return address was our home in Tallahassee.

I opened the envelope and unfolded the page. Before I began to read, I glanced at the salutation at the bottom and felt a shiver of apprehension at the sight of my father's typed signature.

> Dear Mr. Clark,
>
> I am writing to inform you that my wife Lillian passed away yesterday from a brain aneurysm. It happened unexpectedly when she was at home in the kitchen and she died a few hours after reaching the hospital.
>
> I am writing now to ask that you respect the promise you made to her and that you do not contact Fiona for any reason. We are both very distraught, and because she is not aware that I am not her real father, I believe it would cause her undue pain and dishonor her mother's memory if Fiona ever found out, because it's not what Lillian wanted. Most importantly, I need Fiona here with me. She is all I have left, and she lifts my spirits on the bad days. I couldn't possibly go on

without her. If you have any feelings left for my wife, and if you have any compassion for me, given that you are responsible for what happened to me, you will continue to honor Lillian's wishes until I am gone.

Sincerely,

Fred Bell

My blood ran cold. "Oh my God."

"What is it?" Marco asked.

"This letter . . . it's from my dad. He's telling Anton about my mother's death, but he knew . . ."

"He knew what?"

I couldn't breathe. I could barely think straight. "That I wasn't his daughter. That I was Anton's." I glanced up and frowned with shock and bewilderment. "If he knew about that, he never let on to my mom. She thought it was her secret. All her life, she was trying to protect him from the truth, but he knew . . . he always knew . . . and he pretended to believe that I was his."

"But how could he have known," Marco asked, "if your mother didn't tell him?"

"Maybe because everyone says I look so much like Anton," I replied. "It wouldn't take a rocket scientist to figure it out, given that he knew they'd had an affair and he was away in Paris. But why would he pretend not to know? Why would he never confront my mom about it?"

I read the letter a second time, which caused a fresh flood of anger to surge through my body. "And then he kept the truth from me because he wanted me to stay at home and look after him. He says it right here in black and white." Lowering the letter, I turned to Marco. "I always felt so guilty about keeping that secret from him. I did it because I was protective of him, just like Mom was, and I didn't want him to be hurt, but he knew the truth all along. And he didn't care that I might want to know I had another father. That I might want to meet him."

Marco shifted into a lower gear as he slowed down at a sharp turn. "We're about five minutes away from Montepulciano. What are you going to do?"

I slid the letter back into the box. "As far as my dad is concerned, I'm not sure, but as far as the will is concerned . . ." I met Marco's gaze directly. "I'm going to give these letters to the lawyers and tell them everything that Francesco told me today. That should take care of any suggestion of undue influence. It's proof of what Anton really wanted, and he deserves to get what he wanted for once, because he certainly didn't get it during his lifetime. Then I'm going to go knock on Connor's door and tell him to stop tearing my house apart."

I replaced the lid on the shoebox, though I knew there was still one more letter at the bottom. But I was not prepared to read it yet, because the seal had not been broken and it was intended for my mother. The return address said *Anton Clark, Maurizio Wines*. According to the postmark, it was mailed shortly before my mother's death. It was stamped *Return to Sender*.

CHAPTER 26
ANTON

June 12, 2005

Dear Lillian,

I just finished reading your letter and I will write the same thing I write every year: Please let me come and help you. Let me meet our daughter. I don't know how it would be possible to explain it to her, but maybe there is a way? Please let me share your burden. I would shoulder it all if you would let me.

Even as I'm writing this from a thousand miles away, I can feel your reaction. You're afraid I'm going to break my promise to stay away. Please, don't let yourself worry. That is the last thing I would ever want—to cause you any fear or concern. I gave you my word. I will never reveal that I am Fiona's real father, and my word is true, but I need to say something I have never said to you before, because I never wanted to add to your burdens. Maybe it's the wine tonight. I've probably had too much, and the moon is full, which always makes me think of you. But here it is: With every day that passes, I feel like I am slowly dying. Your letters break me apart because I share your sorrow—the guilt over what happened to Freddie and the agony of being separated from you. I wish we could be together to comfort each other, but maybe that's not what we deserve. Maybe the fates have decided that we stole a lifetime of happiness that one summer. We used it all up and there is no more left for us.

Since you left Tuscany, nothing is the same. There are no words to describe my loneliness which grows worse with every passing year. The loss of you was devastating, but it came on top of the loss of my children. What man could survive that? As you know, Kate was brutal in the divorce. Connor and Sloane have no interest in coming to visit me and I still don't understand what I did wrong as a father. It was Kate who left me, not the other way around, and I believe now, without a doubt, that she only married me for my money. All I ever wanted was to be a normal family and raise our children here, on the vineyard. I think Kate must say bad things about me . . . I don't know. Or maybe the children just prefer the city and their new stepfather, who's richer than I ever was. I am lost. I love them and I miss them. I wish they would come here. I'll keep asking. I'll invite them again next week.

You asked about my artwork. The answer is no, I haven't picked up my paintbrush since you left because whenever I see beauty in the world, I don't want to capture it because it reminds me of you and my children and everything that's gone. There is no one to share it with.

Maybe this is my punishment for falling in love with a married woman. I wanted too much, and what happened to Freddie is the cross we both must bear. You are drained and worn out, and I am without you and without my children . . . Connor, Sloane, and Fiona.

I am sorry for all this. I don't want to add to your burdens. Whatever the case, I am in awe of your strength, your sacrifice and devotion to your husband, so I will soldier on, waiting for the day when we will see each other again.

But I must ask . . . perhaps it's time for a brief reprieve? I miss you, Lillian, and the waiting is tearing me apart. Please consider it. If you could put my promise to you into a drawer and push it closed, even just for one day, I would come to you. No one would have to know. No one but us.

Yours,

Anton

CHAPTER 27
SLOANE

Tuscany, 2017

Seated at the dining room table with the lawyers, Sloane was first to finish reading a copy of her father's final letter to Lillian Bell. The room was quiet as a tomb as Connor, Fiona, and Maria continued to read. When Fiona set down her copy, Sloane turned to her, and her voice shook as she spoke. "I guess this is the proof you were looking for."

Connor was still reading, his face twisted into an infuriated frown.

Mr. Wainwright folded his hands upon a file that contained the original copies of the letters, sent over a span of eighteen years. "It shows, without a doubt," he said, "that Mr. Clark possessed genuine feelings of love for Fiona's mother. This will make it very difficult to overturn the will."

Connor finally finished reading the last letter and tossed it onto the table. "How do we know these are even real?"

"It's Dad's handwriting," Sloane said.

He pointed at Fiona. "There's a lot of money at stake here. She could have forged it."

Mr. Wainwright held up a hand. "I spoke to Francesco Bergamaschi, who confirmed that the letters were genuine. He also confirmed Mr. Clark's final wishes."

"Who the hell is Francesco Berg . . . whatever his name is?" Connor asked.

"He was your father's driver and personal assistant for many years," Mr. Wainwright replied.

Teardrops pooled on Sloane's eyelashes. "I remember him. He used to drive us into town for ice cream when we were little. Remember?"

"That guy?" Connor replied. "He must be senile by now. You trust what he has to say?"

"We believe the letters speak for themselves," Mr. Wainwright informed Connor, with a note of impatience. "The will stands."

A tear spilled from Sloane's eye. She quickly wiped it away, but Connor noticed and turned to Fiona. "Do you see that? That's the kind of father he was. A vindictive bastard to the very end, cutting his own kids out of his will just to spite us. Look what this is doing to her."

Sloane couldn't allow Connor to speak for her, because he didn't understand how she felt, nor did he have the slightest appreciation for the things she loved—her children, this winery, the London house. He was her brother, and she would always love him, but deep down, they had nothing in common. She had to be honest.

"That's not why I'm crying," she said shakily.

"What's the problem, then?" Connor asked irritably.

She gestured toward her father's final letter to Lillian Bell. "I didn't think that kind of love was possible. I've certainly never been loved like that."

Connor leaned back in his chair and shook his head at her. "Great, sis. Well done."

"And he wasn't vindictive," she added. "Even if he was, it's our own fault for making him that way. Didn't you read what he said in that letter? We were terrible children. We believed all the lies Mom told us about him. We believed it because we were selfish, and we didn't want to miss out on our friends' parties in LA. We never gave him the benefit of the doubt. If we had come to visit him once in a while, we might have seen that he wasn't the two-timing womanizer that Mom made him out to be. Maybe he would have confided in us about all this. Maybe he would have been happier." She buried her forehead in a hand. "I can't believe he's gone and I never knew him. I'm not surprised he did what he did. As far as I'm concerned, what we got in the will is more than we deserved."

Connor shoved his chair back and stood. "I don't care what these letters say. I still think she did something to make him rewrite it, because she was no better than us. Why did she deserve it more than we did?"

"Because she was a good daughter!" Sloane replied heatedly. "She's been at her father's side her entire life. She was devoted to him, and Dad knew it! What did we ever sacrifice for anything?"

Connor stood for a moment, glaring at her. "You're going to have to buy me out of that house in London, Sloane, because I never want to set foot in it again." He headed for the door.

Sloane watched him go and realized that she was shaking all over. With trembling hands, she wiped the tears from her cheeks, then noticed suddenly that everyone at the table was staring at her in silence.

"Thank you," Fiona said.

Mr. Wainwright cleared his throat and pulled another file from under the one that contained the letters. "Now that that's out of the way, we'd like to begin the process of transferring the deed for the winery and all the corporate holdings over to you, Ms. Bell. And Maria, we also have the deed for your villa here. There's a fair bit of paperwork. Do you both have time to get through this today?"

Fiona and Maria exchanged a look.

"I do," Fiona replied.

"Me too," Maria added.

"Excellent. Let's get started, then." Mr. Wainwright opened the file.

~

After the lawyers left, Sloane was upstairs in her bedroom, curled up in a fetal position on the bed. Evan and Chloe sat on the sofa with earbuds, swiping at their tablets.

A knock sounded at the door, and Fiona walked in. Sloane sat up, dabbed her eyes with a tissue, and fought to pull herself together. Evan and Chloe glanced up briefly, then back down at their screens.

"Hi," Fiona said. "How are you doing?"

"Horrendous," Sloane replied. "But please don't think I'm crying because you got the winery and I didn't. I don't blame you for that, and it's not what I'm thinking about right now." She watched Fiona move more fully into the room.

"What are you thinking about?" Fiona asked.

"That I don't know how I'm going to get past the fact that I ignored my father all my life. I let him down terribly." She glanced at Evan and Chloe, who were oblivious to the conversation. "I don't know what I would do if they let me down like that. If they didn't want to see me. I won't do that to Alan, no matter how angry I am with him. I'll make sure they continue to have a relationship with him, and they can judge him for themselves as they get older."

Fiona sat down on the edge of the bed. "I don't know your husband, but I will say this for him. He's lucky he married you. You're a decent person, Sloane." She glanced at Evan and Chloe on the sofa. "You know, my dad always told me to look forward, not back. He had to do that because he was forced to let go of the life he knew before the accident, when he could walk and do other things like dress and feed himself. But now I realize that it also included my mother's affair and how it broke his heart and how he had to accept responsibility for his part in it, for what was wrong in their marriage in the first place. At least I hope he accepted some responsibility. Either way, he had to focus on how he was going to live with the cards he had been dealt and make the most of the years he had left." Fiona lowered her gaze. "The doctors didn't expect him to live very long."

"He must be an amazing man," Sloane said. "He wrote books?"

Fiona's eyes lifted. "Yes. He finished his first novel here in Tuscany, but he always believed he only got published because of what happened to him. They used his situation to publicize the book, and that's why it sold so well. He wrote two more—he was able to dictate—but they didn't sell nearly as well as the first one. I think it was a blow to his confidence, because all he ever wanted to be was a novelist."

"That's unfortunate," Sloane said.

"At least he found purpose with a different kind of writing—articles for a charitable foundation he and Mom started for spinal cord research. That was how he looked forward, not back. He was able to pivot and make a change. See a different future for himself and get on board with it. It's turned out to be the thing he's most proud of."

Sloane sat up straighter against the pillows on the bed. "You're lucky that you have a strong relationship with him. You won't have any regrets about that. You'll always know that you were a good daughter. I feel like I ruined that for myself, and my dad must have hated me."

"No. He loved you. I know he did." Fiona stared at Sloane for a few seconds. "That's why I'm here. Would you mind taking a walk with me?"

"Now?"

"Yes, and let's bring the kids." Fiona stood up, moved to the sofa, and waved her hands in front of their faces. "Calling all children. Lower your tablets. It's time to go outside."

"What for?" Evan asked, tugging the white buds out of his ears.

"Have you been inside the wine cellars yet?"

Uncertain, he turned to Sloane. "Have we, Mom?"

"No, you haven't been there," she replied.

"Then let's go," Fiona said. "Trust me, you'll love it. It's like something out of Harry Potter."

"I love Harry Potter," Chloe replied. "I saw all the movies. Hermione's my favorite."

"I like Hermione too," Fiona replied.

Evan and Chloe set down their tablets and followed Fiona and Sloane out of the room. Together, they left the villa and walked down Cypress Row to the little medieval hamlet and chapel at the bottom of the hill. Fiona led Sloane and the children into the stone building where the wine cellars were located, down the circular steps to the dimly lit labyrinth below. Massive oak barrels lay on their sides in the largest cellars, and beyond that, they moved through narrow passages with dusty bottles of wine stacked on either side of the corridors.

"Your uncle Connor and I used to play hide-and-seek down here when we were your age," Sloane told them.

"Can we do that?" Evan asked.

"I don't know," she replied. "Ask your aunt Fiona. It's her winery."

Fiona turned and walked backward, smiling, spreading her arms wide. "Of course you can! Why do you think I brought you here? You can come here anytime you like, as long as you don't pull a plug out of one of those big barrels we just passed, or you'll flood the place."

"We won't," Chloe replied.

Fiona led them to an ancient oak door at the end of the last corridor and dug into her purse for a key. "This is a very old hiding place," she said, inserting the key into a wrought iron lock and pushing the door open on creaking hinges.

Rapt with fascination, Sloane, Evan, and Chloe followed her inside.

"What's all this?" Sloane asked, moving along groups of wine bottles stacked against the walls on wooden slabs.

"It's a very special room," Fiona explained. "These are collections from the harvest year of a child's birth. It was a tradition started by the Maurizio family, who owned this winery before your father did. Some of the bottles are very old, as you can see. Look at the dates on the plaques. But come over here." She beckoned to Sloane. "This collection is for you." Fiona removed the plaque from a hook on the wall. "Your father wanted you to have this. There are bottles here for Connor as well. I'll make sure he gets them."

Sloane stared at the dusty plaque with her name and date of birth written on it and couldn't fathom what she was looking at. She picked up a bottle and rubbed the grime off the label. "My goodness. This artwork . . . it's one of his paintings. I remember when he used to paint when we were small. I would paint, too, in his studio. He'd let me use his brushes and oils. I'd make a terrible mess, but he was never cross with me. He told me how talented I was."

Sloane's heart lurched painfully at those fond memories.

Fiona moved deeper into the room. "Come over here. There are two more recent collections you should see."

Sloane read the names and dates on the plaques. Mesmerized, she turned to Fiona. "These are for Evan and Chloe."

"Yes."

Sloane picked up a bottle, saw another of her father's paintings, and bowed her head with grief. "I should have brought them here. They should have gotten to know their grandfather and seen what he created."

"They're here now," Fiona replied.

"But it's too late." With another rush of sorrow, Sloane set the bottle back in place.

"It's not too late. You can tell them about him, show them pictures, and share stories you remember."

They looked around for a few more minutes, examining some of the older bottles.

"I know this is difficult," Fiona said in a quiet, understanding voice. "I've noticed that you keep saying what a good daughter I was, but what you need to know is that I wasn't perfect either. I've been feeling the same way as you, wishing I had come here and gotten to know Anton when he was still alive. I'm always going to regret that I didn't make that effort, but I was too busy resenting him because it was easier and less complicated."

"That's how I felt," Sloane said. "It was easier not to face any of that."

"And though it's important to look forward, not back," Fiona added, "I also think it's important to reflect on past mistakes and learn from them. It helps you move forward in the right direction."

Evan approached and tugged at Sloane's sleeve. "Mom, can Chloe and I go explore?"

"Sure, as long as you don't leave the building without telling me."

"We won't."

As soon as the children were gone, Fiona regarded Sloane curiously. "Have you made any decisions about your marriage?"

Sloane sighed. "That's a tough one. Connor thinks I'd be crazy to divorce Alan, and he doesn't think I'll go through with it. Lord knows I've never followed through before, but something feels different this time. Maybe it was coming here and remembering the person I used to be. Or meeting you and seeing how relaxed you are about the money. Whatever the reason, I feel like I can't let the prenup keep me from doing what's right. Money shouldn't be the reason I stay with Alan, at the cost of my dignity and self-esteem. I want to be a good mother—the kind of woman who's not a doormat and can't be bought. I want my kids to know what it means for a woman to be strong and independent. I just hope I can figure out how to be that kind of woman. I feel like I've been locked away in Alan's ivory tower for the past ten years, and I'm terrified of what will happen when I leave it. I don't know what to expect, and I don't know how to do any of this on my own. I've never even had a job."

"You've been a mother. That's a big job."

Sloane shrugged, as if she didn't think it would count for much out there in the real world.

"Well, it's never too late to start fresh," Fiona replied. "On that note, I have something to tell you."

"What's that?"

Fiona strolled to the collection of wine with Sloane's name on it. "This place is part of your heritage, and your children's, and I'm your half sister. Evan and Chloe are my niece and nephew. So I asked Mr. Wainwright to write a new will for me. I'm setting it up so that you, Evan, and Chloe will be my heirs and inherit this place one day."

Sloane wasn't sure she'd heard Fiona correctly. "What did you just say?"

Fiona faced her. "I don't have children of my own, and I'm not sure I ever will. If I do, we'll cross that bridge when we come to it and divide the winery up appropriately, but for now, I want to make sure this stays in the family."

Out of the blue, a childhood memory emerged from somewhere deep in Sloane's consciousness. She felt her father's strong arms scooping her up to carry her on his shoulders across an olive grove. She had felt safe and loved in those days, comfortable and at home. She realized she hadn't felt that way in many years.

Fiona continued. "And believe me when I say that I want you to come here and visit as often as you like. Your rooms in the villa will always be yours. I mean it, Sloane. I've been an only child my entire life, and this has been an incredible experience for me . . . coming here and getting to know a part of my life I never knew existed. The villa can be a home for you, or a second home if you want to live in London or LA or wherever."

Sloane inclined her head. "You're not planning to sell? Connor thought you might. That's what he would have done if Dad had left it to us."

Fiona looked around at all the bottles stacked up against the walls. "I admit, I did think about it. It didn't take long for an agent to call and make an offer, but I never called him back. Now I know what I want. I want to keep this place because it feels like home. And if your husband won't give you the money to buy Connor's share of your London house, I'll give it to you. You won't lose it."

"Seriously? Fiona, are you sure?"

"I've never been more sure of anything." She moved to the collection with her mother's name on it. "Our father made an exceptional wine, and this place was special to my mom. She was never able to come back here, but she dreamed about it until the day she died. I think if she were here, she'd want me to enjoy it and share it with you." Fiona picked up one of her mother's bottles and dusted off the label with the palm of her hand. "I say there's no time like the present. How about we enjoy this bottle, right now."

"Now?"

"Yes. I feel like celebrating. I want to raise a glass and toast to the fact that I have a sister and a niece and a nephew—and a brother, if he ever decides to lay down his sword. What do you say? We can go sit by the pool and pop the cork."

Sloane smiled. "That sounds wonderful. Let's go find the kids."

Together they walked out, and Sloane held on to the bottle of wine while Fiona closed the big oak door and locked it securely behind them.

CHAPTER 28
FIONA

The flight home across the ocean was far less plaguing than the red-eye I had endured on my journey to Italy. Somehow, I lucked into a direct daytime flight from Rome to New York, with a brief one-hour layover at JFK, no delays, and I flew first class all the way. Whenever the flight attendant offered me something delicious to eat or refilled my glass of wine, I couldn't stop pinching myself. I kept waiting for the other shoe to drop.

Time in the air also provided precious opportunity to reflect upon what I had learned about myself since my arrival in Tuscany. I was relieved to know the complete, unspoiled truth about how I had come into the world. It had not been an assault upon my mother or any other form of seduction or ravishment. It had been an act of love, and even the keeping of secrets had been an act of love, in its own complicated way, stirred together with guilt. A wife had hidden something from her husband to protect him from further heartbreak following a terrible trauma. She had buried the truth to give him a reason to live. She had sacrificed her own desires in the process.

I now understood that my silence had been a continuation of that act of love—to protect the father I'd always adored and idolized for his courage and fortitude in challenging circumstances. At all times, my mother and I had placed his happiness and well-being above our own. We did everything in our power to shelter him from further injury, both physical and emotional.

Had it been a two-way street? Had he done the same for us?

No. I understood now that he had not. He had allowed us to make those sacrifices, and he had been doing that to my mother since the day they met—long before her infidelity and the tragic accident that changed his life. In the beginning, he'd needed her to support him while he wrote his book—not just financially but emotionally as well. He needed her to provide for him and build him up and ignore her own dreams. When she wanted to have a child, he was reluctant because it would have gotten in the way of his writing, and it didn't matter to him that my mother had deep, genuine longings for motherhood.

After the accident, his needs morphed into something else. He needed her, and me, to remain at his side and never leave him. He needed us for his own physical and mental survival.

As I looked out at the breathtaking view of white cottony clouds just below the aircraft, I didn't know what to do with my thoughts and feelings. It was a complicated situation, and I had no idea how Dad would react when I told him where I had been for the past week. What would he say when he found out I had been to Tuscany and uncovered all his secrets—and that I had lied about where I had gone?

I supposed I was in no position to judge him for keeping secrets. I had kept secrets too.

~

After collecting my bags at the airport, I took a cab home and walked into the house where I grew up. Instantly, I detected the familiar sound of light fabrics spinning in the dryer in the laundry room. It was a constant in our home: the washing and disinfecting to guard against infections. Having been away for a week, I realized how much the house smelled like a hospital.

I dropped my keys onto the breakfast bar, then moved down the hall to my father's room, where he was sitting up in bed and Dottie was giving him a shave.

"Hey there," I said from the doorway.

Dottie jumped with surprise and set the razor down on a stainless steel tray. "You're back!" She moved to hug me. "How was your trip?"

"Amazing," I replied. "Exhausting. Enlightening."

"I want to hear all about it," Dottie said, "but I should let you two say hello first. He's only half-shaved, as you can see."

"I'll finish up for you," I replied, for I had shaved Dad many times. I knew the drill.

"Wonderful. I'll go pour myself a cup of tea."

Dottie left us alone. I moved closer and kissed the top of Dad's head. "Hi, Dad."

"Hey, sweet girl," he replied. "I'm glad you're home. How was the flight?"

"Wonderful," I said. "No delays. And the sky was blue over the Atlantic. I could see for miles."

Standing at his bedside, I picked up the razor. The scent of the shaving cream was as familiar to me as the humid Florida air.

"How did you make out while I was gone?" I asked.

"It's never the same without you," he replied.

I dipped the razor in the basin of water and carefully shaved along his jawline and under his chin. "It's good to be back. But it was an interesting time away. I learned a lot." I paused a few seconds, concentrating on my task, then rinsed the razor and tapped it a few times on the edge of the basin before I continued. "We need to have a talk, Dad."

His Adam's apple bobbed, and I looked into his eyes. They narrowed at me with concern.

Or was it fear that I saw?

Before speaking another word, I finished the shave and patted his face dry with a soft towel. He was quiet the entire time.

After I put away the shaving supplies, I sat back down. "What I want to talk to you about is pretty important," I finally said. "But first, there's something you need to know. I wasn't honest with you last week. I told you that I was going to London for a conference, but that was a lie."

"A lie?"

"Yes. I didn't go to London. I went to Italy."

His mouth clamped shut, and his eyebrows pulled together in a frown. "Why?"

"Because Anton Clark passed away," I explained. "He had a heart attack, and he died."

My father's face reddened, and he blinked a few times. "Anton Clark . . . ?"

I took a deep breath and let it out slowly. "Dad . . . please. You know who he is. Don't pretend that you don't."

He seemed at a loss for words, so I paused and tried again.

"I've known the truth about Anton since Mom died," I explained. "A few hours before she passed, she told me that he was my real father, but she begged me to keep it secret from you because she was afraid it would hurt you to know that I wasn't really yours." I bowed my head. "She knew how much you loved me, and I knew it too. You were a wonderful father to me." I took a deep breath and looked up again. "But you knew the truth all along, didn't you? Yet you pretended not to. Why?"

A muscle twitched at his jaw, and he turned his face away, pressing his cheek into the pillow. "I don't want to talk about Tuscany."

I sat forward in the chair and took hold of his hand. "I'm sorry. I know those aren't pleasant memories for you, but we have to talk about it."

"I don't know why you're doing this," he mumbled, "why you're bringing it up."

All I could do was try to explain the situation as best as I could, because we needed to be honest with each other for once. I was so tired of lying to him. "I know it's hard, Dad, but I need to understand what you knew and what you were thinking and feeling all these years."

"Why should it matter?"

"It matters because I love you," I said. "And because I'm angry with you for keeping Anton out of my life. If we're going to move forward, I need to understand what was in your heart . . . and what was in your mind."

He shook his head and squeezed his eyes shut.

I tried again. "I know that it must have been very difficult, because Mom betrayed you and you were raising a daughter who wasn't really yours—a daughter your wife lied to you about. Don't you think it's time we talked about that?"

He remained stoic.

"Please talk to me, Dad, because I went to Italy for another reason, and it's important that everything is out in the open from now on, because I can't go on living a lie. Not with you. You're the only father I have left." When he continued to look the other way, I told him the truth. "Anton named me as a beneficiary in his will."

Finally, Dad turned his head on the pillow and looked at me, but still, he didn't speak.

"That's why I went there," I continued. "I stayed at the winery, and I met his family—his two children, who are my half brother and sister. Dad, he left me everything. The whole winery. All his cash. Everything."

My father's brow furrowed with a deep frown. "He did what?"

"I know. I was shocked, too, because I never even met him, and he made no effort to contact me. All this time, I thought he was a terrible person. I didn't want to meet him out of loyalty to you, and I thought maybe he raped Mom or something, but that wasn't it, and it turns out you knew that." I watched Dad carefully. "You knew that Anton loved Mom and that he spent the rest of his life missing her and that he kept a promise to her—that he would never reveal to you or me that he was my real father. Not as long as you were alive."

The lines on Dad's face deepened into an even darker frown.

"But you always knew," I said, pressing on. "Mom's enormous secret wasn't really a secret at all."

He shook his head. "I didn't know."

Disappointed beyond all imagining, I shut my eyes. "Oh, please don't lie to me, Dad! I *know* that you knew, because I read the letter you wrote to Anton after Mom died. You asked him to continue to stay away."

Dad could do nothing but blink up at me while his cheeks flushed with color.

"Why didn't you tell Mom that you knew?" I asked. "Mom and I spent our entire lives trying to protect you from the truth, and because of that, I never had the chance to meet my real father, and I thought the worst things about him, which he didn't deserve. Now that he's dead, it's too late for me to meet him, and that's going to haunt me forever."

Dad's eyes filled with tears. "I didn't say anything because I was afraid I would lose you."

"Like you were afraid of losing Mom?"

"Yes."

"Because you needed her? To take care of you? To be your nurse?"

It was cruel and I knew it, but I was glad I had said it. I needed to know the truth.

"No," he replied. "I loved your mother, and I loved you too. I couldn't imagine my life without you. I didn't want to be left behind. I didn't want you to leave me."

I rested an elbow on the chair and watched him for a few seconds. Memories flooded my mind—climbing onto his lap when I was very small and turning the pages of a book so that he could read to me. Riding around the house on his motorized chair, laughing. Later, when

I was older, I talked to him about my swim classes and the parties I went to. I shared everything with him, and he listened with fascination.

Even then, I had understood that I was his window into a world he could no longer experience. It gave me purpose and filled me with a sense of value that never compared to anything else I ever did in my life. No one loved me like he did. I knew how much I meant to him . . . how important I was to him. I represented the life he couldn't live for himself. I was his entire world.

"I know you loved me, Dad," I softly said. "And I loved that you needed me. You made me feel so important. But didn't you ever once want to give something back to me? To put my happiness before your own? I was only eighteen when Mom died, and I had to take her place, keeping your spirits up, becoming your sole reason to live. It was a tremendous responsibility for me then, and I can't lie—it still is. I'm thirty years old, and I've never been able to maintain a long-term relationship with anyone because my whole existence revolves around making sure that you're okay, that you're not going to give up and let yourself die. Mom worked so hard at that, trying to make you feel happy every day, and now I understand where her fears were coming from." I hated saying these things to him, and my voice shook as I spoke. "Because you told her that you would die if she left you."

His voice went quiet with defeat. "Where did you hear that?"

It all came tumbling out. "I met a man in Italy named Francesco. He was Anton's driver and closest friend. He was Mom's friend, too, and he drove her to the hospital in Montepulciano after you were taken away in the ambulance." I paused. "Please tell me the truth, Dad. Would you really have given up? Or were you just trying to guilt Mom into staying with you?"

He swallowed hard and offered no reply.

"Mom thought you didn't want to have children, and then you ended up with a kid who wasn't even yours. Talk to me, Dad. Tell me that you didn't just want us to take care of you. Or that you weren't trying to punish Mom or punish Anton by keeping me away from him."

"I did love her," Dad said again. "But she didn't love me, not the way she loved him. She never loved me like that. And there were days I hated her for it, and I blamed her for what happened to me. It was her idea to go to Tuscany in the first place, and if she hadn't had the affair . . . if she hadn't sneaked out and gone to the villa that night . . ." He paused and squeezed his eyes shut. "What happened to me was her fault. There were days I wished I'd never met her."

Recognizing the anger that still burned in him, I sat back and waited for him to collect himself and continue.

"And I hated Anton more than I ever hated anyone. No one believed me when I said he ran me down on purpose. Not even your mother. Especially her, which only twisted the knife. They said it was an accident . . . maybe it was . . . either way, I still blame him. And yes, I did want to keep you away from him to get back at him. There's a part of me that's glad he's dead. There. You wanted me to be honest, so I've said it. I'm not proud of it, but there it is."

"Dad . . ."

"That doesn't change the fact that I loved you more than anything, and I couldn't live without you, because when you came along, you brought joy with you, and joy was something I never expected to feel, ever again. It didn't matter that you weren't mine, and I knew that if your mother went to Italy to be with Anton, she would take you with her, and I couldn't let that happen. And that day in the hospital, I *did* want to die. I wasn't trying to manipulate her. I swear it. Later, when I couldn't forgive her, I told myself that she deserved to pay a price for what she did. She was unfaithful and she'd had an affair, and because of that, I ended up like this." He looked away and grew quiet. "I lost everything. I became a burden to everyone."

"You weren't a burden."

"Yes, I was. And I tried to forgive her. Honest, I did. Year after year. But I just couldn't, so I did whatever I had to do to make sure I didn't lose you. Especially not to Anton."

"But I wouldn't have left you," I assured him, feeling my anger rise up again and fly into the open. It had found a path through the dense forest of my love and compassion. "Even if I had met Anton, you would have always been my dad. I just wish you had been honest with me. I wish you had helped me to meet him. He was my biological father, and he wanted to meet me, but you wouldn't allow it, and now I'll never get that chance. And I never got to know my half brother and sister either. If Anton hadn't died, I still wouldn't know about them. How can I ever forgive you for that, Dad?"

I began to weep with the agony of learning that the man I believed would do anything for me had denied me the greatest gift of all—the gift of his trust in my love for him. And the gift of my biological father's love. For the first time I saw, with perfect clarity, the full extent of my father's wounds beyond the physical—the deeper ones that had weakened his soul at a very young age when his own mother had deserted him. Then his wife had intended the same thing. I saw the world through his eyes, as a place where love was a destructive force, where it left behind a twisted, mangled wreckage, which was how he viewed his life.

Dad watched me with concern. "Please, pumpkin, don't cry. I can't bear to see you cry."

I looked up and wiped away my tears. "Then why did you do what you did?"

A part of me hated him for what he had kept from me. I wanted to lash out at him.

Another part of me pitied him for the love he had not let into his life because he feared its destructiveness. He had been possessive, distrustful, and jealous.

"I'm sorry," he said. "I knew it was wrong, but I was afraid of what would happen if you knew. And now I'm afraid I'm going to lose you anyway."

Seeing the total unqualified despair in his eyes, I forced myself to reach out and take hold of his hand, because I didn't want to become like him—a person with a soul that couldn't forgive. A person with a heart that couldn't trust in love or have faith in a loved one's loyalty. I wanted to see the best in him. I needed to believe that he cared for me and that he could put my happiness, for once, above his own.

"I never expected to live this long," he continued to explain, his voice breaking into a sob. "I hated being a burden to you, but I thought you and your mother would be free of me eventually. I always expected that you would meet Anton one day, after I was gone. I expected it from the beginning, so every new day with you was a blessing. I stole what happiness I could because I thought it would be brief. That was my mistake. I waited too long. If only I had known how long it would take for me to die, I might have acted differently."

"Please don't say that, Dad. I never wanted you to die." I stared down at our joined hands and tried to see through my anger to what he had just confessed. I thought about his fears and insecurities and began to feel the first small traces of forgiveness, like one or two isolated raindrops that made you look to the sky before a downpour.

"I was selfish," he admitted. "I know it, and I wish now that I could go back. If I could, I would tell you to go to Italy and learn where you came from. I would tell you to follow your heart. I swear, that's all I want for you. I want you to be happy, even apart from me, because I couldn't bear it if you stopped loving me."

I bent forward and kissed the back of his hand. "I'll never stop loving you, Dad. You were a good father to me."

"Except for this."

I nodded. "Except for this."

Total forgiveness was not going to be easy. This much I knew. It was going to take some effort, but it was better than the alternative, which would leave me hating my father and resenting him. I couldn't live like that. I didn't want to feel anger in my thoughts for the rest of my life. I wanted to wake up in the morning and feel blissful at the sight of the sunrise. I wanted to feel grateful for the kind father who raised me, who had made me feel loved.

We sat in silence for a moment. After a while, I sat back and pondered everything I now knew about both of my fathers.

"I have a question," I said, wiping away the last of my tears. "How did you know about the promise Anton made to Mom? How did you know that he would keep the secret, even from me? Did she tell you that?"

"No," he replied, "we never spoke about Anton after the accident. It was as if it never happened. She never mentioned him or talked about Tuscany again."

"Then I don't get it. How did you know?"

He paused, as if considering whether he should answer the question. "Years ago, when you were still a baby, I asked one of the night nurses to go through your mother's desk and see if there were any letters from Tuscany. She found a half-written letter to Anton, and she showed it to me."

I wanted desperately to understand. "You didn't try to talk to Mom about it?"

"No," he replied. "I was afraid that if she opened up to me, it would be like opening a floodgate. She would tell me the truth—that she loved him and wanted to be with him—and I would have no choice but to let her go."

All at once, I realized the consequences of the secrets we had kept from each other. My parents had never really known each other on a soul-deep level, not since my father's accident. They had lived in a constant state of denial and had hidden everything from each other.

Where did that leave me now that everything was out in the open? I stood up and paced around the room.

"What will you do?" Dad asked, watching me intently, nervously. He pressed the button on the bed to raise himself to a more upright sitting position.

"I'm not sure," I replied. "I just found out I inherited a fortune, and I have a half brother and sister and other family members living in London. My head is still spinning."

Dottie appeared in the doorway just then. She held a Mickey Mouse mug and was bobbing a tea bag up and down on the end of a string. "So spill the beans, Fiona. I want to hear everything. Did you see the queen at Piccadilly Circus? Or William and Kate at Harrods?"

I gave Dad a look, then responded to Dottie's question. "No, because I didn't go to London. I went to Italy."

"Italy." She looked bewildered. "But I thought the conference was in London."

I strode toward her. "It's a long story. Why don't you come in and sit down with us? We'll tell you everything. Won't we, Dad."

He nodded as she entered the room.

~

I was up early the following morning and found Dad in front of the computer in the den, surfing the internet. Dottie was off, and Jerry was in the kitchen.

"Good morning," I said, still in my pajamas and slippers. I took a seat on the sofa under the window.

"Good morning," Dad replied, turning his motorized chair around to face me. "I was just doing some research."

"About what?"

"Wineries in Tuscany. Maurizio Wines in particular."

I understood the magnitude of what he was telling me, because I knew how he had always given images of Italy a wide berth. They did not evoke pleasant memories for him.

"And?"

"And I think you have just become a very rich woman."

I tipped my head back and looked up at the ceiling. "Yes, I have, and I still can't believe it. Now that I'm back here, it doesn't even seem real. It feels like a dream."

Dad wheeled himself closer. "But it's not a dream. You are the daughter of a very successful businessman."

"That may be true," I replied, meeting his gaze. "But I am also the daughter of a strong and brave survivor who beat all the odds that were stacked against him."

"I survived because I was selfish," Dad replied.

"In some ways, but not all. You weren't acting selfishly when you looked at me like I was the best thing that ever happened to you. You made me feel special and loved. That's what I want to remember, Dad. It's what I need to focus on."

"Me too," he replied. "And you were special. You still are. Because if you can sit here in this house and forgive me for everything that I . . ."

"Stop, Dad," I said gently. "Of course I'm going to forgive you. How can I not? Life is rough for everyone, and it's complicated. It's full of hairpin turns we don't see coming. You know that better than anyone. You suffered a terrible trauma. And we all make mistakes. Mom certainly wasn't perfect. She left a fair bit of destruction in her path."

"Yes, but she gave me you."

"And she gave me you."

I realized in that moment that I was going to have to find a way to accept how my life had played out and let go of the frustration and regret about not meeting Anton. This was my reality going forward. What good could come from grappling forever with "could have beens"?

Every life was full of "could have beens." The best we could do was make the most of what was and what had been.

At least I finally knew the truth about my mother's life, and I was no longer lying to my father. There was a tremendous relief in that—in the purging of secrets and the guilt that accompanied them. I felt somehow lighter, as if I had used a shovel to excavate my soul.

Dad and I regarded each other in the rays of the early-morning sunlight through the window, and I believed he felt lighter, too—that he was relieved to have let the truth out of its long confinement.

"What are you going to do with the inheritance?" he asked.

I thought about it for a moment. "Well. That's an interesting question. I should probably tell you that I received an offer on the winery, and I did consider selling. It was a lot of money. Ninety million euros." I shook my head in disbelief.

"Fiona . . ."

"I know. I can barely conceive of that much money. Selling it would have probably been the easiest thing. Then I could have come home, stayed here with you, and we'd have more money than we'd know what to do with. We could buy a bigger house and pay off the van . . ." I rubbed the back of my neck. "But Dad, I loved being there. I can't explain it, and I hope this isn't hurtful to you when I say it, but I feel like Tuscany is in my blood. I loved the people and the way of life. I loved learning about the vineyards and the wine-making process and, of course, drinking it." I gave him a sheepish smile. "And I have a half sister named Sloane, and she has two children, and I want to get to know them better. If I keep the winery, I could learn how to run it and . . ." I faced him and spoke openly. "I could move to Italy and build a pretty amazing life for myself there."

Dad stared at me intently, and I understood that this had always been his greatest fear and worst nightmare—that he would be left behind. Alone. That Mom would leave him for Anton, and I would disappear too.

I turned on the sofa to look out the window and watched the young palm trees in our yard as they blew in the wind, swaying and bending. My future lay before me, unpredictable like the force and direction of the wind at any given moment. I didn't want the wind to be destructive. I wanted it to lift me up and carry me, to give me the push I needed to figure out what I was supposed to be doing with my life. I wanted it to lift us both.

Then I turned back to face Dad, and my indecision seemed to hang in the air between us.

With a note of conviction, Dad touched the button on the joystick and drove his chair closer. "Then you should do it. Go and make great wine in Italy. And don't worry about me. I'll be fine here, as long as I know you're happy. You'll call?"

I stared at him with a strange, buoyant feeling, as if I had just fallen from a great height and bounced like a balloon.

"Of course," I replied, leaping immediately into the promise of a new future. "And I'll come home often to visit. I'll make sure that you have the best of care whenever I'm away. Dottie . . . she's devoted, and she loves you."

"I love her too."

My heart softened, as it always did with my dad. "Or you could come with me," I suggested. "It's a big house and—"

"No," he said flatly. "I don't want to go back there."

This I understood.

Rising from the sofa, I sighed and took hold of his hand. "Please don't feel that I'm leaving you, Dad. I'm still your daughter, and I'll love you forever. But I need to do this. I need to go out there, into the world, and figure out what I'm capable of."

"I want that for you too," he replied shakily, with tears in his eyes. "I'll miss you, but I'll be so proud."

I kissed him on the forehead and hugged him, then wiped the tears from my own eyes and prepared myself for a new beginning.

EPILOGUE
FIONA

Tuscany, one year later

Maria found me in the studio, paintbrush in hand, standing before an easel that had once belonged to Anton. It was a tool he had carried across unknown distances to paint colorful fields of sunflowers and poppies or sunsets over Tuscan vineyards. I hadn't done that yet—painted outdoors—but I had learned to never say never. Perhaps one day I would venture outside to paint Tuscany as well.

Until then, I was overjoyed to have a studio of my own, surrounded by boxes full of my father's canvases, for which I had great plans. I was discovering that, like my mother, I had a rather good head for business. One of my current projects was an upcoming art auction, which would showcase my father's paintings while raising the profile of Maurizio Wines. I planned to donate the proceeds of the auction to the local hospital in Montepulciano.

Today, however, my focus lay elsewhere—on the canvas before me, illuminated by a muted light filtering in through the windows from an overcast sky.

"How's it coming?" Maria asked as she walked in.

"Come and take a look." I was never shy about showing my works in progress to Maria, because she seemed to love everything I painted, which fueled my confidence and creativity. "Although there's not much to look at just yet," I added.

She stood beside me, contemplating the canvas, which was mostly blank. "You're only just getting started."

"*Sì*. I've been sketching. But can you picture it? Try to imagine here"—I waved my hand over the middle section—"when I start adding the colors of a sunset."

"I'm sure you'll make it very beautiful," she said. "I don't know how you do it. I'm always surprised and amazed by what you come up with."

"So am I," I said with a laugh. "It's just trial and error most of the time."

Maria looked out the window at the tall cypresses swaying in the wind.

"So what's up?" I asked, studying the angles of a few charcoal lines on the canvas.

Maria sat down on the windowsill. "I came up here to tell you that Sloane just called."

My heart gave a little leap. Sloane and I had grown close over the past year. She often called to talk about her divorce from Alan, and sometimes she vented about her challenges as a single parent. I was not a parent myself, so I enjoyed the vicarious experience when it came to my niece and nephew. I was sympathetic and in awe of Sloane's strength and patience in dealing with everything.

"What did she want?" I asked, wondering why she had called the villa when she usually called my cell phone directly. I suspected it had something to do with the fact that it was on this day, exactly one year ago, that Anton had passed.

"She wanted to surprise you," Maria replied, "but I told her I was terrible at keeping secrets."

I laughed as my cell phone rang in my pocket, causing me to jump. Quickly I retrieved it and answered. "Hello?"

"Hi," Sloane said. "It's me. Let me guess. Maria is standing right next to you. She couldn't resist, could she?"

I laughed. "You know her too well." I moved around the easel and winked at Maria.

"Did she spoil it?" Sloane asked. "The surprise, I mean?"

"Well . . . kind of . . . yes."

I heard the sound of Evan's voice in the background asking Chloe if she had any more bubble gum.

Sloane paused before she spoke again. "Okay. So here's the deal. I'm at LAX with the kids, and we're at the gate, waiting to board an overnight flight. We arrive in Florence tomorrow."

I pressed my hand to my heart. "That's wonderful. I can't wait to see you."

"Me neither."

She broke away from our conversation to ask Evan and Chloe to watch the suitcases for a few minutes. Then she continued. "We'll be there by late morning. We want to visit the cemetery and look at some old pictures I asked Maria to dig out. Maybe we can all do that together."

"I'd love that."

"And it'll be a nice visit for the kids before they start school in London," Sloane added.

"Are they excited?"

"I think so. Nervous, too, but I'm sure they'll love it. They already have friends in the neighborhood. I'm just glad to be moving into the house, finally. Our stuff arrives next Tuesday."

"What about Alan?" I asked. "How's he taking it, now that you're actually leaving for good?"

Sloane was quiet for a moment. "He's still trying to talk me into staying in LA. He even offered to give me the house—as if it was a huge concession and I should bow down and be grateful for it. Meanwhile, he's on Tinder. Imagine that. Oh, Fiona, I'm so over him, and I don't care about his house or anything else he's had his dirty hands on. I'm looking forward to telling you everything over a bottle of wine and a gigantic plate of pasta tomorrow night. Can we do that?"

"Of course." I paused. "What about Connor? Have you heard from him lately?"

"No, but Mom says he's dating the producer of a cooking show. Good luck to her."

I chuckled.

"I'm sure I'll hear from him when they break up. That's usually how it goes."

I nodded. "How about a pickup at the airport tomorrow? Should I send Marco?"

"Don't worry about that. Maria already asked him to fetch us. Wait a second . . ." She paused. "It sounds like they're calling our zone for boarding. I have to go. I'll see you soon."

"All right. Safe travels."

~

Later that night, after dinner, I returned to the studio, switched on the chandelier, and wandered leisurely to one of the large wooden crates that held Anton's canvases. Carefully, I pulled one out, unrolled it, and found myself staring with contentment at the exquisite artistry before me. In simple terms, it was a landscape, but what I saw with my heart was Anton's appreciation for the beauty in our world and for the extraordinary love he had known.

As I admired his graceful brushstrokes and his brilliant mix of color, I felt a connection to him like never before. My father. Winemaker and artist. I also understood my mother's love for him and her love for this place, her passion for the vineyards and the people of Tuscany. In the painting, I saw my future, years from now, working with the crews to prune the grapevines and study the soil, to plan the harvests. I knew in that moment that I would spend my life preserving something beloved and valuable.

At the same time, I would build something new, looking forward, not back. I was already working on a special blend of wine to commemorate Anton's love for my mother, which had never been celebrated before. I would paint the label myself.

And though I tried to let go of certain things and live without regret, I was beginning to accept that regret would always be a part of my life. I was only human, after all, and as much as I wanted to, I couldn't escape it. What I decided was that I would not let it consume or define me. For the most part, I was at peace with how my life had unfolded, and I would embrace my regret—and my ability to work at forgiveness—as evidence of my humanity. I would wake up each morning and count my blessings.

Rolling up the canvas, I smiled, then slid it back into the wooden crate with the others. I then returned to my own work in progress on the easel. Tilting my head to the side, I narrowed my eyes, taking in the shapes and proportions of my sketch. I tried to envision the color palette and saw blue, yellow, and orange for the setting sun and different shades of white for the clouds. Silver for the wing of the airplane. It was a rather heavenly view.

Yes, there was much promise there. I had every reason to believe it was going to be a beautiful painting.

ACKNOWLEDGMENTS

Special thanks to our dear friends Natalie and Darrell Munro for suggesting that we take a trip to Tuscany together and tour some wineries. What an adventure it was as we navigated our way around the Italian countryside. You were wonderful travel companions.

The winery in this book—Maurizio Wines—is a fictional composite of a number of vineyards that we visited, so I must thank our many tour guides, who provided invaluable information and histories that served as inspiration for the scenes in this book.

Thanks also to my friend Benedetta Holmes for your generous and careful reading of the first draft of the novel and for your indispensable help with the Italian translations and other elements of the Italian setting. I will always be grateful for your friendship.

To my cousin Michelle Killen (a.k.a. Michelle McMaster)—thank you for your loving friendship and for remaining my talented and irreplaceable critique partner for a quarter of a century. And to my cousin Julia Phillips Smith—you mean so much to me, and I don't know what I would do without your help every single day!

Thanks also to my agent, Paige Wheeler, for your continuing professional excellence and for being the person who is always in my corner and working hard behind the scenes. To Alicia Clancy, my editor at Lake Union, for being so good at what you do and for coming up with the concept for this book, which you called *The Will*. It was a spark that lit a fire in me and sent me on an incredible journey, both literally and figuratively. And then your editorial comments and suggestions made this book so much better on so many levels. Finally, to the Lake Union marketing team—you are this author's dream come true!

Thank you, Kimberly Dossett, for your sharp and thorough attention to all the little details surrounding my writing career.

Finally, thank you to my husband, Stephen, for being amazing in every way, to our daughter, Laura, for making us proud and adding so much love and laughter to our lives, and to my mother, Noel, for your love and support each day. What a wonderful life you gave me.

ABOUT THE AUTHOR

Photo © 2013 Jenine Panagiotakos, BlueVinePhotography

Julianne MacLean is a *USA Today* bestselling author of more than thirty novels, including the popular Color of Heaven Series. Readers have described her books as "breathtaking," "soulful," and "uplifting." MacLean is a four-time Romance Writers of America RITA finalist and has won numerous awards, including the Booksellers' Best Award and a Reviewers' Choice Award from the *Romantic Times*. Her novels have sold millions of copies worldwide and have been translated into more than a dozen languages.

MacLean has a degree in English literature from King's College in Halifax, Nova Scotia, and a business degree from Acadia University in Wolfville, Nova Scotia. She loves to travel and has lived in New Zealand, Canada, and England. She currently resides on the East Coast of Canada in a lakeside home with her husband, daughter, and mother. Readers can visit her website at www.JulianneMacLean.com for more information about her books and writing life and to subscribe to her mailing list for all the latest news.